CENTER OF GRAVITY

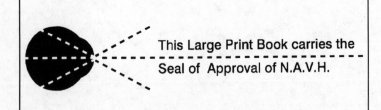

This Large Print Book carries the
Seal of Approval of N.A.V.H.

CENTER OF GRAVITY

LAURA MCNEILL

THORNDIKE PRESS

A part of Gale, Cengage Learning

GALE
CENGAGE Learning·

Farmington Hills, Mich • San Francisco • New York • Waterville, Maine
Meriden, Conn • Mason, Ohio • Chicago

GALE
CENGAGE Learning

LIBRARY OF CONGRESS CATALOGING-IN-PUBLICATION DATA

McNeill, Laura.
    Center of gravity / by Laura McNeill. — Large print edition.
        pages cm. — (Thorndike Press large print Christian mystery)
        ISBN 978-1-4104-8143-6 (hardcover) — ISBN 1-4104-8143-3 (hardcover)
        1. Large type books. 2. Domestic fiction. I. Title.
PS3613.C58623E58 2015b
813'.6—dc23   2015020734

Published in 2015 by arrangement with Thomas Nelson, Inc., a division
of HarperCollins Publishing, Inc.

Printed in Mexico
2 3 4 5 6 7 19 18 17 16 15

For John David

PROLOGUE:
AVA

When your children are stolen, the pain swallows you whole. Logic fades, reason retreats. Desperation permeates the tiniest crevices of your mind. Nothing soothes the ache in your wounded soul.

Right in front of me, my sweet, charmed life fell to pieces. Everything destroyed — a hailstorm's wrath on a field of wildflowers. All I'd known . . . gone. Foolish me, I'd believed in magic, clung tight to false promises. The lies, spoken from tender lips, haunt me now, follow me, and whisper into my ear like a scorned lover.

What's left is emptiness.

Give up, a voice urges. *Let go.*

No! I argue back. My children aren't gone. Not yet. Precious and delicate, tiny fossils, they exist in glass-boxed isolation. Hidden. Protected.

And so tonight, I run. Blood pulses through my legs, my muscles protest; my lungs scream for more oxygen. Thick storm clouds brew in the distance. The rain falls in blinding sheets. The force of it pricks my skin like needles, but the pain only makes me push harder.

I will rescue them.

Lightning flashes across the wet driveway. I skid to a stop and catch my breath, pressing a hand to my heaving chest.

They're here. My children are here.

Thunder booms and crashes, nearer now, and the wind whips my hair. A gust tosses tree branches to the ground. Birds cry and flutter to safety. An escaped sand bucket spins, clattering on the blacktop.

I grasp the railing and pull myself up the steps. At the top, the door is shiny-slick with water and humidity. Mother Nature howls and drowns out my knocking.

"Hello! Can you hear me?" With my palm open wide, I slap at the barrier, willing it to open. I will rescue my children. I will rescue them . . . or I will die trying.

CHAPTER 1
JACK

ONE MONTH EARLIER
WEDNESDAY, MARCH 24

Every day, somebody somewhere needs a hero.

Think about it. The mom lifting a two-ton truck to save her son after a car crash. The dad — who can't swim — who jumps in the water anyway to pull out his drowning daughter. The guy who kicks down the door of a burning building because his friend's kid is trapped inside.

All of a sudden, getting hurt doesn't matter. There's no thinking twice. Just a gut-pumping, jump-off-the-cliff, no turning back.

For these regular people, thrown into crazy life-or-death situations, there's that one big moment. Then they go back to work, their jobs, or school.

And it's someone else's turn.

I'm only in the third grade, but I've been

9

waiting for my whole life.

Waiting for my chance — my moment to be a hero.

An ear-piercing shriek yanks me back to the school playground.

My best friend Mo runs up, breathless. "Emma Dunlop's stuck up in the oak tree." He bends over, chest heaving in the humidity, and puts both hands on his knees. "She's freaking out."

Shielding my eyes, I grit my teeth. The tree's as big as a monster, with twisted brown branches that extend like arms, thick emerald leaves at the fingertips. Spanish moss hangs from the lowest limbs, the ends curling like a snake's tail.

Though I can't see her through the tangle of limbs, I picture Emma hanging on tight to the rough bark. Shaking. Really scared. Trying not to look down at the brick-red clay.

I run a hand through my hair.

She's in trouble. And I know why.

Legend says a man's head — a genie — is hidden in the leaves and branches. Weird, rough pieces of wood make up his face. He has knots for eyes. A bump for his chin. It's for real. I've seen it.

All the kids know the story. If you touch the genie's nose, your wish will come true.

Of course my dad doesn't believe in stuff like that and says I shouldn't either. He's a PhD and does an important job at the college. So I guess he knows what he's talking about.

But that's not going to save Emma now. I start to jog, then full-out sprint. At the base of the tree, I push through a crowd of my classmates. Third and fourth graders, gaping, heads tilted, mouths open like baby birds. When I reach the trunk, I squint up and find Emma's brand-new saddle shoes dangling high above me. I see pale, thin legs and the crisp edges of her plaid jumper. And despite everyone talking and whispering, I hear Emma crying. It's a whimpering wail, like a hurt animal.

"Y'all go on back inside now. Go back to class," my teacher says, pushing the group back an inch or two. I end up jostled next to the school librarian, who's holding her hands like she's praying.

Our eyes meet. Mine flicker away.

"Don't even think about it, Jack," she warns.

But I kick off my shoes anyway and grab hold of the trunk. Deep down in my belly, I make myself act like I'm not scared. I don't like heights or even hanging upside down from monkey bars. But Emma needs me.

And no one else is doing a thing.

Ms. Martin gasps, but she knows she's too late. I'm out of her reach before she can react. I think hard about one of my favorite superheroes, Daredevil. He's like an Olympic athlete and a master of martial arts. He's blind but uses his other senses to fight crime, beat up bad guys, and save the girl. If he can do it . . .

When I look back down at the ground, my stomach churns like I've eaten too many Snickers bars and guzzled a two-liter of Coke. I push the feeling away. *Climb, Jack,* I say to myself. *Just climb.* When I start to move my legs again, the first few feet are easy. Soon I'm above everyone's heads.

"They're going to get a ladder," the librarian calls out. "Come on down here, Jack Carson, right this instant. Lord have mercy!"

At the sound of her screech, Emma wobbles. Her saddle shoes kick and knock some bark from a branch. *I can't come down now. She's slipping.*

"They've called the fire department," my teacher adds. "Truck's on the way."

I pretend I don't hear her and move closer. My head starts to hurt. My ears are ringing. But I take a deep breath and hold on tight to the tree, concentrating on Emma.

12

She's tiny, a first grader, with brown corkscrew curls and a yellow bow pinned to the side of her head. Her pink cheeks are streaked with dirt.

"Hey, Emma," I say, making my voice calm. "Whatcha doing up here?"

She flushes pink. "I wanted to make a w-wish. For my birthday."

A breeze ruffles the leaves, cooling the sweat on my forehead. My hands, gritty with dirt and bark, inch closer. I can almost reach her. "Well, let's make sure you get to your party."

"But I haven't found the genie." She begins to cry, which makes her body wobble. The branch moves up and down, and she starts sobbing harder.

"Emma," I say. "It's okay. I'll help you."

She snuffles and blinks a few times. "I'm scared."

"I know. Me too," I tell her. "But I won't let you fall. Give me your hand."

Her palm is slippery wet. I grip it and try to smile so that she's not so nervous. "Slide your foot toward me. Then the other one."

I watch Emma drag one foot about an inch. She tries the other one but gets her shoe caught on a bump. I inhale sharply, the scent of dirt and sweat filling my nose.

"Wait. Don't move," I say, squeezing her hand.

Sirens wail. The crowd below grows bigger. I swallow hard. *Daredevil. Be like Daredevil.*

"Hold on," I tell her. "I won't let go."

After what seems like forever, Emma moves her foot closer.

"Can you think of something great, like going on vacation or your birthday?" I ask.

"Or getting a pony." For a moment, she sighs dreamily.

"Right," I say. "Now, let's go."

We begin to climb lower, inch by inch, but my arm muscle cramps. Emma hesitates. I squeeze her hand. I need to get her down. And fast.

"Emma," I whisper. "Look to the right."

The face of the tree genie is right there.

"Oh," Emma breathes.

"Touch his nose, quick."

She reaches out a finger and brushes it, then giggles. Right then, another gust of wind blows through the branches. Her curls tickle my cheek. I almost want to laugh. But I can't. Not yet.

Climbing down is simpler now; the limbs are wider, sturdier. The voices right below us are louder. The last big branch, large enough to hold both of us, is about ten feet up from the ground. We stop here, gasping for breath.

Firefighters are waiting underneath us with a blanket. An ambulance is there with the back door open. Teachers are waving their hands. And saying something.

Jump. They want Emma to jump.

"All right." I use my most grown-up voice. "Emma, I need you to do one more thing."

Her chin moves up and down.

"They want you to let go. So they can catch you."

Emma's arms and legs get stiff. Her eyes widen, and we both swallow a gulp. We're taller than the high dive at Spring Hill Swim Club. I try not to sway when I look at the ground.

"Maybe pretend," I tell her, thinking fast, "that you're a butterfly. Or an eagle."

"How about a unicorn?" She gives me a lopsided grin.

I bite my lip. *Enough with the horses.* I want to get down. This rescue stuff isn't for sissies.

Emma looks at me.

"They're waiting for you, Emma. On the count of three, okay?"

When the firefighter below calls out "one," she jumps, and her uniform billows open like a plaid parachute. She lands square on

15

the blanket and beams in delight. A firefighter reaches in, grabs Emma, and scoops her up.

Emma waves good-bye to me as the firefighter carries her to the ambulance.

"Think you'll get the pony?" I yell after her.

She shakes her curls. "I can't tell you my wish. It won't come true!"

Emma's mother runs up then, crying, hugging, and kissing her.

With Emma okay, the grown-ups turn back to me. Most of them have their arms crossed and don't look happy. No doubt the principal is ready to dish out a detention or two.

"Dude, your dad's going to freak when he finds out," Mo says and rolls his eyes. "He hates your superhero stuff."

"Don't remind me." Inside, I feel sick. I know that I am supposed to get good grades, play sports, and be polite. My dad isn't a fan of making big scenes.

"It was pretty cool anyway." Mo cocks his head. "Who are you today?"

"Daredevil."

"Nice." He grins and leans against the tree below me, waiting. "You coming down now, superhero?"

I lean back against the trunk, waiting for

the firefighters to come back with the blanket. "Yep."

"Go ahead," Mo dares me, raising an eyebrow and grinning.

I hesitate, thinking I'd be crazy to jump. But superheroes take chances, don't they? I'd seen Daredevil jump from this height before. So holding my breath, I let go. Somehow, though, I twist midair and land smack down on my face. Hard.

The belly flop knocks the breath from my lungs. Time stops.

The smell of cut grass makes me want to sneeze. And someone's wearing really, really bad perfume. At least I'm not dead. Everyone is shouting and my ears hurt. There are hands touching my legs and arms. I roll my head an inch to one side. All I can see are shoes. A pair of black heels come closer.

"Jack, sweetheart, can you hear me?"

I push myself up with one arm and swipe at my hair with the back of my hand. "Sure thing," I answer, jaw set at the ridiculous question. Even superheroes stumble sometimes.

"Jack —"

"I'm fine." To prove it, I try to jump up and get to my feet. But like Superman with a mound of Kryptonite in the room, I am so weak that I almost fall over.

The office lady's mouth stretches wide and yawns.

My brain won't work. What is her name? Two of her now? Ink-stained fingers snap in front of my nose. My brain starts to rewind. My knees give out. Everything slides to the right and goes black.

CHAPTER 2
AVA

WEDNESDAY, MARCH 24

Life never quite turns out the way you plan. Take my first attempt at gourmet cooking. The twelve-week-long class was a wedding gift from my husband, Mitchell. I think he secretly hoped the instruction would uncover my amazing talent and I'd be the next Giada De Laurentiis.

So armed with a new apron, thick, glossy new cookbooks, and dazzled by my new home's professional kitchen — full of gleaming stainless steel utensils — I bounced fearlessly into the day of instruction.

I proceeded to set both oven mitts on fire, much to the horror of nearby students. The next week, my crème brûlée singed into a charcoal volcano. Week number three, the heady scent of cloves caused a wave of nausea so strong I had to run outside and gulp fresh air. I turned out to be pregnant, of course. So much for the Food Network and my budding career as a chef.

Since then, we keep a fire extinguisher handy, and I work from a collection of standby, no-fail recipes. We've decided that I do excel at comfort food: chicken salad, tacos, and oatmeal cookies. Tonight's plan: fresh vegetables and pasta.

With baby Sam on my hip, I maneuver down the clean, gleaming aisles of Fresh Market, chatting on the phone with our contractor.

"Heart Pine?" I echo, leaning over to pick up fresh broccoli florets. "Isn't that . . . really expensive?" I pause and wince when he tells me the cost.

At Mitchell's request, our contractor is building us an amazing staircase in the foyer of our hundred-twenty-year-old home. Crafted to mirror late eighteen-hundreds décor, it will be quite the showpiece. Lovely and very, very expensive.

"So the down payment? You'll need it this afternoon?" I ask, selecting a ripe, ruby-red tomato and holding it up to the light like a jewel.

The contactor confirms that he will, in fact, need quite a large sum. I almost drop the fruit but manage to set it carefully in the buggy. Mitchell hasn't left me the cash or a check. To withdraw it from my household account would take every last penny. The pennies I've been saving, in secret, for the boys' swing set. The swing set I haven't told Mitchell about yet. Mama always says it's easier to ask for forgiveness than permission, after all.

I stop wheeling the shopping cart to rub the back of my neck. "And if we miss you today?"

His answer is clear. He'll be gone, out of the country, for a week. We'll be behind schedule, and Mitchell will be less than pleased.

"I'll meet you at the house in thirty minutes."

Throat tight, I hang up and check the time on my phone. Sam breaks the tension with a giggle and presses his cheek to my chest. He's flirting with the produce clerk, a cute redhead with big blue eyes. Sam's the most sweet-natured child, and his blond curls, pink cheeks, and dimples draw a bevy of admirers. Of course, as his mother, I'm unduly biased. He's always had my heart.

As I lean to press my lips to his head, my cell buzzes again. *It can't be the contractor again.* With a small sigh, I answer and press the phone to my ear. "Hello?"

Urgent and clipped, the voice on the phone stops my world. A comet screaming toward Earth, bent on near destruction.

It's about Jack. My third grader. There's been an accident.

I leave the groceries, stammering out an apology to whoever can hear me. My shopping cart, filled with organic chocolate ice cream, soymilk, and Mitchell's favorite whole grain bread, sits behind us, forgotten. On my budget, it was wishful thinking anyway.

I dash for the automatic doors, which open with a hiss and a jolt. Luckily the parking lot's not crazy, and I make it to my Jeep in a matter of steps.

As I buckle him in, Sam gurgles and bats at my face, wanting to play. With a shaking hand, I rub and kiss the top of his sweet head, move his very necessary fuzzy brown bear close, and shut the door. I sprint to the other side of the Jeep, jump in, and almost lose my shoe.

My Jeep's old engine cranks on the first try. *Thank you.* I give the dashboard an affectionate pat. *This is no time to be temperamental.*

The wheels groan and grab gravel, throwing it like confetti as I drive out of the parking lot. Sam claps his hands at the clatter of stones and pebbles. My cell phone slides to the floor, out of reach. The slip from the dry cleaners falls between the seats.

Around a curve, the folded pink heart I keep tucked in the visor flutters to the seat beside me. Jack and Sam's homemade valentine. Construction paper, glue, and crayon — more precious than any gift. Two small stick figures, a taller one in the middle with a hair bow. I press two fingers to the soft paper and say a prayer.

The road rushes under the wheels. I rearrange snippets of the frantic conversation. *Gash. Some blood. Breathing fine. Emergency room.* A few more miles to the hospital.

I flash back to this morning. Packed sack lunch, flop of dark hair across his bare forehead, navy backpack slung over one shoulder. A surge of pure love courses through my heart. A stab of worry steals my breath. I force myself to focus.

The traffic light ahead flashes green to yellow. Intersection's clear. I push the accelerator to the floor, glance in the rearview mirror. Air from the open window catches Sam's wisps of hair. He smiles, showing off his first few baby teeth, and reaches a chubby hand at the rays of sunshine streaking by, trying to catch the light.

Thump. Thump. The Jeep jerks to the left. I guide the wheel, hold it steady, and take my foot off the gas. When I pull over and brake, the abrupt stop sends up a dust cloud.

"Uh-oh," Sam says.

I unbuckle, jump out, and survey the damage. A glance at the tire confirms it. Flat. Dead.

Hands on my hips, I bite my lip.

Tentatively, I grab the jack from the back of the Jeep, the weight of it solid and heavy in my hands. I can fix this. After all, in my former life, as a school counselor at Mobile Prep, I was the problem-solver, crisis manager, and shoulder to cry on. I always handled situations. And I didn't need help.

Then my eyes fall on Sam as he babbles and blows bubbles in the backseat. I hesitate, gripping the metal between my palms. As the sun beats down on us, heating my skin, my pulse begins to race. Maybe I was fearless because I didn't know any better. I wasn't a mom then. I didn't have two children depending on me. Trusting me to do the right thing, be on time, and not screw up.

I catch a whiff of gasoline and hear the faint rumble of an engine behind me as I open the red Jeep door and stretch for the cell phone. I dial quickly, hoping that my husband answers.

"You've reached Mitchell Carson . . ."

A heavy footstep crunches on the pebbled pavement behind me. I hang up and whirl around, nerves already frayed.

"Ava?"

Disbelief hits me. I take in the broad shoulders and smartly pressed uniform and erupt with emotion at the pure, dumb luck of finding Officer Mike Kennedy next to my broken-down Jeep. Between sobs, I squeeze out an explanation. "Jack . . . the school . . . accident."

Mike holds up a calloused hand to stop me. He's rescued me more than once. "Whoa! Slow down, Ava." His forehead wrinkles. "He's at Springhill Medical Center?"

Throat tight, I nod, trying to process what to do, what to say. Fingers trembling, I reach for the pink heart. Something to hold on to. A piece of Jack.

"I'll take you." Mike opens my door. In no time, he transfers Sam and his baby seat to the patrol car, straps us in, and gets back on the road.

The scenery whips by, a blur of trees and signs. I clutch my phone tight and try Mitchell again. *Voice mail.*

"Can't get through?" Mike asks.

I drop the phone into my lap and shake

25

my head.

Mitchell's job pulls him in ninety different directions at once. My husband's a newly minted college vice president of advancement and somehow balances all of his responsibilities with finesse. My heart still stops when I see him. My husband has the voice, the look, and the irresistible charm of a George Clooney twin.

It's not all roses, though. With baby Sam, our marriage is more difficult than I ever expected. Life's busier, more exhausting, juggling diapers and soccer games. We're both getting less sleep. But that's normal, right? Our date nights, which used to be weekly, are nonexistent. Making love during stolen lunch hours doesn't happen anymore. And instead of talking about the symphony or the latest bestseller, we discuss schedules.

I push the thoughts away. Everyone goes through a rough patch. I glance over at Mike instead and study the scar below his hairline. Ten stitches from a nasty tumble near the creek bank when we were just children. He never cried.

"Jack will be okay, Ava. He's a tough kid," Mike assures me, eyes on the road. His thick-knuckled hands rest on the wheel. Protect and serve. His mantra as long as I've known him. Even as a child, he knew he wanted to be a police officer. Mike has always been reliable, predictable, steady. A rock. Even on the worst days.

We pull up to the ER doors. Mike slams the cruiser into park. Police scanner static fills the air with letters and codes. "Hey, duty calls," Mike says. "I'll get a tow truck over shortly. Go in there and find your boy."

I scoop up Sam, unbuckle his seat.

Hold on, Jack.

CHAPTER 3
JACK

WEDNESDAY, MARCH 24

EMTs put me on a stretcher, shove me into an ambulance, and slam the thick, metal doors shut. The engine cranks up, spewing a cloud of exhaust, and we scream out of the parking lot, sirens going, all of the lights flashing.

If I were The Flash, we'd be there already, since he thinks and moves at superhuman speeds. No stopping for red lights or sticking to roads or speed limits. I'd never have to do this crazy roller-coaster ride to the hospital. I grip the sides of the stretcher as the driver turns like he's on two wheels. Everything, including me, leans to the right. We speed up, swerve to the left, and stop suddenly in front of the emergency room.

I squint at the bright sunshine as the back doors fly open. The EMTs pull me out of the ambulance, push me down a painfully bright hallway, and park me in the ER. The

Flash would have just jetted through the walls using vibration. Problem solved. But since I'm in the ER, and not a science lab that'll be hit by lightning, the chances of me turning into the new Flash today aren't great. There's always next time, right?

I press my neck against the pillow, shifting to look around. Everything's white, shiny clean, and new. It's almost like a fancy hotel, except for the machines and little buttons making robotic beeps. There's a gross antiseptic smell, too, but I decide it isn't so bad after a while. My jaw hurts a lot, though, and there's thick tape and a big bandage on my chin. A tall, silver IV pole and tubes sit next to the bed, but luckily no one's come in to stick me in the arm yet.

A few seconds later, a burly man in scrubs walks in and throws a salute my way.

"How's our favorite stunt man?" he booms. The floor almost shakes. His hand clasps my shoulder and squeezes. Make him golden orange and built from stone, he'd be exactly like Ben Grimm, *The Thing* of Fantastic Four.

"Hey, Dr. Max."

Behind his thick glasses, one huge gray eye winks. He bends closer to get a better look at my chin. Dr. Max peels back the gauze and whistles out loud at the gash.

"Good job. Part of our frequent-flyer program now?"

"Frequent-what?" I tilt my head, and the paper behind my neck crackles.

"Never mind," he laughs. "What's the latest count?"

I rattle off my list: "Um, one broken leg — tree house; two sprained ankles — soccer; three bruised ribs — swing set; a fractured wrist — monkey bars; sixteen stitches in my left arm — chain-link fence; seven more on my right hand — glass window." I pause. "Did I miss anything?"

"I think you've got it covered." Dr. Max glances at my chart and smiles at me. "Any more visits and we'll have to put a plaque on the wall with your name on it."

The idea kind of makes my stomach churn. "Uh." I think of when my mom died. It rained and everything smelled like dirt. Everyone was crying, except me. I made myself into a rock so I didn't have to feel anything.

I rub at my eyes, hard, and try to forget it. It doesn't work.

"Don't you do plaques like that for dead people?" I ask.

Dr. Max raises his eyebrow. "Ah, Jack." He winks. "Don't worry about that. Your plaque would be of an honorary nature — a special award."

"Oh." I consider this and lean back against the fluffy pillow. "That sounds okay."

Dr. Max scribbles something on a chart. "Keep that gauze on there now, the lidocaine will help numb the area. We'll give it a few more minutes to work."

Dr. Max and I both look up as an office lady from my school pulls back the nubby curtain and steps inside. She smells like roses and baby powder, even from a few feet away.

"Anne dear, is someone from Jack's family on the way?" Dr. Max asks.

My memory snaps back. Of course. Miss Anne from school and Dr. Max are married.

She bobs her head and tugs at a thick rope of pearls. "Any moment now." She looks worried and small, standing nearby in her navy blue dress.

My stomach lurches. "Who's coming?" I ask, pressing against the bed to sit up taller. "Please tell me you called my dad. It's kind of a rule. He likes to know everything first, even if he can't make it."

"Um, sweetie," she says. "The principal had some trouble getting in touch with your dad. But your mom will be right here." Miss

Anne stumbles. "Ava . . . I mean your step-mom."

I grin. "Ava adopted me," I say. "Well, we adopted each other. That's what she says. It was final and all last week. Dad took us out for a big dinner to celebrate."

"Jack, I knew Ava when she was just a little girl in pigtails. She's a keeper." The overhead pager crackles. "Listen, champ, I'll be back in a few minutes to put in those stitches." Dr. Max salutes again and disappears into the hallway.

"I'm so happy for you all." Miss Anne claps her hands. "Now, if she'd just come back to school . . ."

I roll my eyes. "Not gonna happen. My dad won't let —" I stop. A warning sign flashes bright red — TMI — too much information. "She's staying home with Sam."

"Of course." Miss Anne, who's staring at me, coughs into her hand. "Yes. Right. I'm sure your father knows what's best for her and the baby. We just miss her."

I gulp and grip the sheet. For a second, I think about life without Ava.

"Yeah, I would too."

CHAPTER 4
AVA

WEDNESDAY, MARCH 24

The Springhill ER lobby swarms with people, a busy hive of activity, with nurses buzzing from station to station and at least two dozen people waiting in the lobby. When I give my name to the woman behind the front desk, there's a swell of chatter from a family in the corner and a blare of music announcing the latest CNN headlines on the flat screen above our heads.

Sam begins to fuss, emitting the baby whimpers that immediately tell me he's overstimulated and exhausted. I hug him to my chest, bouncing him up and down, and begin humming "The Itsy-Bitsy Spider" in his ear.

Poor little guy. I get it. The noise and confusion, mixed with the scent of day-old coffee and sweat, is enough to push me over the edge.

I step back, trying to ease my way into a

quieter corner, and promptly crush someone's toe with my shoe. "I'm so sorry."

The man behind me flashes a brilliant smile. "My fault," the stranger apologizes. "It's a zoo in here and I wasn't watching where I was going."

Our gaze locks and I find myself temporarily mesmerized. His eyes are the most intense silver-gray I've ever seen, like a sliver of moonlight.

"Mrs. Carson?" The receptionist announces.

"Oh!" My body floods with relief, and I hug Sam and rush toward the exam rooms. As one of the ER workers leads us down a hallway, I glance over my shoulder to say good-bye, but the man with the silver eyes has disappeared.

We step into a bustling ER, maneuvering around nurses and doctors.

"Ava! Sam!" Jack calls out the moment he sees us.

I paste on a brave smile, taking in the streak of blood on his shirt, the purple bruise staining the side of his cheek, and the dirt in his hair. None of it matters. He's all right.

"Hey." I kiss his forehead, inhaling the scent of fresh grass and earth. I bend my head to get a better look at Jack's chin. The

34

skin gapes at the corners of the gash. "Oh my."

I glance down at Sam, who's lodged a finger between his gums and is staring intently at his older brother. "Ja," he says.

Dr. Max laughs and holds up his blue-gloved hands. "That's what I thought. You're just in time for the big show."

I step back from the bed, casually, so as not to embarrass Jack, but inside I quiver with relief. I can't imagine a day, a minute, without Sam and Jack. Everything that defined my "before kids" life somehow seems irrelevant.

I stroke Sam's downy-soft head and drink in the scent of baby lotion. Before he was born, other moms always shared stories about the fierce love that surges in a woman the moment she gazes on her newborn's face. How childbirth pain disappears, replaced by an intense need to care for and protect this amazing creature at all costs. It's so true, but the remarkable thing is this: no one mentioned it could happen the other way around. The same bond can form — just as deeply, just as strongly — when a child without a mother finds you first. It happened with Jack, which makes me doubly blessed. A precious baby and an adorable son. How lucky can one woman get? They're my world. Which is probably why Mitchell teases me relentlessly that he's neglected.

In fairness, I've pointed out several times that a spouse has to be *home* to get attention. His reply? He wasn't quite ready for baby number two. A fact he divulged right about the time morning sickness hit me full force.

A little. Too. Late.

I hold Sam a little tighter, melding his body to mine. I'm positive Mitchell will come around. Sam is his legacy. Just like Jack.

The sound of an ambulance siren reverberates outside the building. A ruckus of crash carts and moving bodies erupts in the hallway.

"Ready, champ?" Dr. Max nods at Jack while he leans him back on the table, then looks up at me. "He reminds me of you, Ava, back in high school. A little bit of a free spirit, eh?" He begins suturing Jack's chin.

"What happened?" Jack shifts his eyes to me. "Tell me!"

"Hold still, babe," I mock-threaten, wagging a finger. "And Dr. Max, you're under a gag order. No spilling any secrets. It's been one of those days."

Dr. Max raises an eyebrow as he stitches. "What happened?"

My neck prickles as I shrug. "Flat tire," I say, curving my lips into a smile to hide the worry. "Thank goodness for Mike Kennedy."

Dr. Max grins, snipping a piece of thread. "Police escort, eh? Nice. Not everyone gets one."

"Ha-ha." I wink as Jack smirks and rolls his eyes at me from the table.

"You made it here, didn't you?" Dr. Max looks at me, then back down, as he finishes another suture.

"More than I can say for Dad," Jack mutters under his breath.

This stabs at my heart. "Jack," I chide, then soften my voice. "I'm sure he's busy finishing up plans for the sports complex." I glance down at his face. "Your dad's been working so hard getting it together."

"That's what everyone says."

Dr. Max straightens up and claps Jack on the shoulder. "Well, we're done. No coming back here for at least a year. And make that a social visit."

"I'll try." Jack jumps to the floor. "See, good as new!" He pretends to give Sam a high five. His brother claps in delight. "Dr. Max, can I play Friday? Last game of the

37

season."

"Bandage that chin up really well if you do," Dr. Max says sternly. "There's a chance you could rip the sutures. However, I'll leave that decision up to Ava and your dad."

"Thanks so much, Dr. Max." I reach out to squeeze his huge, rough hand, then turn to buckle Sam into his car seat carrier.

"Anytime." He rumples Jack's hair. "Look after Ava here, and your brother."

Jack grabs his backpack and throws it over one shoulder. "No problem. I will." In an unprecedented public show of affection, he interlaces his fingers with mine.

The floor gleams as we walk out. In the tiles, I see our wavy reflection. Sam cradled in my arms, me in the middle, Jack at my side. Connected.

Outside I take a deep breath of the warm spring breeze. The air, thick with honeysuckle, seems to welcome us.

"Let's see if we can grab a cab to the repair shop," I suggest. "It's not far."

"Sure, but what's Dad gonna say?" Jack frowns.

I pause. "About the Jeep or your chin?" I ask, readjusting Sam's carrier in the crook of my arm.

"My chin," he replies. "I'll bet he'll be pissed."

Stiffening, I frown. "Jack, don't say that word," I say. "Upset, maybe. Annoyed, probably. He's under a lot of pressure at work, but he loves you. He'll get over it. He always does."

"But why does he get so mad sometimes? It's not like I'm trying to get in trouble." Jack stares at his feet as we start to walk again.

My chest tightens. "You know, I guess your dad wants everything to be perfect." I wrap an arm around Jack and give him a quick squeeze. "And that's a tough assignment. Perfect."

"He's not," Jack shoots back, his face dark.

I put a finger to my lips. "It's true, but don't tell him that," I say. "It'll be our little secret."

Jack grimaces instead and kicks at the sidewalk. He stares into the cracks, traces the edge with the toe of his tennis shoe. In that moment, the frightened kid I met nearly three years ago reappears. Confused. Hurt. That Jack doesn't come around often these days.

"Hey, think about this instead. That scar will make you look all grown up, actually. Tough. Clint Eastwood-y. *Dirty Harry.*"

"Um, Clint Eastwood's old, Ava." Jack untangles himself and tries to make a serious face but ends up laughing. "Maybe Robin or Nightwing."

My shoulders relax. "Okay, okay." I pretend to pull away from him. "Just trying to make you feel better."

"Thanks." He chuckles. "It's kinda working."

I stop walking and face him. "Jack Carson, I love you no matter what."

His face softens. The words, somehow, are magic, a salve. "No matter what?"

"Absolutely." I solemnly cross my heart. Corny, but I don't care. "I promise."

CHAPTER 5
AVA

WEDNESDAY, MARCH 24

At exactly six o'clock, my husband walks in the door, smiling and apologetic. Somehow, after a full day at the office, Mitchell still manages to look close to perfect. Suit unwrinkled, every hair in place, devastatingly handsome.

"Sorry I missed your calls, sweetheart," Mitchell says, arching his brow. He closes the door and loosens his tie. "Can you believe my cell was in my briefcase? The ER folks finally called the office."

When Mitchell strides over and takes me in his arms, I melt. His hands find the small of my back and pull me close. My fingers trace his muscled back

"Hey, stranger," I murmur and kiss his lips. He smells delicious and earthy. "Dinner's almost ready."

Mitchell turns to examine Jack's bandaged chin. "Hey, big guy, let me look at that war wound." My husband draws his head back in mock horror. We all laugh.

I gaze at the two of them. Jack is, without a doubt, Mitchell's mirror image: coal-black hair, same strong jaw, eyes deep and dark as the night sky.

Mitchell crosses his arms. "No more superhero stuff, you hear me?" he says. "Save it for the game Friday. Gotta win, right?"

"Yes, sir." Jack grins and grabs an oatmeal raisin cookie off the cooling rack.

Mitchell bends down and tugs a lock of Sam's hair. The baby babbles in delight, then utters a confused cry as his father abruptly turns his back and walks away.

I grip the counter, blinking after my husband.

Next to my feet, Sam whimpers, a sure sign he's about to launch into a full-out meltdown unless I intervene.

I squat down, pick up Sam, and smile brightly before I press him to my chest. "It's okay, love," I murmur as I nuzzle his soft skin. Sam settles down as I rock him back and forth.

When I look up, Mitchell is watching me, forehead creased. When our eyes meet, he grins and resumes a jovial tone. "So an exciting day all around," he teases.

My stomach knots, but I fight the anxiety. We need a nice, quiet evening.

"A little too much excitement," I say, adjusting Sam onto my hip so that I can pour the sweet tea. "Frantic phone calls and an ER visit aren't my idea of fun." I set the salad on the table and wink at Jack. "No more of those, young man."

Jack smiles through a mouthful of cookie.

"This kid's been full speed since the day he could walk," Mitchell says. "We've always been rough and tumble, haven't we, son?" He grins at Jack. "When I helped coach pee-wee soccer, you were a terror on the field. Those were some good times!"

I lift Sam into his high chair, then glance at Jack, who's not saying a word. He's staring off into space, chewing the last bite.

"Jack?" I prompt.

"Good times," he echoes, slides into his seat, and gives me a tired smile. Jack provides instant replay to Mitchell on Emma's big rescue from the oak tree, and his second trip to the ER this year. He downplays the chin gash and rattles off a dozen reasons why he should be allowed to play goalie in his last soccer game.

Before I get a chance to motion for him to stop, Jack tells his father the story about my flat tire and Officer Mike helping us out.

43

Mitchell's face darkens.

A chill snakes up my back. "It was nothing," I say lightly. "Let's eat."

We dig into dinner, and for the first time today, everyone around me is completely quiet, save for the clinking of silverware. In a matter of minutes, the tender pork chops, fluffy corn bread, and bowl of buttery black-eyed peas have all but disappeared. Jack pushes back from the table, stands up, and stretches.

"Homework?" I ask.

"Yes, ma'am." Jack starts heading for the bedroom. "And I need to find some pictures for a school project," he calls from down the hall. "Could you help me later?"

"Sure," I reply. "It's not for tomorrow, is it?" I hold my breath and smile at Mitchell.

"No, ma'am," he yells back. "Next week." Jack closes his bedroom door.

"Whew!" I press my hand to my forehead.

As I get up from the table, Mitchell stands and pulls me close. He presses his lips to my forehead, murmurs into my hair, and slides a hand down my back. "My sweet Ava. Poor thing."

"Wish you could have been there today."

"I know," Mitchell answers, his voice gruff. "But, see, it's better that you stay at home. One of us is always available."

"I know. I'm thankful." I untangle myself and pick up Sam to wipe his face. "But I do miss the kids at the school. The day-to-day. The adult conversation. You know they said I could come back whenever I wanted."

Mitchell frowns and leans into the doorframe. "It's not really a good time, Ava."

"I know." I purse my lips and carry Sam to the bathtub, start running the water.

When we first began dating, Mitchell spent every spare moment with me. We'd drive to Dauphin Island and walk on the beach, spend an afternoon poking around in shops downtown, or spend a Friday evening visiting art galleries in Fairhope. We talked about children and the future. We discussed politics and religion, the state of education in Alabama. Where we saw ourselves, personally and professionally, in five and ten years.

Mitchell wanted to know everything about me. My hopes, fears, and dreams. What frightened me, what I loved. The attention was overwhelming and wonderful; his concern for me was mesmerizing. Mitchell wanted nothing more than to take care of me.

Looking back, I realize that I was the one doing most of the talking and sharing. If I asked a tough question, Mitchell would change the subject. If I pressed him about his mother or father, he'd pretend he hadn't heard me.

After the wedding, I was certain he'd relax and settle into our relationship. I just knew that Mitchell would open up and share his secrets. But fast-forward, and nothing's changed. Two years later, there's so little I really know about my husband.

Mitchell follows me to the bathroom, taps his fingers on the wooden doorframe. "What happened with the contractor?"

I feel the heat of my husband's stare but concentrate on lowering Sam into the bath-water. "I couldn't meet him. There wasn't time," I add. "With Jack, and the tire on the Jeep . . ."

My husband exhales. There's a beat of silence. And another.

"You need to sell the Jeep. It's ten years old. Get something practical. An SUV. A minivan. A Mercedes."

"I like my Jeep," I protest.

Mitchell exhales. "*Mike Kennedy* had to give you a ride to the hospital."

I lather Sam's slippery body and swallow. "Mitchell, he was just helping out."

"Oh, right. Officer Mike, always to the rescue." He rolls his eyes.

"Please, don't be like that," I whisper and

glance down at Sam, who's splashing happily. "He helped *your* family today. Give him a chance. We've turned down, what, three dinner invitations from Mike and Marley?"

My husband's shoulders relax and his frown disappears. "I just love you so much, Ava. I want you all to myself, sweetheart."

I can't help but smile. "I love you too. And you have me all to yourself. See? Wish fulfilled."

Mitchell lowers his voice. "I don't trust many people," he reminds me. "It's just my nature to look out for you and protect my family. You're so important to me. You're my everything. Just remember that, okay?"

"Okay," I echo and smile brightly to reassure him.

Mitchell softens at my affirmation. He nods and steps out. "I'll be in the library."

I wrap Sam in a towel and dry him off. Mitchell's just stressed. The more pressure he's under, the more quickly he flashes to anger. It's been worse lately because of the sports complex project. But the capital campaign is almost finished. One more donor to go.

Sam yawns. I slip him into his fuzzy pajamas in his bedroom and cuddle him on my lap. After *Goodnight Moon,* then *Runaway Bunny,* he drifts off to sleep.

Gently, carefully, I lay him on his back in his crib. *Good night, sweet baby.*

Jack tiptoes in, throws his arms around my waist. "G'night." He yawns and turns to leave, then trips over something hard.

"Whoa!" I catch him midfall.

He leans over, picks up a book, and screws up his face. Jack holds it out and stares intently, like it's a book on Jack the Ripper. Not even close. The story is about a mouse.

"What is it?" I whisper.

Jack shakes his head, his eyes tearing. "Nothing." He sticks the book under his arm, leaves without a backward look, closing his bedroom door behind him.

In Sam's room, I stand still, completely bewildered. When Jack doesn't reappear, I steal into the library, grab a pillow, and hug it to my chest before sinking into the love seat next to Mitchell. "They're finally in bed."

For a moment, I let my eyes wander along the wall. My collection of pregnancy books, baby manuals, and volumes of child-rearing advice take up two shelves. There are photos of Sam, Jack, Mitchell, and me. Candid shots, Christmas morning, the beach, soccer games.

My husband looks up. "Something the matter?"

"It's just strange." I sigh. "Jack stopped by Sam's room. This book I bought was lying on the floor. When he saw it, he got really upset, took it, and shut himself in his room."

Mitchell raises an eyebrow. "What book?"

"Just something I picked up the other day. Great illustrations. *Beach Mouse Magic,* I think it's called. Not like it was *Goosebumps* or pop-up vampires."

Mitchell readjusts on the seat to look at me squarely. "Do you remember me telling you his mother was an artist?"

A bitter taste fills my mouth, the sting of grapefruit. "Of course."

His gaze drops. "Well . . . if it's the same series I'm thinking of, Karen did the illustrations."

"Oh no." I bite my lip and want to cry. Tears sting at the corners of my eyes.

"Karen used to read those books to Jack every night. Before she left."

Wiping at my cheeks, I hesitate for a moment, then tuck myself close to my husband. We sit, breathing in sync, lost in our thoughts.

"It wasn't on purpose," I finally say. My mind tumbles end over end. First Mitchell and his jealousy about Mike. Now Jack is upset too.

"I know."

"I never would have —"

"Shh." Mitchell stops me. "Don't worry. He'll be fine."

I put my head on his chest. "I'd never hurt him like that," I murmur. "Never."

CHAPTER 6
MITCHELL

THURSDAY, MARCH 25

I click through the Seaside, Florida, website, bookmarking idyllic beachside properties and scanning reviews of best places to dine and shop in the quaint Gulf Coast community. The postcard-perfect photos of azure sky and powder-white sand make my heart pang for Ava.

I miss my wife. The house, our children, my position at the college — everything competes for our time together. We have a few stolen moments, usually at midnight, in bed. Even then it's not unusual to be awakened by our one-year-old, Sam.

A long weekend away from everyone and everything is exactly what we need. Our own little cottage in paradise, where we'll recharge and reconnect. It's been forever since we've been really alone — two years — and that was for our honeymoon in Baja. I close my eyes and picture jagged sandstone rising from an ocean of indigo blue. Ava's tanned shoulders aglow under the sun's heat. We're surrounded by golden sand and can taste salty air on our lips.

We made love. Passionate, intense, and fierce at times. My fingers tangled in her red-blonde hair, pulling at the strands. Her soft skin, scented with cinnamon, was euphoric. My mouth sought her full lips hungrily, my hands tore at her cotton sundress. The gold clasps of her tiny bikini broke apart, clinking as the pieces hit the floor.

As I pressed my weight onto her, my mouth traveled down her shoulder, finding her perfect breast, and the curve of her hip. I took her with such intensity that the world fell away. I could no longer hear the chirp of birds, the crash of waves, the breeze rustling palm trees outside our window. We were one.

We've talked a dozen times about going back. To be fair, she knows a multitude of important issues are stopping me. With the new position at the college, there's always one more hurdle to jump, another fire to put out.

Tonight, however, I can breathe and plan out details for a weekend away while she's off with Sam at a neighbor's baby shower.

Narrowing my eyes, I glance at my watch. It's about time she should be getting home.

My neck prickles when my cell begins ringing. One glance tells me it's the school.

"Dr. Carson," I answer, striding over to the window, pulling the thick, silk draperies back to peer out into the darkness. The street's quiet, save for a lone neighbor walking his English bulldog. Streetlights pool silver on the newly-poured sidewalk, illuminating my edged yard, the slope of just-cut green grass.

"How could they? Where is it?" I demand. The curtains fall from my hand, and I turn away from the street.

The college mascot for Springport College has disappeared. The Spartan statue is a landmark, a glorious monument rising from the center of a marble pedestal. With his sword and a shield, the statue must weigh a quarter ton. It would take a legion of men and a massive truck to carry it off.

"Dammit." My footsteps pound back and forth, shaking the house. "It had better be back on campus in the next hour. I'll find out who did this and have them arrested. When I'm done, they'll wish they were never born."

When I hang up, I yank on my sport coat, readjust my tie, and call for Jack. When he

53

doesn't answer, I throw open his door, startling my son, who's deep into a Batman comic book, and wearing headphones. I reach in, grab him by the sleeve, and pluck the Beats off his head.

"We're going into the office. Now."

My son blinks up at me, clutching his comic book. "But I'm old enough to stay home by myself," Jack sputters.

I shake my head and let go, not giving the ridiculous declaration the courtesy of an answer. When I turn on my heel, he follows.

Downstairs I grab my gun from the safe and slip it into my briefcase. Springport campus safety officers don't carry weapons, and although it's unlikely, the last thing I want to do is come up against some meth addict who someone has mistaken for a student. Being an army brat has taught me to always err on the side of caution.

I slide into the Range Rover and grip the steering wheel, waiting for Jack to climb inside. When the door closes behind him, I crank the engine, flick on the high beams, and we take off, wheels kicking up stones as we turn out of the driveway.

The leather briefcase slides a few inches, closer to Jack's feet. Close enough for him to see inside. My son shifts in his seat. Without turning, I can now feel Jack's eyes drilling two perfectly round holes in the side of my head.

At a red light, we jerk to a stop.

"What's that?" my son asks.

My head begins to throb. "Protection." I turn the wheel and head up the hill that leads to the college. It's only about a mile away now.

Jack sinks lower in the seat, pressing himself against the door.

When we drive past the gates, I see the flashing lights.

Chapter 7
Jack

THURSDAY, MARCH 25

Dad slams the truck into park. "Stay here," he tells me and gets out. His door stays open, letting in gusts of cold, black air. He doesn't take the duffel bag or the gun.

Shivering, but not from the cool night, I watch as he walks over to the policemen. Mo's dad, Mike, is there in his uniform, along with some other sheriff's deputies I recognize from around town. I squint and try to see better, but can't tell if they've caught anybody.

Where are the college kids being questioned by the cops? Being led away in handcuffs? Or shoved up against the back of one of the squad cars?

If Thor showed up, he'd toss his enchanted hammer, Mjölnir, at the guys who took the statue, and they wouldn't have a chance. If anyone got away, he could slow them way down by starting a lightning, wind, and rain storm. All he has to do is pound the hammer's handle twice on the ground. If the bad guys decided to take on Thor, Mjölnir deflects bullets, and his Belt of Strength makes him practically unbeatable.

As a Norse god, Thor can also fly and move stuff — like a statue — and has the ability to pass through time. If my dad really wanted to get rid of whomever stole the Spartan, Thor could use his superstrength to launch them out of the Earth's atmosphere.

When I lift my chin up and look around, though, there's no huge muscled guy in a blue suit and red cape carrying a leather-bound hammer. I tuck my feet up under my legs and hug my knees to my chest. It's too bad. 'Cause I think Thor and I could be best friends.

For a long time, my dad talks to Mike. There's nothing for me to do but wait. I can't even listen to the radio because I don't have the keys.

After a while, I'm so bored that I lean my head against the truck and stare up at the sky. The moon's huge; it looks like every star in the universe is out. Even though the night looks magical and the air smells like just-washed sheets, I just want to go home. I close my eyes and think about my soft blanket, big pillow, and warm bed.

In my dream, someone is calling my name. "Jack! Jack, wake up, honey!"

I recoil as something grabs me. Blinking back sleep, I see Ava shaking me. Her face is all crunched up and she's holding Sam, who doesn't look happy either. Officer Mike stands beside her, arms crossed against his barrelchest, forehead crinkled up.

Before I can say a word, Dad stalks right up to Ava, his eyes flashing black with glints of silver. A sure sign he's angry.

"Excuse me," he barks at Officer Mike, who pauses before tipping his hat to Ava and stepping away.

"Listen," he begins, grabbing at Ava's shoulder.

Ava steps back and shakes her head. "We're going home, Mitchell."

My stomach corkscrews. Ava opens the truck door and waves at me to jump down.

"But, Ava —" My dad stops then and clenches his jaw.

Sam starts wriggling like a porpoise. His face screws up like he's just about to start wailing. It's way past his bedtime. I don't look at Dad, I just stare straight ahead and get into Ava's Jeep. She's got the top up and the heat blasting, so it feels about a hundred degrees warmer.

After she buckles Sam in and hands him his fuzzy brown bear, he quiets down. I give him my finger to hold, and he squeezes it with both hands, telling me "Ja-Ja-Ja" like a story. His curly hair is wild tonight, and there's a drooly shine on his bottom lip.

When we pull into the driveway and wait for the garage to open, Ava shakes her head one more time.

"Your dad shouldn't have dragged you out tonight." She turns around and looks at me.

I'm warm now and feel safe, so I smile and shrug. "No big deal," I say.

"Jack," she tells me. "Your dad doesn't like kids — anyone — messing with 'his' stuff on 'his' campus." Ava makes quotation marks with her fingers, but she's not making fun of him at all.

I nod. Yep. My dad has a temper sometimes. Like a button you press, and everything explodes. I'm used to it. She's not as much. Ava can say stuff, though. I can't. I lick my lips a little. "Was that . . . in his briefcase . . ." I don't want to say the word.

"Yes." She nods and closes her eyes tight. She puts a hand on her forehead and brushes hair from her face. "Believe me, I'm not happy about it."

In the back, Sam starts to kick. He's

impatient to be set free from all of the buckles and straps.

"Let's go inside, okay?" She ruffles my hair and tilts her head. "Don't worry about it. I'm going to get your brother to bed. We can all use some sleep."

Ava grabs Sam. I head for the house, brush my teeth, and change clothes. I grab another blanket and try burying myself under a mountain of covers, snuggling down deep.

I wake up again when I hear my dad come home. Ava must have been waiting for him in the kitchen, because I can hear them talking right away. And it's not happy words. My insides twist tight, like cooked spaghetti wrapped on a fork. I try not to listen, even put my head under the pillow, but then I can't breathe.

"What were you thinking, Mitchell?" Ava asks him.

My dad's voice muffles. I only catch half of what he's saying. "Going to protect . . ."

"Protect who . . . from what?" Ava cuts him off. She's totally upset, because she's all out of breath like she's about to cry. "From a bunch of kids . . . playing a silly prank? Really, Mitchell?"

My dad mumbles.

"And you were going to use — that gun?"

A chair scrapes against the floor in the kitchen and I can't hear my Dad.

Ava's voice gets louder. "I don't care. D-do you know that Jack asked me about it? He's only eight, Mitchell. Eight."

There's a bang, then, like something got slammed down on the table. My whole body jumps. Holding my breath, I pull the sheets up to my chin.

"What sort of *example* does that set for him?" she lowers her voice.

"The right kind," my father shouts back at Ava, and a chair scrapes against the floor.

It's dead quiet in the house now. Spooky-silent. I'm hoping they don't come into my room. If they do, I'll pretend to be asleep. Some of my friends say that their parents fight all of the time. I guess I'm lucky because Dad and Ava don't do it much.

I squeeze my eyes shut and try to think about soccer. About tomorrow's game. Maybe I'll score a goal. And the team will cheer for me. And that will make my dad happy.

If he'd just say he's sorry, Ava would be happy too. My dad's wrong this time. Even I know that. But he doesn't apologize. And I don't think that he ever will.

CHAPTER 8
JACK

FRIDAY, MARCH 26

The whistle shrieks. Time out. I float back to Earth and the soccer game. The team huddles up. We're ahead 4–0, so everyone's relaxed and a bit cocky. Coach urges us to keep our heads in the game. We clap once, yell, "Team!" and get back in position. I glance at the bleachers. Dad's there, proud smile, his arm around Ava, Sam in her lap.

Focus. I crouch down and shield my eyes from the sun's glare. My gloves rasp against my knees. A bee buzzes in circles around the goal posts. A cheer erupts from the other side. A player in red breaks away from the pack. His legs pump as he rushes toward me. The ball is a blur as he dances around defenders and breaks downfield.

Adrenaline courses through my arms, and I tighten every muscle to spring. I coil and ready myself to move, a trigger. We size each other up. He darts to the right; I match his movement. He cuts left, then back. I mirror him, hands outstretched.

A breeze gusts across the field, catches the ragged edges of the bandage on my chin. My face throbs and I hesitate. The ball stops under the kid's foot. He rears back and kicks with force. I glue my eyes to the ball's trajectory and leap to block the kick. Too late. My fingertips brush the leather. It falls behind me as I crash to the ground. The whistle blows.

I eat dirt. The game is now 4–1.

My teammates gather around. Mo offers a hand and pulls me to my feet. "S'all right, man. Tough break." Someone else slaps me on the butt. Another punches my shoulder.

I shake it off, brush blades of grass from my uniform, and wait. The clock ticks down another ten seconds. Halftime. We jog off the field. Before I can grab a Gatorade and collapse on the bench, Dad corners me. He towers over me and the other players like a giant on the field. He's still wearing his navy suit from work. His shoes gleam so much I can almost see my face in the shiny reflection.

"Jack, what was that?" he mutters under his breath.

Someone throws me a thick, raspy towel. I wipe sweat from my forehead. "A mistake."

"Is that what you call it?" I don't want to look up at him. His eyes get all dark and spooky when he's mad.

I shrug and sling the towel around my shoulders. A few teammates listen in, hanging close by to hear. My throat aches. I can almost taste the tangy, sweet Gatorade, but I have to wait, even though the last thing I need is my dad giving me pointers.

He played ball at Alabama and therefore believes he is the all-knowing God of all sports. And he cares about winning. A lot. Coming out on top. Being number one.

Dad tells everyone we're two of a kind, how we think the same way, like the same things. And it's somewhat true; up until the point he starts barking orders. It's like he can't just watch. He has to outthink the coach, the other team. If I interrupt, the lecture gets longer. I've learned this much: stand there and act interested.

Tweet! Coach blows the whistle, red-faced, motions for a team meeting.

With a raised eyebrow, Ava catches my eye from the sidelines. I push up the corners of my mouth so she doesn't worry about what Dad is doing. She gives me a thumbs-up.

"Gotta go, Dad."

"Fine, fine." He grabs my shoulder, pulls me close. It's so I'm the only one who can hear. "Pay attention. Start using this." Dad taps my forehead.

His touch thuds against my skull, and I recoil into myself.

"I'm not —"

He cuts in, puts his back to the coach, and lowers his voice. "Don't argue with me. Make excuses. That's a coward's way out." With that, my father turns and walks away.

Coward?

Stinging with disbelief, eyes lowered, I jog to the pack and take my place, wishing the whole time someone or something would swoop down onto the field and help me out.

It really happens on this show called *The Fairly Odd Parents.* Magical "godparents" Cosmo and Wanda — little people with wings and halos — follow this kid, Timmy, around, grant his wishes, and get him out of messes. How cool is that?

If some wish-granting relatives landed on the field right now, I know what I'd do. First, I'd ask to play soccer like David Beckham, just for one game. Score enough goals to make my dad's mouth hang open, and get awarded MVP. Then once I'd wowed my father, I'd make him pay more attention to what's important. My grades, Sam's first steps, the dinner Ava slaved over to make just right. I promise I won't even complain if she fixes broccoli.

Last, I'd have Wanda and Cosmo whip me up a memory eraser; pocket-sized, so bad thoughts and dreams just fade away, kind of like the faces on my old, worn-out Justice League T-shirt.

Going, going, gone.

CHAPTER 9
MITCHELL

FRIDAY, MARCH 26

I walk back to the stands, shielding my eyes from the afternoon sun as the second half begins. Ava's waiting, forehead furrowed, bouncing Sam on her knees.

"Everything okay?" she leans close and whispers. Her hair catches the sunlight as she gazes up at me. Her clear green eyes, flecked with gold, look like jewels. My wife is beautiful. Even more so when she's concerned.

I break into a smile. "Of course." I clap my hands together and rub them for warmth. The breeze sneaks down the collar of my jacket, giving me a chill.

Ava turns back to the game, letting out a little squeal when Jack makes an attempt on goal. The ball grazes the keeper's glove and rolls away from the net.

"Next time!" I shout, cupping my hand so that Jack can hear me. I grip my knee. He either won't acknowledge my encouragement or can't hear me, though I choose to go with the latter.

A smart child listens. And learns much from his father, especially. From the simplest tasks — crossing the street, telling time — to the most complex — excelling at sports, developing good study habits, and preparing for a successful career. You can't start too early.

I tilt my head toward Ava. "I tried to give Jack some motivation out there. Told him to get his head in the game and focus."

My wife raises an eyebrow. "How'd he take that?"

"Aw, he's a trooper," I say. "Look at him now." I point out to where Jack is driving down the field, passing back and forth with his teammate.

"It's important for him to know that I care. That I'm watching," I add. "I'm here at the game, cheering him on."

Ava nods and gives me a small smile, then hugs Sam to her chest. "Both of your boys love you."

I reach out, squeeze her fingertips, and lean close. "I won't be like my parents."

It's a story Ava has heard a million times. In the solar system of all relationships, my mother and father resembled an off-kilter

68

sun and planet, each rotating on its axis, but never in complete alignment. Too close, get burned. Too far, freeze to death.

When the pressure became too great for my mother, she imploded. My father, a great athlete, escaped by lecturing me on sports and conditioning. When on leave from the army, he'd take me to my own games, talking strategy and technique until he dropped me off at the locker rooms.

If I succeeded, I'd get a smile, a slap on the back, or a wink. If I failed, my punishment was silence. Black and deafening. For days. Which is why I challenge Jack, talk to him, motivate him through my words and my presence. I'm here. He matters. We're a team.

I can't become my father. It *has* to be different this time.

CHAPTER 10
GRAHAM

FRIDAY, MARCH 26

My nephew scored his first goal tonight. He's elated, and his team's dominating the field. He made striker this year and is clearly a valuable asset to the forward line.

I grin, clap, and whistle, making the shrill pitch sound over two soccer fields.

Truth be told, this soccer game is my first crack at any social life in Mobile, Alabama, outside my nephew's birthday party. I scan the crowd for my brother, but it's halftime and he's buried ten people deep.

It's a warm afternoon, even for March, with the air off the Gulf of Mexico hanging thick and heavy overhead. The sky, painted postcard blue, is punctuated only by the occasional wisp of clouds. I lean against the trunk of a thick oak, my hand gripping the rough bark. My knee throbs from standing so long. For the millionth time, I curse my next-to-useless joint and dig in my jeans for

Advil. The concession stand is close, and the sweet, spicy scent of grilled hot dogs fills my nose. Balanced out with a tall, icy cold Coke, it's the closest I'll get to heaven this morning. At least that kind of temptation won't get me in trouble with anyone, except a cardiologist.

And I don't need problems. Of any kind. Yeah, I know. I'm different. A paranoid lawyer with a conscience. If you're asking why, the long version is complicated, but the quick answer is Vicodin. Those pills could erase Mother Teresa's devotion to Calcutta. Convince a person to sell his soul.

I know, because I did it. Ruined everything, had my law license suspended. Managed to keep my Harley and worked my ass off to regain a shred of self-respect. Thanks to my brother and Narcotics Anonymous, I'm clean two years, three months, and one day.

After a torn ACL playing flag football on spring break from law school, I got hooked on pain pills. Because my grades were stellar, I still managed to land a job at a big downtown Birmingham firm. The salary paid for my habit until the day I showed up to try a case under the influence.

It was only through the grace of God that one of the partners noticed and sent me straight home. His caveat? Check into rehab that week. I was later politely and quietly asked to resign, but didn't lose my license. I could have lost everything. Mobile is my second chance. And I'm not going to screw it up. This time I'm one of the good guys.

I take my place in line, check for my wallet. The baby in front of me catches my eye and starts to babble in my direction. He's adorable and chubby with the sort of blush-pink cheeks grandmothers like to pinch. The woman holding him has long hair, shining gold-red in the fading sunshine.

It hits me then. The woman and her baby. From that day in the hospital.

It's her turn at the counter. "Hey, y'all. One Coke, a hot dog, and a small popcorn."

It's clear she knows everyone. They banter back and forth while she reaches for her purse.

She hesitates, studying my face with wide bottle-green eyes. "Have we met before? You look so familiar."

"Springhill Medical Center," I remind her. "I think you crushed my foot."

Her face lights up and she starts to laugh. "That's right," she replies. "My son, Jack, was getting stitches that day. Of course he's right back out on the field."

I watch as she gestures to the soccer field.

She's all-American beautiful. Delicate features, long eyelashes, and a sprinkle of freckles. Her son is a mirror image.

"I'm Ava Carson and this is Sam." The baby lifts his arm in my direction.

I lean forward, catching Sam's fingers. With a soft grip, I move his tiny palm up and down. "Graham Thomas. Nice to meet you, Sam. And your mommy."

The baby grins and chortles. Ava giggles and nuzzles the baby. "Sam, are you making conversation?"

"You bet," I joke, wanting, somehow, to keep the conversation going. "He's lamenting about junk food calories and the nation's rising obesity level."

"Really?" She raises an eyebrow and grins. "You got all that from my son?"

"You should hear what else he tells me," I joke.

We both laugh as the girl behind the counter calls out Ava's order. I ask for my own Coke, grab her tray and balance it on one hand.

"Let me." I pay for my drink and follow her to a set of picnic tables.

She pauses on the end of the row and our eyes lock again. Ava looks away quickly, and I catch the flash of a huge diamond on her left hand. Right. *Behave, Graham.*

"Want to join us?" she asks, tilting her head and pulling Sam close on her lap. She sweeps a stray strawberry blond hair from her cheek, slips it behind one ear. She wipes her hands on a napkin and unwraps the hot dog. "So, you're new in town?"

"Is it that obvious?" I remember the Advil, pop it in my mouth, and sit. Sliding my drink close, I leave space enough for her husband and Big Foot to settle in.

She flashes an apologetic look. "Sorry. Might as well wear a sign and flashing lights."

While we make small talk, I notice Ava watching the parking lot. She begins to look worried, and I shift my eyes in that direction. Next to a black Range Rover, a tall, dark-haired man is on the phone, pacing, deep in conversation. He's dressed in an immaculately pressed white shirt, red tie, and dark slacks. I glance down at my beat-up khakis, until I realize Ava's watching me.

She takes a dainty bite of hot dog, closes her eyes blissfully. "This is so amazing," she murmurs, smothering a big smile. "Nothing like a big juicy hot dog. Don't let anyone see."

When I move to block her from the crowd, she grins.

"Thanks. It's my tiny bit of rebellion." She pauses and presses a napkin to her lips. Her voice is soft and musical, with a touch of a honeyed southern accent. "You know, anything this good has to be horrible for me. Ladies should only eat lettuce."

"That's a rule?" I play along.

"For the last two hundred years," she teases. "So where do you work?"

"I run my own business. Just getting started." *She probably hates lawyers.* No need to spoil this. I hand her a card, face down.

"Great. Thanks." Ava tucks it away. A whistle blows, long and loud. Game time again. Her eyes dart from the ball field to the Range Rover.

She puts a hand to her lips. The next thing I know, the man by the Range Rover opens the door, climbs inside, and guns the engine. The tires dig into the dark red dirt, kicking up small clouds of dust as he drives away.

What the hell?

"You'll have to excuse us." Pink-cheeked, Ava stands up and hoists Sam to her hip. His tiny foot grazes the popcorn, spilling the contents of the bag. Puffed kernels scatter around her hot dog and Coke as she steps over the bench and hurries away.

I can't help but watch her leave. The

sunshine on her hair, the curve of her hip, the way her arms wrap around the baby. She's talking to Sam, tilting her head to look at his face. Then, she steps into the crowd and disappears.

Damn. My appetite vaporizes. Ava's husband must be out of his mind.

CHAPTER 11
AVA

FRIDAY, MARCH 26

Sam, rag-doll tired and fussy, finally plops his head on my shoulder. A dull ache travels down the small of my back. It's growing dark, and the cicadas greet the evening with a loud, chirping chorus. The final glow of tonight's brilliant sunset, dark reds and purple, fades into the night through the branches of giant oak trees high above us.

I'd turned down several rides home, thinking my husband would be back any minute. It's been almost two hours. Dinnertime, and the thought of grilled steak sets my stomach rumbling. I'm afraid to even ask Jack if he's hungry, as I have nothing to feed him or Sam. I'm stuck at a dusty soccer field with a baby, an eight-year-old, and no vehicle.

I am baffled, hurt, and a little scared. For a moment, I think about how easy life used to be before I was a wife and mother of two. People tell you that marriage and mother-

77

hood are the hardest job in the world. Naive me, I didn't believe it.

As if he can read my thoughts, Sam whimpers, reaches for a handful of my hair, and pulls. I take it as a reminder to be thankful for my blessings despite the mess I'm in. Message delivered. Gently, I untangle the strands from his chubby fingers, rubbing my nose with his and making him laugh. "Love you," I murmur.

It's then I notice that Jack has edged at least three feet away. Shoulders hunched, he's scuffing the dirt with the toe of his cleat. Biting my lip, I step closer and rub his damp head.

"Good game today, honey," I say. "You really tried hard."

Jack shrugs and doesn't answer. The loss was devastating, and his silence pierces my heart.

I try again. "You're sure your dad didn't say where he was going?" I ask.

He frowns and continues poking the dirt. "Nope."

An invisible wall shoots up between us. This is the old Jack. Lonely, lost, and wounded.

As the school counselor at Mobile Prep, it was my job to know about the kids who needed extra attention, the students who were failing, the teenagers having trouble at home. In Jack's case, it was simple — he was new to the school — and didn't quite fit in yet.

The week school started that year was insane. Over the course of five days, a pregnant teen from a devout Catholic family confessed she'd made an appointment for an abortion. Our salutatorian — with at least a dozen full-ride college scholarships — joined the Marines but couldn't figure out how to break it to his parents. Worst of all, someone stuffed peanuts into the sandwich of a highly allergic kid. Guess who wielded the EpiPen? That's right. Yours truly.

Jack Carson wasn't nearly as overt. He didn't draw any attention to himself, walled off the world, and didn't make friends. He wasn't adjusting. He wasn't happy. It was time to check in with his father about my concerns. When I contacted Dr. Mitchell Carson, his cheerful assistant answered on the first ring and put me through.

"I'm so glad you called," he said, his deep voice resonating in my ear after listening to a brief explanation. When I asked if he'd like to come by the school and discuss any issues in more detail, Mitchell didn't hesitate.

"I'm between meetings," he replied. "Give me ten minutes."

Good as his word, Dr. Carson arrived with time to spare. He filled the doorway with his broad shoulders and an air of confidence that commanded attention.

"Jack is a wonderful child. I love him dearly." Mitchell sat down and smoothed his tie. His dark eyes were steady. "What I'm about to share should help explain some of his behavior."

I listened, intent on absorbing every detail. Jack's mother died in a tragic car crash. They were college sweethearts. Mitchell's own father passed away soon after — another huge loss almost too much to bear.

"When the position at Springport came open, the timing couldn't have been better," Mitchell told me, the sparkle returning to his eyes. It was exactly what he'd been searching for. He and Jack moved to Mobile. Since then he'd been valiantly attempting to juggle the new job, a new home, and getting to know staff, students, and community leaders. And of course, taking care of Jack.

"Life as a single dad," Mitchell told me, "is more difficult than running a college." He sat back in the chair and shook his head, rueful.

Mitchell did say Jack had signed up for soccer, which was encouraging. They had gone hiking and fishing just last weekend. Anything to help, he explained. Anything to get his mind off his mother and grandfather.

"It sounds like you're doing all of the right things," I told him. "Giving Jack your time and attention means a lot, especially after such losses."

When I asked about any specific issues, Mitchell didn't get the slightest bit defensive. Depression, mood swings?

On the contrary, his father insisted. And his grades were fine.

"I'll watch out for Jack and stay in touch," I promised.

"I appreciate that," Mitchell said and checked his watch. "I've got to get back."

"If there's anything else, just let me know." We both stood up. I handed him one of my cards. Mitchell took it, and then hesitated.

"Well, it's probably harmless," he replied. "But Jack's developed this fascination — with superheroes." Mitchell confided this like we'd shared a secret. "I wanted to mention it."

"Thanks for telling me," I said and paused for a moment. "It's not unusual, you know," I said.

Mitchell nodded.

"It's natural for kids to look for heroes; real or imaginary," I added. "Everyone needs a little hope when life gets rough, don't you think?"

We both fell silent.

"It's like Jack wants to save the world," Mitchell finally said, looking thoughtful.

I smiled. "Don't we all?"

We're still waiting for Mitchell. *Clink! Clunk!* Jack kicks at loose stones, head down. Puffs of dust cloud his ankles. I don't press Jack further about the game or his father. If he needs to talk, I'll be ready to listen.

Sam stretches and babbles. His voice echoes across the empty soccer field, just as Mitchell's Range Rover rolls into sight. Thank God.

Jack double-times it to the truck and jumps inside. I heave the door open with one hand and buckle Sam in tight. The crickets chirp a farewell song as we drive off into the silver-edged moonlight.

The truck rumbles toward home. Usually, Mitchell reaches for my hand, gives my fingers a squeeze. This time the distance between us is wide and cold. I trace the outline of the window with my finger, trying to decide what to say.

Finally, I break the silence. "Want some?"

I offer my pack of gum to Jack. He grabs a stick, unwraps it; I do the same. When things get stressful, it's our reminder. A simple trick Jack and I share. The 5 on the package says it all. Take five minutes. Breathe. *This too shall pass.*

Jack picks up his iPod, sticks in his earphones. Sam dozes in the back.

Mitchell stares straight at the black road ahead.

"So, honey, where were you?" I finally ask. "You didn't pick up when I called. The kids are exhausted. Jack has school tomorrow."

He doesn't reply.

"I tried a few times," I continue. "We were getting worried." I let my finger graze his arm. "You didn't forget about us, did you?"

Mitchell snaps back, forceful and sharp. "I'm off managing a major incident at the college, and you want to complain about me being late? That's perfect." He grips the wheel.

Shaken, I pull down the sun visor and check the boys. Jack slams his eyes shut. *He's listening.*

"Sorry. Let's not argue." I bite my lip and lean back. "The kids are still awake."

Mitchell nods and slides his arm across the seat. He squeezes my hand tight, his version of a peace offering.

He clears his throat. "Spoke to the contractor today."

I swing my head to look over at my husband. "Really? I thought he was gone."

Mitchell manages a small grin. "Never underestimate the power of determination. And payment in full, up front, for pushing our job to the front of their priorities. I just made them an offer they couldn't refuse."

I suck in a breath of air to calm the fluttering in my chest. "Oh, that's great!" I say, a little too brightly. "When will he start?"

"Monday." Mitchell doesn't offer any other details.

And I don't ask.

We're almost home. The canopy of trees opens wide to reveal a black velvet sky. In the distance, stars sparkle like diamond dust.

Our home seems to rise up from the ground as we round the corner, its white pillars glowing in the moonlight. The porch, wide and long, sprawls across the front of the manicured lawn. It's lovely, and too large for my tastes, but the zip code and country club location are necessary for his position at the college, Mitchell insisted.

We pull into the long driveway and the Range Rover settles to a stop.

Thirty minutes later, kids asleep, I steal

into the kitchen on tiptoes, uncork some wine. When I peek around the corner, I see Mitchell buried in a section of newspaper. "Want something to drink?"

He shakes his head, straightens the page. Mitchell rarely indulges; always been the type of man to grab beer at a barbecue and carry it around an entire evening. He says he doesn't like to lose control.

I pour myself a glass anyway, take a sip to calm my quivering nerves, then position myself in the chair across from my husband and stroke the knee of his pressed khakis. "Would you tell me what happened, please?"

Mitchell takes his time answering. He directs his gaze at me, then the window. "I'm hurt you'd insinuate I'd ever, ever, forget to pick up you or the boys. That's not me. Never." He clenches his fist. "My father may not have been around much. My mother . . . she couldn't —"

"Mitchell, don't," I say softly. I'm not certain if the army or his father get more blame for his unhappy childhood. His mother ended her loneliness by taking her own life.

"Well, I wouldn't do that." He shakes his head and shuts his eyes.

"All right. So what happened?"

Mitchell sits up, puts both elbows on his

knees, takes my hand in his. Heaves a sigh. "Elijah Marston pulled out of the campaign."

Shock tingles through me. This is a huge blow. "What?" Elijah Marston is a Springport grad with more money than Bill Gates. Mitchell had been certain about Elijah. His ace in the hole. The savior of Springport, he'd joked.

Mitchell nods, then taps his chin with two fingers. "He called me tonight. Said I had to drive over so that we could talk."

Elijah lives an hour or more away on a sprawling horse farm. No wonder Mitchell had been gone so long; though it didn't explain not calling me.

My mouth can barely form the words. "And now what?"

"That's it. He wanted to tell me right away." Mitchell frowns.

"I'm so sorry, honey." Tears sting my eyes. "That's terrible news. What will happen with the sports complex? There's no way to make your deadline now."

Mitchell pushes off the sofa. He draws himself up to his full height, stares down at me. "It's not over, Ava. I'm not giving up that easily. You, of all people, should know that."

"I didn't say —"

And just like that, he turns into a stranger. "Forget it." He stalks into the kitchen. "I think I'll have some of that wine after all."

"Okay," I murmur. *Good idea.* I pick up my glass and tilt it; watch the wine swirl, and tell myself Mitchell's mood has nothing to do with me. It's stress, just a bump in the road.

A cabinet opens and shuts. A drawer.

"By the way," Mitchell calls to me, off hand. "Can you pick up the dry cleaning tomorrow? I need that blue shirt. The one with the point collar."

I make a mental note. "Sure thing. Before I get Jack."

The faucet runs. A glass clinks on the counter. I hear Mitchell curse under his breath.

"Need something?" I get up and walk into the darkened kitchen. I flick on the lights, bathing the room in a soft glow. It's my favorite room in the house, with its high ceilings, crown molding, and gleaming stainless steel appliances. The boys love to hang out here while I cook, Jack sitting at the counter doing homework, Sam in his high chair eating Cheerios.

When I see the look on Mitchell's face, though, the charm and nostalgia of the space disappears. He glowers at me. "Did

87

you have to drink it all?" He gestures to the bottle, fingering the cork.

There's a beat or two of deafening silence. *What?* I examine the container. *Empty.*

"Or did you have some help?" Mitchell narrows his eyes. "That guy at the soccer park. I'm sure he'd love to share a glass or two."

"Mitchell, what are you talking about? That's not even reasonable."

"Right."

"You don't trust me?" I'm tense, and bewildered. Gone is the calm, collected guy who can charm even the grumpiest tollbooth operator. The man who buys flowers for no reason from city street vendors. Who loves me.

"You're home all day — you can do what you want."

I resist the urge to throw the comment back in his face. *You're the one who wants me home. The one who wrote the resignation letter, signed it, and mailed it without asking me.*

"Mitchell," I level my voice. "Listen. You're upset about the sports complex. You're worried about finding another donor. Keeping the project on track."

He stiffens. "Is that so? I'm glad your telepathy's working." Mitchell takes the wine bottle, rinses it. "It'll sure come in handy."

I lean closer, try to reach his hand.

With a menacing look, he shoves me away. My hip jams into the edge of the counter. I'm so shocked I nearly lose my balance.

He tosses the bottle. It crashes into the recycling. "Maybe I'll just ask your mother for a big donation. She and George certainly have the money." He muses darkly. "And Ruth might support me. More than her own daughter."

Glowering, Mitchell reaches above my head. He rummages a hand toward the back of the cabinet. He grabs a thick, dark, squat bottle, pours enough for just about anyone to exceed Alabama's legal limit of intoxication. Hendrick's Gin, straight.

"And while we're at it," he hisses, "stay away from Mike Kennedy."

I shrink back. "What?"

"Really?" He tosses back the shot and slams his glass on the counter. "Why don't you read my mind now, Ava?"

Without so much as a glance, he stalks from the room.

CHAPTER 12
AVA

SUNDAY, MARCH 28

Worry pulses through my veins, matching the patter of rain on the kitchen window. As the rest of the house sleeps, I stare out at the morning sky, painted in thick swaths of steel gray.

Thunder grumbles in the distance, echoing distaste, and a tree-branch crack of lighting follows moments later. I squint at the yard, illuminated in shades of silver-white.

Swallowing a shiver, I turn and face the espresso machine. At the touch of a button, the device whirs to life, grinding and brewing. As hot liquid fills my cup, the smell wafts through the house, intense and caramel-sweet.

"Ava."

I whirl around. Mitchell's standing three feet from me.

"Oh, you frightened me!" One hand on

my chest, I grip the counter, steadying myself.

My husband doesn't blink or smile. "Ava, where's the bread I asked you to buy?" Mitchell peers at the pantry shelves.

The whole-wheat loaf I left at the market. With the milk. I bite my lip and open the fridge. Take out red grapes, a few crisp, green apples, and cheese as my frantic breathing slows.

"Mitchell —"

"Sweetheart, you forgot?" He doesn't wait for a reply. "What about the dry cleaning?"

I hesitate. "There was nothing to pick up," I tell him. "They checked twice."

Mitchell holds a hand up to stop me. "There must be some mistake."

I don't answer. Instead, I adjust the cutting board, take a knife, and start to slice the apples. The blade slides through the firm, crisp fruit. Slices fall to the side in an even pile.

"Any receipts for me?"

I shake my head no, and see Mitchell glance in the mail holder, where I'm expected to file proof of any purchases. Every week since Sam was born, he has taken the receipts and tallied the total. His rationale? To make sure I'm not spending too much on the boys. Or myself.

This morning the slot is empty. I haven't spent a dime.

Mitchell doesn't believe me. "You must have forgotten that too. Listen, it's clear you can't handle things on your own. Hire someone."

My throat constricts. I inhale and blow out, then silently count to ten.

"Mitchell, even if I needed the help — which I don't — there's no way to afford something like that."

"Really? I think your budget is quite generous."

If Mitchell wasn't so seriously off the mark, I might laugh. I decide I'm better off negotiating than tossing back a negative comment. My monthly "household allowance" — Mitchell likes to call it that — is a few hundred dollars. Hardly enough to cover standard groceries, let alone gas or anything extra. My gaze travels into the hallway and out into the foyer. We'll have workers here tomorrow, banging and hammering.

I don't mind the noise. It's the outlandish amount of money being spent on house renovations meant to impress board of trustee members, not to make me happy. If I had a fourth of what he's paying them, I wouldn't have to scrape and scrimp, buying off-brand diapers and picking up pennies in parking lots.

"I could go back to work," I say and begin chopping again, knowing I'm treading into dangerous territory. I cut harder, faster. "What about part-time?"

"Out of the question."

"Even a few hours a week?" The words fly out, despite my brain flashing a neon caution sign. I am pushing it. Deliberately. And I already know the answer.

"Ava. I'm not going to play games. Or listen to you beg me about this trivial —"

The knife slips and catches the tip of my finger. "Oh, ouch." I hold up my hand to examine the cut, then press to stop the bleeding. "This is not trivial. This is *my* life."

My husband sets his jaw, crosses his arms. "Funny, I thought it was *our* life."

"Mitchell, just wait. I need to get a Band-Aid." The bathroom is clear across the house. I have a first-aid kit in the car, steps away inside the garage. "Could you grab the door, please?"

Mitchell opens it for me, and I head for the Jeep's passenger side. On my way around the vehicle, I notice a bag hanging in Mitchell's Range Rover. A dry cleaning bag, with his blue shirt. The shirt he asked me to pick up. I squint into the window to make sure I'm not seeing things.

"Ava." Mitchell's deep voice follows me into the garage. "Sam's up. Jack too. And you have a visitor."

I stiffen, snatch a Band-Aid out of the glove compartment, and wrap it around my finger.

"Who in the world?" I step back into the house and ask Mitchell, as Sam toddles toward me as fast as his legs can carry him. "Hey, babe." I take Sam in my arms, give him a smooch, and set him down.

When I look up, my husband is shaking hands, jaw tight, with Officer Mike Kennedy in the middle of our kitchen. Mike is dressed in full uniform, his gun belt strapped around his hips. His face breaks into a wide smile when he sees me.

"Mike, what a surprise!" I gulp and maintain my distance. "Jack, can you come get your brother for me?" I glance at Mitchell, who's maintaining a mask of polite detachment.

Jack dashes in, scoops up baby Sam and waves at Officer Mike. "Hey, sir!"

"Nice to see you, son." Mike leans down to examine Jack's bandaged face. "How's the chin?"

"Good, it was nothing. Few stitches is all." Jack grins, leaving the room with his brother.

"Be right there," I call after him and step closer to Mitchell, nudging up against his arm. "So to what do we owe this honor? Just in the neighborhood? Catching any bad guys?"

Mike's lips twitch. "Special delivery. I found this in the cruiser." He holds out his hand and opens his palm to reveal my pink paper heart.

"Oh, I've been looking for that," I exclaim and pick it up carefully. "Thank you so much. It's my Valentine's Day card from Jack and Sam."

"Thought you might want it back." Mike tips his hat. "Hope y'all have a good day."

Officer Mike and Mitchell amble toward the front door. I hear Mitchell laugh and Mike say something in return. The crunch of gravel tells me he's on his way out the driveway.

When Mitchell returns, any traces of pleasure have vanished. "That was interesting."

"I must have dropped it in his car when we were on the way to the hospital."

"A convenient excuse."

My palms grow tacky with moisture. "Mitchell, that's what really happened."

"Ava." He heaves a sigh. "This is so tire-

95

some. The truth would be so much easier. You obviously have something special going with Mike Kennedy." Mitchell snatches a blue receipt from his coat pocket and waves it like a flag. "He paid for your damn tires. And the tow."

I gesture in the air, aghast. "I didn't ask him to. He took care of it while Jack was in the ER. You didn't answer your phone, remember?" My temples begin to throb. "Can we drop this, please? Mike put that on his account. I'm going to take care of it."

"In more ways than one?"

"Mitchell? Really?" My lungs, punctured with his words, struggle to expand.

"I asked you to stay away from him. And here he is in our house."

My finger is throbbing, but his accusation cuts me to the core. Words fly out of my mouth like angry bees from a jostled hive.

"You can't forbid me to see a childhood friend —"

"If you loved me, you'd do that for me." Mitchell's gaze burns through me.

I ball my fist and press it to my lips. I have to get him to see reason. "I do love you. I've made a home with you. I'm the mother of your children. I try, Mitchell."

His lips twist into a sneer.

"So if we're talking about love and respecting each other, why is the dry cleaning I was supposed to pick up hanging in *your* truck?" I ask.

My husband frowns. "My truck?" He hesitates, then points a finger at me. "Oh, that's a good one. I walk out with Mike; you slip the bags into my truck." He pretends to laugh. "So you did remember. You just thought it would be fun to play games? That's mature."

"That's not true." I frown and cross my arms. "Why don't I call the dry cleaners? I'm sure someone will remember."

Instead of lashing back, Mitchell straightens his shoulders and turns away. "Really, Ava. I'm not going to dignify that with a response."

Heart thumping with anxiety, my mind goes blank. Mitchell doesn't turn around. "If our marriage is so awful, if you really don't trust me," I finally say, "then maybe we both need space. Is that what you want? Time apart?"

Mitchell walks away.

I lean over the counter. Tears drip and splash onto the ceramic squares. I'm horrified at myself for losing my temper. My vision's so blurry even my fingers can't find the fruit. Upstairs, there's a heavy thump on the bed. The bedroom closet opens and closes, drawers slam open and shut.

At my feet, Sam clings a hand to my ankle and begins a hiccupped cry, a sure sign that my baby needs to eat — now. I kneel down and pick him up, cradling Sam's warm body to my chest. "Let's get you some breakfast, honey."

Before I can get to my feet, I hear his footsteps on the tile floor. Mitchell stands still in front of me, blocking the light from the window. With an overnight bag in hand.

"Ava," he begins and then hesitates, "this is not what I want. But perhaps the time apart *you're* asking for will give us both the chance to see more clearly."

My throat burns hot and dry. I can't speak.

"I'm going to the office until I can think this through," he says, monotone, robotic. "In the meantime, I'd appreciate you not discussing any of this with Jack or your mother."

He yanks open the door, heading for the truck without a backward glance. There's a sudden, metallic crank and the whir of the garage door opener drowns out every other sound.

I sink against the nearest wall, making my body into a tight tangle of arms, legs, and baby. A flurry of emotions attack, vultures at a carcass. Disbelief. Agony. Failure. Holding Sam tight, I sob into my sleeve.

CHAPTER 13
GRAHAM

MONDAY, MARCH 29

The door slams hard enough to rattle my empty coffee cup. A teenager races through the front door. Breathing hard, he ducks down near the bookcase, crouches on the floor. The pungent odors of whiskey and perfume billow from his dusty overalls.

"All I was trying to do was get across the street," he mutters. "And some asshole nearly runs me over in his Range Rover."

I blink in surprise. "Did he hit you?" I ask, leaning forward, trying to make out any injuries.

The teenager scowls. "Nah. I made it okay."

I frown and rub at my forehead. "So I take it that's not why you're here?"

The kid shakes his head. The office crasher shifts his eyes, sweeps the room. He pushes a stray lock of dirty-brown hair out of his face, pulls at the neck of his camouflage T-shirt.

I ease back in my chair, letting my arm drape over one side. "Want to sit down?" I ask and motion at the seat across from my desk.

After a morning of twisting paper clips and making sure the office phone has a dial tone, the interruption is a welcome distraction. Much better than popping Advil like candy and trying to ignore my aching leg.

He slides into the chair and starts to grin, but then thinks better of it. "I kinda got into the Jack Daniels last night. Then I got a wild hair to ride Daddy's new John Deere. I took her down Main Street."

"*Her* the tractor?"

"No, sir." The kid rubs his forehead. "Her being my Becky. Becky Marshall."

Marshall. Marshall. I pick up my mug, take a drink.

He grins. "Um, yeah, she's the DA's daughter."

I nearly spit out the coffee. "How old?" I sputter. My pen pauses above the page.

"Sixteen next week. She's a looker, now, my Becky." He crosses his arms, smiles to himself. "That she is."

I want to choke him. "Property damage?"

He taps his forehead. "The corner store,

Mac's grocery, missed the telephone pole . . ."

List made, details recorded, I take a breath. Being new in town, I need the clients, even a mess of one like this kid. Farmer's son, first offense. Just a joyride with major consequences. "So," I ask, "how'd you end up in my office?"

"Because if my Daddy finds me, he'll kick my tail. My sister was pretty sure he won't look here." He glances around my office. "And you don't have coffee regular at Miss Beulah's like all the cops and judges and them."

I stifle a laugh. "They probably don't much take to outsiders."

The farmer's kid grins. "Especially one who rides a Harley."

"Is that a fact?" I eyeball Mr. Smart-Ass.

The alcohol-induced cockiness vanishes. He turns pasty-white. "Don't mean no harm."

"None taken." I pretend to look over my calendar, empty as a tomb. "After checking my schedule, I believe I can find time to take your case."

"Thank you, Jesus," he breathes into his hands and wipes his face.

I stifle a grin. I'll take any assistance at this point, even from unknown and unseen forces. "First, you're going to have to bathe, comb your hair, and put on some clean clothes. Okay?"

The kid bobs his head. "But I can't go home. I told you Daddy'll kill me. I've missed my chores, blew off school, messed up things bad."

My mouth twists. "Seems like your father will tear your hide anyway — it's just a question of when."

"I reckon," he agrees. "But I'd rather face the law before I head home."

With a quick glance at his stature, I can guess the kid is about my size. "Can you manage to walk into that house behind the office and get a shower? There are clothes on the bed — or get Miss Becky to drop some off?"

His eyes widen.

"It's my place," I explain. "You can sleep on the couch if you don't have anywhere to go. We'll sort all this out in the morning."

Bug-eyed, he digs a wad of bills out of his overalls and sets the crumpled mess on my desk. "It's not much. A few hundred. I hope it's enough. I'll get paid next Friday."

My first paying client. A tractor-driving delinquent with a dad who probably resembles Arnold Schwarzenegger. A man who will also want to kick my ass when this is all over.

"We can settle up the rest later." I stuff the bills in my middle drawer, then lock it.

"Yes, sir," the office crasher says. "I owe you big."

My head starts to throb. I put up a hand for him to stop. "Listen, don't steal anything," I warn. "And don't drink my beer. You need at least one person on your side. We clear?"

"Crystal."

"I've got thirty minutes to get to my nephew's soccer game." I scramble to find my keys. "And I need some caffeine."

CHAPTER 14
JACK

TUESDAY, MARCH 30

My dad stayed away for two nights. So when the garage door opens this morning, and I hear him come back in, I think it's all over. I actually smile. My stomach quits hurting. Things will go back to normal. It was just a bad dream.

Dad walks in with the workmen, who carry hammers, saws, and steaming cups of coffee in small, white Styrofoam cups. Downstairs, everything smells of wood shavings. Yesterday the piles were so thick in places I could leave an entire golden footprint.

I creep out of my room and peer over the edge of the railing, careful to keep out of sight.

The foyer is cluttered with hammers and saws, the metal teeth sharp and gleaming in the sunlight coming in through the front windows. White drop cloths cover parts of the floor like fallen parachutes. Dad's in the center of the room, dressed in his dark suit and tie. The man he's talking to is short and wiry, his muscles tight and tattooed with blue ink.

My dad hands the man an envelope, shakes hands with him and nods, murmuring something I can't quite make out. As he turns to round the stairs, I scurry back to my room like a badger down a hole. I crawl into bed and pull up the covers just as my father walks past.

When the coast is clear and the bedroom door closes behind him, I sit up and fix an ear to the smooth wall. My stomach gurgles, nervous. I'm craving biscuits and gravy to fill the empty space. Below us, boots clomp and echo. Toolboxes squeak open on their hinges, and there's the sharp sound of a measuring tape snapping back in place.

I close my eyes, trying to listen for Dad and Ava. After a moment, the arguing starts again. I peel away from the wall, nauseous.

Stumbling from my room, I press my hands over both ears and make my way to the end of the hall. There's a set of narrow steps there, leading down to the kitchen. The original owners built it for servants in the late 1800s.

My socks slip on the bare wood, but I

manage not to fall, even though my legs are rubbery and weak. I go straight to the hall closet under the steps and shimmy between the brooms and dustpans. When I pull the door shut, the dark air falls around my shoulders. Since I can't leave my brother, or catch a plane to Canada, it's the safest place to get quiet and think.

Hey, it worked for Harry Potter. Deep in the dungeon-house of Number Four Privet Drive, Harry is forced to live with his awful relatives — the evil, fat Dursley family. Harry's an orphan, treated worse than a stray cat with mange. There's little food, lots of chores, and long punishments. His bedroom, and only escape, is the tiny cupboard under the stairs.

I close my eyes and concentrate. On Hogwarts. And magic. Shifting staircases and wands. I'm in there a long time, until my breath feels hot and sticky in the space. Then footsteps cross the kitchen floor. I nearly leap out of my skin when the hallway door flies open.

"Jack, are you in there?" The glare from the light blocks my dad's face. "I've been looking all over for you."

It's probably a good thing he found me. It's stuffy in here. Terrible monster-starvation sounds growl from my belly. And

I can't feel my right leg.

His hand reaches in and helps pull me out by one arm. I limp to the sofa and collapse on the mountain of thick pillows, sinking my cheek into the one on top.

"Jack."

I lift my head an inch or two. "Sir?"

"Ava and I are having some issues. I'm sure you realize that." He interlocks his fingers, puts his elbows on his knees, and stares at my face.

"Yes." No sense in lying, though this morning I'd like to fake a vomit-fest. Or have fire trucks scream by at ninety miles an hour.

"You're not a baby anymore, Jack. So I'll give it to you straight. Sometimes parents argue. They disagree about things. And that's okay." He sighs. "But when you work hard, take good care of your family, and love your children and wife as much as I do, it hurts when one person isn't telling the truth."

I sit up straight. *He means Ava.* Sucker punch. My gut contracts. The room turns like a Tilt-A-Whirl ride at the state fair.

Dad reads my brain waves. "It's a huge blow. I'm horribly disappointed."

He keeps talking. I stop listening. *I don't want to move. I don't want to start over. I don't want anything to change.*

Our hero, Harry Potter, at this point in the story, would receive a mysterious envelope. An invitation to attend Hogwarts School of Witchcraft and Wizardry. The answer to his dreams! But when his evil uncle finds out, he does everything to stop Harry, including hiding him at sea.

In the book, half giant Rubeus Hagrid storms their rickety shack in the middle of the ocean for a dramatic rescue. Harry heads off to Hogwarts, makes friends, and finds an invisibility cloak along the way. How cool is that?

Of course, he's in trouble every other day, a dead girl follows him, he deals with drooling three-headed dogs, a huge snake, and You-Know-Who. Oh yeah. That's the person who's trying to kill him. But he's got magic on his side. What I wouldn't give to be Harry Potter right now.

"I'm sorry." My dad grips my shoulder and yanks me back to Mobile, Alabama. He stands up, brushes at an imaginary wrinkle on his pants. "The truth can be tough to take. There's a line that's been crossed."

I see his suitcase then. Packed full.

"You're leaving again?" Shock courses through me like I've stuck my finger in an outlet.

He meets my eyes. "For now, yes. I'll be nearby." Dad tells me an address. Explains it has something to do with the college, but I don't want to hear it.

All of a sudden, I'm furious and freak out. "No. Fix it. Both of you apologize. Make her happy. No one has to leave." I'm crying. Big, blubbery tears wet my cheeks, drip on my shirt.

Dad reels back, off guard. He blinks at my outburst. For once, there's no snappy comeback, no words of wisdom, no rehearsed, perfect answer. He opens his mouth, then closes it. Rakes his fingers through his hair. Turns around and leaves. A door opens and closes. Footsteps.

The Range Rover's engine rumbles to life. I race to the window. Taillights snake from the garage and swing out of sight. *He thinks I'm taking Ava's side.* My body shakes like a winter's wind has whipped my bare skin. My knees buckle. I press a hand to the window, my fingers wide. But he's gone.

CHAPTER 15
AVA

I must be desperate. I'm calling my mother for advice. She answers before I can leave Sam's bedroom.

"Ava, is that you?" Her tone arches with a smidge of concern.

"Yes," I whisper back. As I place the phone between my ear and shoulder, I pull the cover over his legs, turn on the baby monitor, and tiptoe from the room.

"Darling," Mama says. "Your throat sounds scratchy. Make yourself some tea with honey."

All at once I'm twelve again, knobby-kneed and awkward, anxious to please. *Stop it,* I tell myself and sit down in the kitchen. I watch the red lights on the small, square receiver travel back and forth with Sam's breathing, the motion of a pendulum.

"How are you?" I stall and wipe down the counter until it shines in the sunlight.

111

Mama winds up her list. "Just dandy, thank you for asking. That awful rheumatoid arthritis is flaring up in my hands, those obstinate squirrels are digging holes around my brand-new trailing verbenas, and all George wants to do is drink coffee with those horrible men who smoke cigars all day and talk about college football."

Some things never change.

My mother clucks her tongue in frustration. "And I'm out the door for a meeting at the country club. Did you need something, dear?"

"Sort of." I hesitate and reach for the small watering can under the sink. After filling it, I move from ivy to fern, African violets to bright pink bromeliads. Mitchell finds all of my plants cluttering, but it's a point I've refused to concede. The greenery soothes me, especially in moments like these.

I hear her breathing quicken. My mother hates, hates, hates hearing about anything difficult or personal when it comes to family. She doesn't want the details — won't spend hours dissecting a relationship's strengths and quirks. She's much better at handing out advice. Still, she's my mother. And I could use some help. A little bit of empathy.

"Mitchell and I. We're having . . . problems." The confession spills like marbles across pavement. I massage my midsection in an effort to settle my stomach.

Mother rattles her keys, a signal of her impatience. "With the house? The plumbing again? Call my handyman and get him out there."

On cue, the workmen in the foyer burst into laughter. I lower my voice and turn my back. "No, Mother. Personal issues. And I don't have anyone to talk to," I say. "In fact, I —"

My mother coughs violently, enough that I have to hold the phone a foot away from my ear. I'm probably giving her chest pain.

"Ava, I'd like to help. I wish I could. But I think you've been watching too many movies. Then again, you've always had a vivid imagination. You're simply overreacting."

"Mother —"

"You listen to me, young lady," she interrupts with hushed urgency. "Think before you do or say anything irrational. Use caution. Unless the damage has been done already." She pauses. "It has, hasn't it? What have you done? Oh, Ava."

Guilt, familiar and heavy, rushes through my veins. My mother is an expert at seeing everything as my fault. For a long time, I believed her.

Gripping the counter's edge, I watch my knuckles turn white. "We might not —"

Mama cuts me off a third time. "Let me tell you this: Mitchell adores you. And women, especially in your position, need to support and love their husbands unconditionally. He holds a prestigious place in the community. He has an image to maintain, responsibilities. As I live and breathe, Ava Keyes, I think you've done enough to tarnish your reputation over the years. Now go fix everything before it gets . . . unfixable."

Judge, jury, verdict decided. Arguing is pointless.

"Yes, ma'am." And I hang up.

I rake my fingers through my hair and sigh. My biological father did a number on both of us; his behavior, his recklessness, caused lasting scars for both Mama and me. Daddy, an account manager and salesman for an international paper company, was a philanderer of the highest breed. Charming, adept at spinning stories, so earnest and likable that Mama always said he could sell ice to the Eskimos. On the outside their marriage looked perfect, but life with Daddy was far from blissful. Even as a young girl, I remember Mama complaining about him staying late at the Mobile Country Club, having expensive dinners out with clients, or racing off to emergency meetings in Birmingham or Huntsville.

Any questions I posed were met with silence from Mama, and as I grew into a teenager, I watched her sink further into depression over Daddy's extended absences. The strange thing was, while he disappeared for days at a time, my father meticulously checked in on Mama. I would overhear their phone conversations, Mama explaining that she'd been to the hairdresser or grocery store, tearfully defending herself if she missed one phone call.

I began to dread my father being home. Mama and I tiptoed around, assessing his demeanor before speaking. If he was happy, Daddy was a joy to be around. I would hope upon hope that he had finally changed; that he'd love me the way other people's fathers seemed to adore their daughters. But it never lasted. If something or someone annoyed him, his black moods could last for days, like molten lava waiting to bubble to the surface of the earth, exploding all at once in a fiery stream of smoke and ashes.

Then one phone call during my senior year of high school changed everything. The blur of events played out like a movie —

Mama dropping the phone, the police coming to the house, calling hours, Daddy's funeral. He'd had a heart attack in Montgomery and died in the ambulance on the way to the hospital. At first I didn't comprehend that it all had happened in his mistress's bed.

The news shook me to the core. My body swirled with shock, grief, and anger. Worst of all, he'd let his life insurance lapse, leaving Mama and me close to destitute.

Much to my mortification, Mama wasted no time finding Mobile's most eligible bachelor. She married George a year later in a lavish ceremony on the grounds of the Bragg Mitchell Mansion. From that point on, between shopping trips, spa days, and vacations to Napa, Mama drilled into my head the importance of marrying well. Choosing a mate with money, a man who appreciated me, who didn't travel fifty weeks out of the year. A man who didn't cheat.

I reacted like a typical teenager — I ignored my mother's advice and ran off to Texas with a boyfriend I thought would love me forever. Instead of happily ever after, I was left alone and humiliated. My mother almost disowned me. My friends ignored me for months. The gossip was brutal and cruel. I couldn't get to college fast enough.

It's a wonder, after Daddy and Dallas, that I ever got married at all.

Still smarting from my mother's lecture, I decide to look for the pictures Jack needs for school. I head for the bedroom and step inside the closet. Above my head, on the tallest shelf, I reach a hand and stretch my fingers, nudging the album to the edge. Finally, it teeters and falls. I catch the book in my arms and sink to the floor.

As I begin to turn the pages, I find a photo or two of Mitchell and discover gaps several pages long. I flip through, faster and faster. The pattern continues. No Jack, no Karen, no family pictures, no house. It's as if my husband's past life has been all but erased.

My chest tight with worry, I turn the album over and shake it. A small rectangle flitters into my lap. With a trembling hand, I pick it up. *Jack.* The photo is tiny and faded but will have to do.

From his bedroom, Sam calls out for me. I jump up from the floor, slip the photo in my pocket, and put the album back on the shelf. Which is when I notice that the gun case is gone. The one Mitchell took to the school the night of the senior prank. He put it back up on the shelf the next day. It's been here since then . . . hasn't it?

I stand on my tiptoes, craning my neck to look. A finger, ice cold, trails down my back. I shiver and cross my arms, frustrated. Sam cries out again. As I jog to his bedroom, I block out my confusion. Surely there's a logical explanation.

Hours later, after school, Jack grabs at the phone when it rings. While he's talking to Mitchell, my mother's impassioned words echo in my mind. *"Think. Use caution. Fix it before it gets unfixable."*

I'm holding Sam in my arms, breathing in his innocent-baby fragrance. Jack hands the phone to me. He goes back to doing homework, pretending he's not listening to our conversation.

Mitchell is polite, respectful, and careful. He lets me know that he paid the contractor in full for the staircase renovations. It's just easier, Mitchell explains, and I find myself nodding in relief at his decision. Then, after a pause, he asks if he can pick up his overcoat. And the boys. Tomorrow. Just for a few hours, he says, after school. He misses them so much.

Like a ghost breezing by me in a darkened hallway, my mother's thoughts nudge me. *He misses them, Ava.*

"Would that be all right?" he asks. "I'll have them back around seven. Just pack their pajamas and toothbrushes. They'll be ready for bed."

And stupid me, I say yes.

CHAPTER 16
JACK

WEDNESDAY, MARCH 31
When Dad swings by to pick up Sam and me, a million questions fly across my brain, like Scooby-Doo chasing clues.

What's happening? Are you getting a divorce? What'll happen to Sam and me?

But I keep my mouth shut.

Ava keeps her bright smile while the workmen are here, four of them in their sweaty, worn T-shirts and frayed jeans. She keeps a pot of coffee brewing and, this afternoon, slides chess pie from the heat of the oven. The top of it glows gold like hay in a farmer's field. The entire house is thick with the smell of warm caramel, the kind you drizzle over vanilla ice cream. As usual, Ava doesn't eat a bite, just passes it out to the men and me on wobbly paper plates.

When the workmen leave for the afternoon and Dad pulls into the driveway, her mood clouds over like a storm that's raced across the sky. Her shoulders curve inward, like she's bracing herself for a blast of wind. Without a word, she hands over his long, tan coat.

Sam, permanently velcroed to her hip, starts crying the moment Dad touches his middle. "No, no," he cries, squawking and tilting his head back, flailing his arms.

Ava turns away, closes her eyes, and gives me a quick hug. She hands over Sam's diaper bag and disappears into the house.

An urge to run after her hits me. My legs twitch, but I force them to be still. It will only make Dad mad, and I can't risk that. I make myself metal instead. Tough, unbendable, blocking out everything, even my brother's cries — even if it's just for a second.

Before I get into the Range Rover, Dad asks me if I've brought a few DVDs, just in case. I show him my personal favorite, *Scooby Doo and the Witch's Ghost,* along with *The Samurai Sword,* and a few others.

Sometimes I like to pretend I'm right there with the Mystery Machine gang, hiding in a dark closet behind the brooms to get away from creepy villains. Making a plan with Fred and Velma to solve the crime.

Sure, I'm old enough to know that monsters and goblins don't exist, but there are bad folks that like to trick other people. Like the time I figured out my ex-friend Stuart stole my baseball cards. Man, he loved them, looked at them every time he came over. One day, gone! All of them, and I didn't want to believe he'd take them.

When I got up the courage to ask, he choked up, turned tomato-red, and denied it. He stopped coming around. Weeks later, on a whim, I took a detour by his house. His mom let me in, smiling, and gestured at the stairs with oven mitts on her hands. Stuart had his back to me, playing some new version of *Call of Duty,* oblivious to my footsteps. And there they were, my cards, in a neat stack by his bed.

I didn't want to find them. Didn't want to know he'd do a buddy like that. I took a step or two, grabbed the cards, turned around, and left. It stung for a while, but I'm over it.

Lesson learned: Monsters don't have to be green or crazy with gnashing teeth. They look like regular people. What's different — what makes them mean or bad — is on the inside.

On the ride over, Sam's sobs turn into an occasional hiccup. I keep my hand in his, and he squeezes my two fingers as we watch out the tinted window. The apartment complex is tall and sprawls out in all directions. It's painted in shades of light green and the panes of glass glow red in the fading light. My heart falls when I realize there aren't any trees or a park for running and climbing. As we drive up, I count rows of silver Mercedes, Volvos, and BMWs.

Inside the apartment, everything's colored a creamy white. The rooms smell like new carpeting, which makes me want to sneeze. The ceilings are high, the walls bare, except for stacks of cardboard boxes. A few tower above my head; mountains of thick brown squares. Sam and I crawl through a few empty ones, white mice in a maze.

As we pass other boxes, labels shout "kitchen" or "bathroom" in neat sharpie marker, but it seems like the movers didn't pay much attention. Nothing's in the right place, everything's askew, which has tweaked my dad into a rubber-band-tight bad mood.

There's a mattress I don't recognize on the floor in one room, a lone pillow and a neatly folded blanket on top with the tags still attached. In the back bedroom, a rolled-up sleeping bag leans against the wall. Camping? A trip? My dad isn't much into outdoor stuff, but these days, you never know.

"Great," I hear him mutter as he attacks the packing tape. While one huge hand braces the cardboard, the other holds a box cutter. He plunges in the silver blade and pulls it back with the ease of a skilled fisherman cleaning his catch.

My stomach grumbles when I imagine a largemouth bass, even an uncooked, dead one. It's been hours since we've eaten. The cabinets echo when I open them. Peanut butter on toast is all I can scrape together. Grocery shopping is not Dad's favorite chore, but I'm hoping he'll make an exception tomorrow.

Sam is tired of crawling through the box maze, so we settle against the only piece of furniture in the living room, my Dad's sofa. As we lean against it, I think that I can smell Ava, a mixture of coffee and cinnamon. I wonder if Sam does too.

Since Dad doesn't move to hook up the DVD player, I decide Sam might want to look at a comic book. I only put one in my backpack, *Superboy* #97, featuring "The Super Mischief of Superbaby!" For fun, I do different voices for all the characters, deep and gruff, high and raspy. Usually, Sam thinks it's hilarious.

Mo says I'm crazy for letting Sam near *Superboy* #97. On eBay, a copy goes for two hundred dollars. Sure, the cash would be great, but tonight I'm desperate to keep Sam happy.

Nothing works.

"No!" Sam slaps at the slick pages. He shakes his head and pushes to climb off my lap.

"But it's Superboy," I argue. "You love Superboy. And look, Superdog." I point to the bottom corner of the cover where a bright red cape and winter-white canine float in the air.

"No, no!" My brother chants. He throws his head back, catches me square in the jaw, inches away from my still stitched-up chin.

"Ugh," I groan and roll him off my legs. "Ow, that hurt, Sam." The noise finally reaches my dad, who stalks over and glares at both of us.

"We're kind of bored." I grimace. "Can't we sit outside on the balcony? It's nice out. You could sit out there with us like Ava does."

"I'm not Ava," Dad snaps. "And we're not going outside."

Immediately I avert my eyes and stare at the ground. Sam starts chanting "Mama" and walking in loopy circles, dragging his hand around Dad's pant legs.

"Maybe he's hungry," I murmur and

cover the growl of my own stomach with one hand. The space inside my middle section echoes Grand Canyon–empty. As much as I've complained about green beans and snap peas, I'd eat an entire plate of them now.

"Later," Dad answers, distracted. His cell phone rings and he immediately takes a giant step over Sam's head to leave the room. Dad paces the thick carpet, then stops at the window, listening. The person who called doesn't make my dad any happier. He hangs up and shoves it in his pocket.

"Dad?"

"What is it now?" He glares at me, then stares past me at the blank wall.

"Did you tell Ava seven or eight?" I trace the swirl of the rug with my finger. "When are we going home?" There's no clock, so I can't check the time, but Sam's rubbing his eyes like crazy, a sure sign he needs to get into bed.

"This is home." Dad's words lash out like Indiana Jones's whip. "Right here." He folds his arms across his chest, daring me to cross him again.

Stunned, I can't open my mouth. I sink to my knees. Sam reacts by toddling over as fast as his legs can go and burying his face in my shoulder. I pat his back and try to rock him like Ava does.

"Now I don't want to hear another word," my father lectures. "Not about food, not about Ava, not about the DVD player. Got it?"

I choke back a sob. "Yes, sir."

"Good." For the first time tonight, my dad looks calm, almost normal. "Go to bed. Both of you. I have a lot of work to do. The crib should be delivered tomorrow."

I start to remind Dad it's been hours since Sam's last diaper change but decide I won't. Instead, I hoist Sam on my hip, find the diaper bag, and try not to breathe too close to my brother's bottom. The smell rivals the knee-weakening power of kryptonite.

We head into the back bedroom. I unroll the sleeping bag and let Sam crawl around on top. The stuffing inside the cover mounds and bends into rolling hills. I reach for wipes, a diaper, and ease Sam onto his back.

"We're going camping, Sam," I tell him. "We can pretend this is the jungle."

He kicks a leg into the air, smiles, and listens to me talk. As I pull and adjust the diaper around his legs and belly, I make soft monkey sounds and swoop my fingers like bird wings. As I wiggle the wipes back into the diaper bag, I take a closer look inside. Under the change of clothes, a pacifier, more diapers, and his fuzzy brown bear, I discover buried treasure.

Granola bars! An apple! Cheerios! I should have known Ava would stash something, just in case. Sam and I take turns grinning and eating with quiet abandon. *Shh!* I put a finger to my mouth. I try not to crinkle the wrapper.

We eat quickly and quietly. Later I drift off with Sam in my arms. His breathing, deep and even, lulls me to sleep. One final thought drifts through my head like clouds across the moon. Ava is not here to remind me to shower, to give Sam his bath, or to read us bedtime stories. But, somehow, she's taken care of us anyway.

CHAPTER 17
AVA

WEDNESDAY, MARCH 31

He's an hour late and still no phone call. I try to read, but my brain muddles the words and sentences. Pressing the spine to my forehead, I rub the smooth cover against my skin, trying to soothe the building stress. The sharp caw of a sparrow outside my window causes me to jolt, and I toss aside my novel, letting the pages fall together, the closing of a fan.

Instead, I pace the expanse of the house, dodging cans of lacquer, stepping over a pile of black-fringed paintbrushes, and picking my way over two–by–fours. I kneel by the tallest pile of wood, examining the curled lines of grain, the shorn edges, jagged and unfinished. Exactly the way I'm carrying my heart in my chest.

I give up and call. The ring pierces my eardrum, but my husband's greeting quells the shrill sound. His voice, mellow and unhurried, heightens my anxiety.

I launch questions, rapid-fire. "Hey, where are you? I don't mean to sound paranoid, but I thought we said seven —" I close my mouth, wishing I could swallow the pseudo-attack of anxious, accusing sentences.

He's so silent I stop breathing.

"Mitchell . . . ?"

He clears his throat.

"What is going on? Tell me, please. Are the boys okay?" I wait for his answer, my heart thudding like truck tires on a bumpy road.

"They're fine." His voice is thick and tight.

I exhale relief. "Thank goodness. So you're on your way?" I take a step toward the window to peek out for his black SUV, listen for the deep rumble of a V-8 engine.

"No."

My knees buckle and I fold into the nearest chair. "Why? Mitchell, what are you talking about? You sound so strange. What's going on?"

Outside the house, frogs croak and crickets chirp. A jet zooms overhead, blinking red lights against the black sky. The world keeps going, business as usual. Inside the door, the walls fold in, misshapen, bent, melting like Salvador Dalí clocks.

"They're staying with me," Mitchell replies.

"For how long? Do you want them another night?" I convince myself the problem is temporary. I misunderstood something, surely. "That's all right, I suppose, but Jack has school . . . Sam has a playdate . . ."

I try to picture my calendar and Jack's schedule hanging on the refrigerator door, but confusion overwhelms my logical train of thought.

"They're staying here," he repeats.

Confusion blurs my head. I press a hand to my cheek. "Mitchell, look, I know I hurt your feelings. You don't have to keep the children longer to make your point."

"I'm not going to argue with you, Ava."

"Argue?" I gasp. "I am asking a question about our children." I cry out like a wounded animal. "I have a right to know what's happening to them."

"Jack and Sam won't be coming back," Mitchell says evenly. "I filed for divorce and full custody of the children. The judge awarded temporary custody to me. There's a hearing later this week. You might want to be there." The phone hums with emptiness, echoing his dismissal. *Of me. As the mother of his children.* "I have to go."

131

My brain screams like the whistle of a freight train. There's nothing I wouldn't do for my children. For Jack.

Before I can plead, beg, or cry out, Mitchell hangs up. The phone clicks and the line goes dead. There's nothing left but static and the rush of desperation filling my heart. My body quakes with fear. Mitchell is abandoning me. As if our entire relationship had never existed. As if we don't have a marriage and two children to raise. As if we never took vows to love each other forever.

I brace myself. The room spins out of control in a drunken haze of pain. A rattlesnake bite without the anti-venom. Quicksand without the rope and someone to pull you out. I am drowning. Sinking. Dying.

CHAPTER 18
MITCHELL

THURSDAY, APRIL 1

Five days and still no decision. The president of Springport isn't at all pleased. "How long is this going to take?" he asks. "I'm beginning to get concerned."

My pulse spikes as the line goes dead. *Concerned.* He's not the only one.

With the utmost patience, on Monday I approached Ava's mother, Ruth, with the prospect of funding the athletic center project. Her initial enthusiasm waned, however, spiraling into dozens of questions, countless suggestions, and ridiculous ideas I've promised to run by the architect. Since that time, no matter what I come back with, she still can't quite give me a commitment.

The proposed athletic center, in the course of a week, has gone from my greatest vision to the massive roadblock sitting between ultimate career success and me. Of course, my wife isn't helping my stress level either, but I have plans to deal with her.

I stand, pressing my knuckles against the chill of the glass-covered desk. My reflection stares back at me, the outline of my face etched in worry. I exhale, pushing tension through my lips. As I close my eyes, I clear my mind and center my thoughts.

Moments later I walk into the huge boardroom, with its mahogany walls, tall-back chairs, and thick Oriental rugs, and settle into my rhythm. Controlled, laser-sharp. Pausing by the huge picture window, I gaze out onto our magnificent chapel, flanked by a rich, green lawn, waving palm trees, and brick-lined sidewalks. Students carrying backpacks hurry past marbled statues. Below us, the wrought iron fountain arcs water into the morning air. Its droplets sparkle silver in the sunlight.

I am the vice president of advancement here. On my campus. Something no one will take away. I rub my hands together, ready to start the meeting. Waving for my receptionist to gather the staff, I remind myself that we're on track for a stellar summer session, class schedules are solid, and more recruitment efforts are under way around the state. As everyone takes their seats, I wait for complete silence.

"Good morning. Thank you all for com-

ing. First, kudos on the website upgrades."
I nod in the direction of the marketing folks.
"Nice job. The parent and family weekend
—"

My cell phone, deliberately set to ring at
8:45 am, starts blaring. A few department
heads stand up, move away from their
chairs. It's protocol to leave the room. Today
I hold up a finger for them to wait. I create
a concerned look, then agree with the nonexistent person I pretend is on the line. For
effect, I rub my forehead and heave a deep
sigh. I make certain to almost whisper my
wife's name.

"Ava. Of course. Certainly. Thank you."

My phone snaps shut with the flick of my
wrist. I set it on the table as if it weighs three
hundred pounds.

"Everything all right, Dr. Carson?"

Evidently my acting isn't too shabby. I
hesitate and force the corners of my lips up
just an iota. "Oh, thank you." I press my
fingers together. "Could we adjourn until
next week? I have some personal matters to
take care of."

A swarm of bodies rushes for the door.
My core team hangs back. Blake Michaels,
head of the business school, speaks up.
"What can I do?" Michaels is, by far, the
least able to keep a secret on my entire staff,

135

thus making him the perfect person to dis-
seminate my story. I estimate warp-speed
delivery.

"That's very kind." I pat his shoulder,
lower my voice. "It's my wife . . . she's a bit
unstable these days. Ava's been stopped a
few times by the police. Drinking and driving with the children."

Horrified looks all around.

"I've all but confirmed that she's having a
liaison —" I let my voice trail off and project
a look of anguish.

No one moves.

I swallow. "Worst of all, she's completely
unstable. Her moods are up and down. One
minute crying, the next laughing. I don't
even know her anymore." I drop my head
into my hands, let my shoulders droop.

Genuine pity surrounds me like thick fog
on an English countryside.

"I've said too much. You're all too kind."
More sympathetic noises and shoulder pat-
ting. "We'll be fine. I'll get Ava some help.
The children are my number one priority."

Vigorous head nodding.

"Thank you again." A sober group shuffles
out of the room at the very moment Ava
appears at the end of the hallway.

Despite my surprise, I arrange my face
into a concerned expression. "Ava," I say

136

under my breath, but loud enough for everyone to hear.

"Mitchell," she calls out, raising a hand in the air in greeting.

My wife walks up, shoulders straight, hair tied back at the nape of her neck. She looks elegant and lovely, makeup attempting to mask the dark circles under her eyes.

I reach for her elbow, drawing her close to me. The scent of her skin wafts around me, hints of cinnamon and vanilla. Any other day it would intoxicate me, draw me in. Today it is repugnant.

"What are you doing here?" I hiss into her ear, tightening my grip.

She ignores me, which only serves to fan my growing annoyance. "Hello, everyone. Hi, Blake." She smiles brightly and offers a hand to Michaels, who shoots her a menacing glare and stalks off. The other staff members murmur hellos, then turn and walk away.

Ava blinks, incredulous, then gives me a sidelong glance. "Did you deliver some bad news to your staff?"

"You could say that," I reply.

She stares after them, brow furrowed. "Can we talk? In private?"

My hand finds the small of her back, and I guide her into my office. "Certainly."

Door closed, Ava glances around the room, taking in my neatly arranged bookshelves, the rich, dark carpeting, the elegantly framed photographs of Springport College buildings on the wall. The room, just cleaned, smells of freshly-squeezed lemon and citrus.

"It's lovely, Mitchell." Her eyes meet mine. "Your office looks wonderful." She gazes out onto the campus, taking in my view of the lush, manicured lawns, wrought iron benches, and tree-lined paths filled with students on their way to class.

I nod, forgetting she hasn't seen it since the complete renovation a few months back. "Thank you."

Ava slides into the chair across from my desk, leaning forward to make sure she has my attention. When I don't say anything further, she draws a breath and begins speaking.

"Mitchell, I'm confused." She tilts her chin. "I love you. I love our boys. This . . . misunderstanding . . . what I said. It doesn't have to go this far."

The words hang in the air between us, stilted and awkward. I won't allow myself to digest them or be softened by pretty phrases. For just a moment, I consider whether she practiced her little speech.

It doesn't matter. I stare back and drop all polite pretense. "My dear, it's what you wanted."

Ava bites her lip and drops her eyes. Her voice lowers and slows. She's choosing her words carefully, as if picking her way around landmines. "I know what I said. I know how it sounded. I'm sorry."

"Really?" I tighten my jaw.

She nods, eyes widening. Ava presses her fingertips together into a prayer, touching them to her lips. "I am. You didn't have to move out or take the children to make your point. We all need to be together. I miss the boys horribly."

Her stab at raw sincerity almost fools me. I lean back in my chair, clasp my hands behind my head. "They're fine."

She hesitates, and I can see the pain and confusion on her face. "They haven't asked for me?" She begins to choke up.

"Not at all. Not a word." I shrug and flick a speck of dust from the polished surface of my massive desk.

"Who is taking care of them?" Ava blinks back tears.

I rock in my chair and glance away. "You don't have to worry about that."

"Mitchell —"

From the corner of my eye, I see her

wrestle to stay in control. It's admirable. I stand up and put my fists on the desk.

"Raise your voice to me again and I'll call security." I reach for the phone.

Ava's eyes dart from me to my hand and back again. She swallows and presses both hands into her skirt. "Mitchell, be reasonable. Let's go to counseling. Come home. Let's talk about this. Figure it out."

I chuckle. "Right. Are you figuring it out with Mike Kennedy?"

Ava jumps out of the chair, her green eyes pinned to my face. She begins to pace in front of the window, then stops, centering the brilliant blue sky behind her. "Mitchell. Please. Listen to me. You know full well Mike's just a childhood friend. That's all he'll ever be."

"I've already had one wife betray me, Ava." I point a finger across my desk. "Karen told me the exact same thing about her agent. Just a friend. Don't you think I know the signs?"

I pick up the phone, watching her as I grab the receiver. Ava presses her lips together and tightens her fists. Her chest flushes pink as a sunset.

"Get me security," I bark.

"Don't bother," Ava says, eyes flashing. My wife lifts her chin, determined. She

stands up and turns on her heel. "I know
my way out."

Chapter 19
Graham

"I take it this wasn't something you expected?" I lean forward and grab a notepad and pen.

In my past life, secretary summoned, I'd have gazed out of my corner office, overlooking a killer view of Birmingham, sipping a latte. But Ava has barely noticed the stacks of dusty books in the corner, the fake paneled walls, the less-than-ideal office with more than a few stains on the ceiling tiles. The rent's cheap, the office sits in front of my tiny rental house, and for now, it's enough for someone starting over.

She shifts her weight, and the wide planks of the wooden floor creak beneath her chair.

"No. Never. He moved out a few days ago. I thought we'd work something out. But then he drops this bomb. He's taken the kids and won't bring them back. He's filed for divorce." Her voice breaks. "And I found out this morning, he's called everyone. Every single attorney in a fifty-mile radius."

"Everyone?"

Ava offers a rueful smile. "Except you."

If he's gone to those efforts, that trouble, the husband is resourceful. Calculating. Definitely revengeful. But I don't say the words out loud. Not yet.

She stares at the wall. At nothing.

I tap my fingers on the top of my worn oak desk. "Listen, it's an old trick. Leave you no options. He's trying to scare you."

Ava attempts a smile, but her face fights any sign of mirth. "It's working."

I don't need her fearful. I need her focused. I train my eyes on her face. "Tell me about your husband."

Ava draws a breath. "He's smart, well-educated. A widower. His wife died in a car accident, so he's especially dedicated to his son, Jack, who's eight." She hesitates. "Mitchell talks about the times they used to go camping. They were involved in scouting, sports." She pauses. "He doesn't have a lot of time for that now. He's the new vice president of advancement at Springport. Lots of responsibility and pressure." She ticks off with her fingers. "Fund-raising campaigns, donor meetings, events . . ."

"Sounds busy." I take a sip of cold coffee

and refrain from rolling my eyes. "Tell me more about the pressure from his job."

Ava grimaces. "Well, it puts him on edge, partly because he wants everything to be perfect. He's always been a high achiever. Heading up fund-raising and marketing for a college like Springport is what he's been working toward since he got his PhD."

I nod. "And how does everyone, including you, handle that?"

She tears up and can't speak. Not so well, I suspect.

"Take your time." I give her a moment.

Ava swallows. "Everything seemed great. We had a wonderful honeymoon. Been married a year and a half. We have a lovely home. We-we're even having a brand-new staircase built." She stops and clasps her hands, shaking her head. "We have Sam, who's one. And I just adopted Jack as my own."

"I see." I make a few notes, and Ava watches me. "Go on."

"Shortly after Sam was born, things changed. Mitchell became a bit distant. Right around that time, his position got a lot more intense." Ava presses her fingertips to her bottom lip. "The board decided the college needed a state-of-the-art sports complex, which would cost upwards of one hundred million dollars. Mitchell thought he had all of the donors lined up. However, someone just backed out."

She frowns.

"What else?" I say.

"He's jealous. Of a childhood friend."

"Any truth to it?" I ask. "It's important."

She shakes her head and her green eyes fill with tears. "I've always been faithful. Always."

"Good. Any weapons in the home?"

Ava shudders. "He has a .45. He took it to work. There's nothing else."

"Okay." I jot down some notes. "Let's talk options. Get a plan together." I rattle off ideas. "First of all, he filed first, so he has the upper hand. Right or wrong, judges here tend to favor this."

Ava frowns, her face pained. "You'd mentioned that on the phone."

"So, as unpalatable as it might sound, and you may want to slug me, have you thought about trying to get him to come home and make the marriage work? Go to marital counseling?" I let this sink in. "If everything goes back to life as normal, he'll have to withdraw the divorce petition and the temporary custody order."

She raises an eyebrow, looking hopeful.

"It's a signal to the court that he forgives

you. Then, later, if you want, or need to, you can always go back and file first."

She pauses and interlaces her fingers on her lap. "He won't. I tried."

"Then we're back to fighting for everything."

Ava blinks furiously, white-faced. "And Mitchell's got temporary custody." She struggles to breathe, inhaling the news like cyanide gas. "I don't understand. Why does it matter who's first?"

I pause, gather my thoughts. "From what I hear at the courthouse, Judge Crane signs off on anything they put in front of him. It's *all* about who gets to him first."

"That's completely ridiculous." Ava's knuckles turn white. "Judge Crane doesn't know me. I wasn't even born when he graduated from law school."

"That's why they have a pendente lite hearing. The judge hears from both sides and makes a decision on custody, which will likely hold until you have your trial."

"And that's tomorrow?"

I nod. "Tomorrow."

She blinks, fiercely gazing out the window, her fury tempered with bewilderment. "Why is it so complicated? How could something like this happen? A baby needs to be with his *mother*." Jaw set, she turns and glares at the diplomas hanging in cheap black frames behind my head, the massive law books haphazardly shelved, and then her reddened eyes find my face. "Isn't there a law? Protecting women — mothers?"

I wince and deliver another blow. "There was, but they've changed it, Ava. The tender years doctrine, the one that said babies needed to be with their mothers, well, it's no more. Unfair to the fathers, lots of people said. It was taken off the books in 1997."

"Off the books?" she repeats.

"I'm sorry." The words offered up mean nothing. They don't even make me feel better.

Ava's cheeks glisten with tears. "I'm not a bad mother. I don't do drugs, never been arrested. I've never even gotten a speeding ticket. None of that matters, I guess."

"Some of it will."

Her face crumples, and I force myself to finish explaining. "Best case, if you both agree and work out a parenting plan, you'll get half the time with the boys. If things get contentious, then it gets tricky. The judge will order mediation and an investigation by a social worker or psychologist. Someone here in town. Plus, you'll have to go to a parenting class."

Ava sinks further into the chair. Her fingers tremble as she reaches for a tissue. One or two translucent squares float to the floor.

"Tell me more about Mitchell. Does he have a girlfriend?

"I don't know." Ava says slowly. "I don't think so."

"Any physical violence?"

She shifts in her seat uncomfortably. She can't meet my eyes, which makes me suspicious. Ava clears her throat. "He has a reputation, an image to maintain. Employs half the county at the college." She lifts another tissue, balls it up. "Like I told you, he's not been himself. More jealous. Angry, sometimes, since Sam was born."

I nod and make a note to revisit the anger issue. "Babies can change people," I say. Not that I have any personal experience in that arena.

"When can I see them?" Ava's voice falters. "The baby. Jack."

"We'll find out soon."

Ava takes a long, deep breath. "All right." She leans over, gathers her purse, and slides her sunglasses on her head.

I stand up and walk around to Ava's chair and offer my hand. She slides a small, smooth palm into mine. Her skin is ice cold.

And she's shaking.

I can't help myself. I draw her close and fold her against my chest. It's a gesture of comfort, but immediately I find myself wanting to protect her. Eager to fight the bastard who's hurting her and her kids. But she has to find it in herself to be strong. There's a flicker inside her, I can see it. She'll need every bit of that fire and more. In battle, I can be her captain, but she's on the front lines. And it's going to get bloody.

After a moment Ava steps back, smoothing her shirt. She takes a breath and looks down at her hand. After a beat, she slides off her enormous engagement ring and places it in the middle of my desk. "Would you take this as a down payment? Until I can get back on my feet?"

I start to protest.

"Please," Ava whispers. "It's all I can give you."

My eyes fall on the ring. Everything it is supposed to symbolize. Love. Trust. Unity. Not a legal retainer. I lock eyes with Ava. "Sure. I'll hang on to it."

She smiles. "Thank you." Her voice is steady. Her eyes are dry now. "And Graham —"

I nod.

She takes a breath and lifts her chin. "Get my children back. Please."

CHAPTER 20
JACK

SATURDAY, APRIL 3

Sam's looking for Ava. He trots on thick baby legs in my dad's new apartment. Quickstep, quickstep, round the corner, cocks his head, and listens.

Nothing.

"Ma-ma," he calls to the stairs. "Ma-ma?" he pleads to the empty hallway. His feet pound the floor in frustration. The deepest, dark green eyes look to me for answers, then cut toward the doorway. Where is she? Where did she go?

I watch him play hide-and-seek with an invisible parent. I know he expects her to pop out from behind a box and scoop him up, cover him with kisses.

It reminds me of *Sonic Underground.* It's this old-school cartoon Ava found for me about a blue hedgehog with superspeed. You find out fast that Sonic's mother, Queen Aleena, is in big trouble. Dr. Robotnik overthrows her kingdom, so she goes "underground" and puts her three babies in different hiding places to save their lives.

A prophecy reveals that they'll all be together again. But not before the children grow, learn the truth, and become part of the Freedom Fighters.

Like Sonic, Sam knows our Ava's missing. Something's not right. And he's not going to quit or give up until he finds her. Since Dad looks more and more like Robotnik every day, joining the Freedom Fighters sounds like a good plan to me.

I think this especially when Isabel, our new babysitter, appears in the doorway with Dad. Wrinkled and dark, round like a bowling ball, she pauses before coming inside. She doesn't seem to speak much English. Dad introduces her to Sam and me, then he takes off.

"All right," he tells Isabel. "Thank you. I have to go back to work."

On a Saturday, I think to myself. I don't say anything, though.

"Yes, sir."

Dad smiles, mostly for Isabel's benefit, I guess. "Have a great day. See you soon." He closes the door behind him. Isabel relaxes a little once he's gone. She looks around. I show her the kitchen. She frowns when she sees how empty it is.

"Isabel fix," she tells me. "We cook next time."

"What kind of cooking?" I ask. I'm thinking of the big Sunday dinners Ava used to fix. Corn bread so sweet it would melt on your tongue, buttery black-eyed peas, juicy pork chops thicker than my wrist. My mouth begins to water.

"You like burrito, quesadilla? Refried beans?" The words, with her accent, sound exciting and different. When she smiles, there's at least one gold tooth. That's kind of cool.

"Uh, I don't know." I scratch my head. "Is it spicy?"

Isabel laughs, making her whole belly shake. "I make mild for you. And for baby." She tries to catch Sam's attention, but he isn't interested in meeting Isabel.

He toddles by, arms swinging. "Ma-ma," he calls to the dining room. The words reverberate through the empty rooms.

He doesn't want me either. I've tried blocks, books, drawing pictures. Nothing works.

"Ma-ma."

"El bebé necesita a su madre," Isabel says, frowning.

Of course I don't speak Spanish, but I

153

agree with her worried expression. Seeing Sam like this upsets Isabel almost as much as it does me.

Across the room, Sam begins to sob. We both run to pick him up. Isabel, despite her size, gets there first. She scoops up his chubby body and clings to him. Behind Sam's soft hair, his head on her shoulder, she peers at me, takes a step or two back.

"Esto no es correcto," she murmurs.

When Sam's sobs get quieter, Isabel turns away, carrying my brother, singing softly in Spanish. The crank of a music box lullaby fills the room.

So. Maybe I'm wrong. Isabel's not a spy. She's probably not a minion working for Robotnik. Maybe she's with the Freedom Fighters after all.

Chapter 21
Graham

MONDAY, APRIL 5

It pours the afternoon of Ava's pendente lite hearing. The weather change makes my knee ache like someone has whacked it with a two-by-four. Puddles soak my socks, and by the time I reach the courthouse my jacket's damp, despite my crappy umbrella. If I see a bearded guy and a big wooden boat, I'm going to worry. It's likely he'd let the lawyers drown.

Judge Crane lumbers toward the courthouse, the slabs of sidewalk protesting under his massive frame. Outfitted in his Sunday best, the judge resembles a cross between Cap'n Crunch and the Pillsbury Doughboy.

According to my sources, I'll be facing off with one of the attorneys who worked behind the scenes to help elect the man. But bias or no bias, there's little point in trying to get another judge. According to

155

local lore, this particular pack might as well be a band of zombies. They eat you alive and they never, ever die.

I duck into the small meeting room. My eyes land on Evan K. Douglas, who is representing Ava's husband. He's a gaunt man, tall, with a long, hooked nose and a thinning hairline. His suit is immaculate and expensive, tailored to fit his slender frame. Smart, Italian leather shoes grace his feet, and they're dry, despite the monsoon outside.

"Douglas." I offer a hand to shake, as is customary, and his thin, clammy palm slides against mine. His limp grip brings to mind clutching a dead fish, and I fight the urge to shiver.

Obligatory duty done, I leave the room to find my client. Ava is in the corner of the lobby, one shoulder against the wall, a leather satchel over one shoulder.

"How are you?"

She looks up, her eyes cloudy but determined. "I'm going on about two hours of sleep, but I'm so wired it doesn't matter." Ava forces a smile. "Ready to get this part over with."

"Good girl," I say and grip her upper arm.

"Thanks." She nods.

I let go of her arm and check the time.

"So here's the deal. Mitchell's attorney and I will go into the judge's chambers; we each get a turn to make our case. You may get a chance to say something or get asked a few questions. If that's the case, we'll call you in. Either way, the judge will make a ruling today and, with any luck, you'll be seeing your kids soon. That's how it usually works."

Usually. I want to cross my fingers behind my back. New town, don't know the judge — there's no telling.

"Okay," she says, training her eyes on my face.

"Be right back." I squeeze her arm. The judge's secretary is in his doorway giving us "the look." It's showtime.

Judge Crane seems to have been built for a larger bench. It's uncomfortable to watch as he sits down and arranges his bulk behind the mahogany table in his office. His arms droop over each side of his armrests. He hasn't bothered to don the black robe, and from the look of the buttons straining on his dress shirt and the sweat beading on his brow, it's unlikely he'll bother.

His secretary shuts the door behind us.

"So what's going on, gentlemen?" He speaks in an irritated rumble of a southern drawl. "Give me the basics, and be quick about it. Don't got all day."

I speak first, edging out Douglas by a hair.

"Your honor, my client needs time with her sons. The younger is only a baby, who's just learned to walk," I begin. "She has a strong bond with the eight-year-old, whom she legally adopted."

Crane nods for me to continue.

"Ava Carson has lived in Mobile all of her life. She was born and raised here, attended school and college here. She holds a degree in education and master's degree in school counseling, with more than ten years experience at Mobile Prep. Her greatest love is children, and she recently resigned her position at the school so that she could stay home with the two boys."

"She quit because —" Douglas interrupts but is silenced immediately when the judge lifts a single finger.

I shoot Mitchell's attorney a sharp glare and smooth my tie. "As I was saying, your honor, my client's whole world is her family. Her young children. She attends the eight-year-old's soccer games, comes to school events, and goes on class field trips. The baby is just a year old and requires attention virtually 24/7, an almost impossible task for a working parent."

Douglas steps forward and cuts in again. "Problem with working mothers?" He raises an eyebrow and glances at the bench. I expect Crane to threaten to hold him in contempt for the outburst, but he does nothing.

"Of course not," I correct myself hurriedly. "And they are to be admired for balancing careers and family life." I swallow. "My point, however, is that Ava Carson *can* stay home with the children. Devote her full attention to the care of the boys. It's the best possible situation — one the two children are content with and know as their routine. Sam, the baby, has known nothing else."

For the third time, Douglas pipes up. "Are you going old school? Arguing tender years?"

"Your honor?" I plead, ignoring the attorney. "May I finish?"

Crane frowns and glances at Douglas, who shrugs, blinking his eyes wide. "My deepest apologies, your honor. I'm having trouble restraining myself after this . . . testimony."

"Ava Carson has been the children's primary caregiver for a year. That's all of the baby's life. She knows their routine. Their wants, their needs. She's with them every day —"

"The older child, though, is Mitchell Carson's biological child," Douglas argues.

"That's eight years, which certainly out-weighs one."

Incensed by the impropriety, I wait for the judge to stop him.

"Judge —"

Crane ignores me and nods his head for Douglas to keep talking. "Go on."

I balk at the slight and absolute disregard for courtroom ethics but restrain myself from interrupting. The last thing I need to do is piss off a judge during my first hearing in Mobile.

"Your honor, you've already awarded temporary custody to my client, who is an excellent father and dedicated servant of the community, Mitchell Carson. We respectfully request that temporary custody remain with him, in his current home, where the children are happy and comfortable." Douglas lifts his chin.

This time, I do interject. "Judge Crane, that motion was filed without my client's knowledge."

The judge murmurs something to himself, then stretches his bear claw hands on the table and stares at the wall.

"She's having an affair." Douglas chortles. "A childhood sweetheart, I believe." This time he and Judge Crane exchange a look.

It's then I lose it. "Douglas, you're out of

line. My client —"

But Douglas speaks louder and begins flipping through his briefcase. "I have letters, testimonials, if you will, from a number of friends of the family." He cuts in with a wave of his thin hand. "They all state that Mitchell Carson is better suited to raise these children than the mother, who clearly cares only about the next time she sees her *boyfriend.*"

My jaw tightens. Douglas flips open a folder, presents three letters from people who appear to work for Mitchell. *Bastard.*

The attorney holds up one piece of paper. "This one says Mr. Carson almost had to call security to have his wife removed from the campus," he says.

The judge snaps it up hook, line, and sinker. Douglas probably has the pope in the hallway ready to canonize Mitchell, and he's Southern Baptist.

Crane hacks to clear his throat. "Heard enough," Judge Crane growls. "Temporary custody stays with the father."

I'm flummoxed.

"Set up mediation," he growls. "Get one of the approved psychologists to conduct a standard custody evaluation, interviews with the children and parents, home visits. If this person agrees to supervise, the mother can get an hour a week visitation at the location to be determined by the psychologist."

I take one last stab at saving the hearing. "Your honor, sir, I haven't finished."

In slow motion, Crane turns his jaw to face me. "This is my courtroom. I'm finished. And that's all that matters. You, sir, are dismissed."

His gavel bangs.

Chapter 22
Lucy

Case file in hand, heels clicking, I blow into the courthouse conference room like a gale-force wind. It's best to assert control up-front, grab attention. Everyone in the room straightens in unison, an orchestra ready to perform.

My mountain of black curls is tamed into a twist behind my head, red glasses on, and I'm wearing a respectable Tahari suit. I'm in charge today, and I'm going to make sure they know it.

I offer a curt nod. "Everyone ready?"

Mitchell Carson, the plaintiff, beams with confidence. He nods, smooths his perfect tie, glances at his Cartier watch. Ava, his wife, sits on the other side of the table next to her attorney, Graham Thomas. She's delicate and small-boned, with bright, clear eyes and long lashes. The room, with its tall white walls, imposing table, and hard-backed wooden chairs almost seems to envelop her tiny frame.

She meets my gaze, though, unwavering. Shoulders back, attention focused on me, hands folded in her lap.

"Let me get one thing straight," I dictate. "I am here for the children and the children only. Not for the adults." I continue with as much intimidation as I can muster. "I expect full cooperation. If we make an appointment, be on time. If there's an issue or a question, I need to hear about it from the attorneys. Understood?"

The group nods in unison.

"I need a minimum of four meetings at my office with the children. These can precede the one-hour supervised visitation with Mrs. Carson."

Silence. More affirmative head shaking.

"I'd like to complete a home visit with each parent. This will be done with the children at each parent's place of residence. My plan is to submit an initial report to Judge Crane in thirty days. His honor will decide then if more visits are needed. Any questions?"

"No, thank you," Mitchell says through a tight-lipped smile. "You've been quite clear with your expectations. We'll cooperate fully, of course. I'm sure your expertise will prove invaluable to our case."

Ava turns a shade of algae-green, fighting to maintain her composure. I look away, down at my case file.

"After I check my calendar, I'll be in touch to set up the visits."

"Thank you so much." Mitchell leaps up, presses a palm into mine, and saunters out the door, his attorney in tow.

Graham pushes himself out of his chair, conferring in hushed tones with Ava as I gather my belongings. With my back to the both of them, I take a quick hit off my inhaler, feeling an almost instant easing in the tightness of my chest. Darn the dust in this old courthouse.

I run a finger along the sharp plastic container, my lifeline, and drop it into my briefcase.

In my twenties, I resented the dependency on it. A few times I tried leaving it behind, with disastrous results. Exertion, dust, and pollen all trigger an attack. Much like a diabetic without insulin and a needle, my body stops functioning when my airways close up.

"Dr. Bennett?"

I turn and hoist my bag over one shoulder

Graham Thomas limps toward me, pausing to shake my hand. "Thank you."

I glance down at his leg. "Recent injury, counselor?" I ask.

He lights up, the smile breaking over his face with boyish enthusiasm. "Karate tournament. I'm a lethal weapon on the mat."

I grin back. *You'd better be in court, too.*

CHAPTER 23
AVA

THURSDAY, APRIL 8

As if he can sense the storm of worry raging in my belly, Graham cracks open an ice-cold can of ginger ale and pushes it across the desk. I take it gratefully, and sip, letting the spicy sweet carbonation roll down my tongue.

"How do you think it went?"

We're back in Graham's office, and I'm grateful to be among the comfortable clutter and the smell of law books and stale coffee. I sink onto the sofa and let my head fall back.

"Dr. Bennett was fine," I say. "Very direct. I hope she's good with the children. She was pretty standoffish today."

Graham sits down at his desk and unwraps a stick of gum, releasing a pungent peppermint scent into the air. He crinkles up the paper into a tight, shiny ball and tosses it. It arcs and falls, the impact making a tinny ping against the metal wastebasket.

"She has to be a hard-ass. She's sizing you both up, getting a feel for the situation. You didn't expect her to ask you to make a lunch date, did you?"

This makes me laugh, the first time in days. "No, not really." I like Graham, genuinely like him as a person, and feel so lucky to have found an attorney so kind, caring, and adorably funny.

"A smile," he says and winks at me. "That's what I like to see."

I feel a blush creeping over my cheeks. "Thanks. I don't think I've even smiled since the day this all happened."

Graham grins back and looks down at his desk. When he glances back up, his face is sober and serious. "Ava, I know this is rough. But you have to keep the faith. Dr. Bennett, by the way, is the real deal. I've checked her background, looked over her résumé. She's got the chops."

I raise an eyebrow. "Meaning?"

Graham presses his fingertips together and swivels in his chair. "Bennett's the key to getting your kids back. If she can see through Mitchell's charade."

"We might need a miracle."

The corner of Graham's mouth twitches in mild amusement. "Listen, what we really need is more time. There's a ninety-day waiting period for divorce with minor children involved. Mitchell's lawyer is going to push hard to get a court date by then. We can slow them down a little with inter-rogatories, a few motions, but that's not a fail-safe. We should request mediation. It's a long shot but worth a try. Agreed?"

"Yes."

He takes a huge breath. "In the meantime, you need to play detective."

I cock my head to one side. "Um, okay?"

Graham cracks his gum and swivels in his chair. "Mitchell's playing hardball. We need ammunition. How much do you know about your husband, really?" Graham asks. "Friends? Enemies? How does he spend free time? What about his mother and father?"

"Whoa," I say, lifting both hands into the air. "I'm not sure I like where this is going. This man is my husband."

"Like it or not, Ava, he's turned on you." Graham exhales and rubs his temples. "Listen. You are a good, sweet person; but this is war. Either play Dorothy on the yel-low brick road and ignore that this man is going to tear apart your life . . ." He lowers his voice a few octaves. "Or trade in your ruby slippers for some steel-toed work boots and let's kick some ass. All right?"

Jagged worry pierces my belly. I blink up at Graham. He's not lying. No amount of hoping, smoothing things over, or wishing this away will solve the problem.

We both stand. He walks me toward the tiny waiting room, where he lifts a wooden windowsill. A moist breeze straight from Mobile Bay blows in from the street, rustling papers. I still haven't answered. The sky's darkened considerably. At that moment, the clouds open, releasing a torrent of raindrops. I stare out the front windows as water pelts the slanted sidewalks, and a nearby tin roof sounds like a snare drum. Steam clouds rise from the asphalt.

"We have to fight hard. I need you on board." Graham says.

I realize this now. Nice has gotten me nowhere. Appeasing Mitchell doesn't work, no matter how hard I try. My boys need me. And I need them.

"I'm a little scared," I admit, raising my eyes to his. I try to make the corners of my mouth turn up. I can't.

He nods. "Of course you are."

Graham stops and looks me straight in the face, more determined than I've ever seen him. He reaches out and gives my hand a quick squeeze, then lets go. "You're tougher than you think."

170

I close my eyes and think of my children. Jack. Sam. The sound of their voices, the way their laughter scented the air with happiness, the feeling of arms around my neck, cheek pressed on mine. How can I not be strong for my children? I will wear their love like armor.

"I'll look around. There are files at the house. And there's always the Internet."

Graham grins. "Good."

I smile back, and it's real this time.

"We'll do this thing together, right?" Graham slaps his hands together and rubs them in anticipation.

A tiny surge of confidence slips into my heart and I hear myself answer.

"Right."

CHAPTER 24
LUCY

I hang back in my office doorway, absorbing the fantastical stories Jack Carson spins for his brother.

"Hey, Sam, did you know that if we had Green Lantern power rings, we could time travel and shoot plasma beams?" His voice lilts and bends, punctuating the words.

"Puh-yu, puh-yu, puh-yu." Jack makes sound effects and I peek around the corner, into the playroom, just in time to see him pretending to shoot laser beams from his closed fist.

I grin as Sam mimics the sounds, watching his brother, a stern look affixed on his baby face. "Puh, puh, puh."

"Green Lantern's ring is one of the most awesome weapons in the universe," Jack continues, his eyebrows furrowed. "It can do almost anything. We could hypnotize someone or throw up a force field." His arms spread wide, as if summoning a glittering orb, brighter than the sun at noon.

Sam listens closely and repeats. "Puh, puh, puh."

I press my lips together, hating to interrupt, but lift my arm anyway. My knuckles touch the door, rapping twice. Both boys look up, startled, though my assistant let them know I was coming. Heather nods at me, stepping through the jumble of toys. When the door closes behind her with a click, I introduce myself.

"Hi, Jack. I'm Lucy." I say, keeping my voice soft and low. "Hi, Sam." I cup my hand close to my cheek and wiggle my fingers.

Sam darts behind Jack's back and ducks his head to hide. He's unsteady and wobbles for a moment, one hand gripping his brother's dark blue T-shirt. In front of him, Jack eyeballs me with trepidation. His dark hair, on the long side, falls over his forehead, hiding the fringe of his lashes.

"Hey," he says, then glances back and whispers to Sam. He scoots around and sits the baby on the floor, pulling blocks over to keep him distracted and entertained.

Keeping my distance, I kneel on the tight loops of carpet, putting myself eye-level with my new client. Jack raises his chin.

"I hear you just had some stitches out?" I ask.

He nods.

Despite my broad smile, I see his shoulders tense. I wouldn't expect anything else.

I've painted the walls soothing colors, lined picture books on the shelves, and added Legos to my burgeoning collection. But it's never enough to erase the small sign outside my office: Lucy Bennett, Psychologist. Or the pervasive feeling that a person's about to be examined like a fossil unearthed from the banks of Mobile Bay.

Eight-year-olds should be outside. On the waterfront. In backyards. Running. Jumping. Battling imaginary dragons. Smelling like the wind, dirt, and fresh-cut grass. Not sitting, enclosed by four walls, with a stranger. Warmth spreads across my chest, deep into my bones. It's my job — my mission — to get him back out there. To his childhood. To his friends. Or, at the very least, back to the best sense of normalcy life can offer.

"Are you a doctor?" Jack asks, breaking the silence. His knees are squeezed up to his chest, one arm wrapped around his shins. Behind him, Sam turns his head and looks at me expectantly.

I smile at the baby, who immediately hides his face again. Instinctively, Jack pats his small, curved back.

"Yes," I answer, "but not the medical kind." I sink to the floor, cross my legs, and rest my hands in my lap. I've made sure to dress casually. My curly black hair is clipped into a loose chignon. I'm wearing my signature red glasses, little makeup, and flat shoes.

Jack tilts his head. "What other kind is there?"

"The thinking, talking kind," I reply with a small smile.

He absorbs this and then wrinkles his nose. "But . . . other doctors think and talk," he says.

Touché. I grin. "You're right, Jack. The difference is that medical doctors deal with physical things. Like when you're sick, you break your leg, you have an earache, those kinds of things. I deal with emotional things — feelings."

"So people who are sad or unhappy?" Jack fixes his round, dark eyes on mine.

"A lot of the time," I agree, leaning closer, meeting his gaze. "Sometimes a parent dies, or there are problems at a school, or —"

"Someone gets divorced," he answers flatly, pinning his eyes to a spot on his jeans.

"Exactly." I take a breath. I don't believe in sugarcoating the truth. "It's why we're here. To talk about things. Work out who should take care of you."

He swallows hard and doesn't reply.

Sam, who's grown tired of his new surroundings, toddles over and crawls in Jack's lap, pulling at his collar and buttons with busy fingers.

I continue, sitting up tall to peek over the baby's head. "So, over the next few weeks, you'll be here a lot, with Sam and your father." I soften my voice to a whisper. "But right now, I'm going to let your mom in. And I'll be in my office." I look at the mirror on the wall. "Behind there."

Jack follows my gaze and nods. "You'll be able to see us, right?"

"I will," I reply. "Or I can stay in the room, which might make everyone feel weird."

"Yeah," he murmurs.

I stand up and walk to my office, motioning for my assistant to let Ava into the long hallway that connects to the playroom. She's been in the waiting room for at least fifteen minutes. It must feel like a lifetime.

As I settle into my chair, I jostle my inhaler with my elbow and send it spinning to the floor. On cue, Ava opens a second door to the playroom. Eyes glued to the scene unfolding before me, I reach down and pick up the small container, tucking it into my palm.

I can't look away. If little Sam could have run on chubby legs any faster to his mother, he would have sprouted angel wings and flown. Ava scoops him up and hugs him so tight he squeals. On the other hand, Jack pulls back, unsure, tentative, like sticking a toe in the winter-cold ocean. He slouches down in the nearest chair and hunches over, placing his chin on his fist.

Her face emanates the pain of rejection, but she refocuses her energy, playing and talking with Sam. When Sam begins rubbing his eyes, Ava pauses. Wordlessly, she pats the carpet next to her and beckons to Jack.

As I am watching, I almost forget to breathe. My chest tightens. Out of habit, almost without thought, I uncap the inhaler, shake it, and direct a puff at the back of my throat. The mist, tangy and bitter, coats the back of my tongue. In moments my lungs expand and my shoulders relax. I set it down within reach. After a beat, Jack slips down beside her. Legs and arms askew, Jack and Sam huddle, two fawns to a doe in the thicket. I can almost hear the birds chirp at twilight. Finally, he breaks the silence.

"I want to go back to the way things were. I want to live in our house together. This sucks. Why can't you fix it?"

Ava thinks for a moment, stroking Sam's hair.

"Jack, you remember that time when Mo came over and you were wrestling and the china cabinet fell over?"

"Yes," he mutters and squeezes his eyes shut. "So?"

"All of the teacups, the ones from my mother, broke into those tiny pieces, right?" Ava pauses and slips an arm around Jack's back.

He nods.

"Well, no matter how much I wanted to, I couldn't put them back together again. Not with glue or tape," Ava continues.

"Uh-huh." Jack purses his lips.

"They'd never be the same, right?" Ava smiles down at Sam, who breaks into peals of giggles.

The baby's laughter just bounces off Jack's stiff exterior. "But with the china stuff, you didn't cry or anything," he accuses and flashes an angry look. "Mo said his parents would have grounded him for life."

Ava takes a breath. "It doesn't mean I

wasn't sad." She puts her hand on top of his. "But, Jack, those were just things. A relationship is different."

He shifts, fingering the carpeting. "How?"

"I-It can only be fixed if both people want to." She pauses and chokes out the rest. "And right now, your dad's not sure."

Jack frowns and sinks his chin to his chest. Then, with a sudden burst of resilience, he attacks. His words rush out, peppering Ava like tiny bullets. "You need to try harder. Make him see it. Promise?"

She flushes. "Of course. I promise."

The scene, through the glass, pierces my soul. I jolt myself back to reality with a sip of hot coffee and a long look at Ava's face. Ava wouldn't be the first really, really good actress I've seen. Anyone can be sweet for an hour. No making judgments. No jumping to conclusions. My job is to observe. Let's see what the rest of the story brings.

CHAPTER 25
AVA

Behind closed doors, my brave resolve fades a little. Without Sam and Jack, the house echoes like a mausoleum in a Hitchcock film. Dark, everything exactly in its place, books perfectly aligned and toys untouched. I run a finger over the rooftop of Jack's Lego fire station, pick up Sam's favorite red airplane with the neon-yellow propeller and press the plastic to my chest.

Back in the kitchen, I slip the pink Valentine heart from my purse, secure it to the fridge with a magnet. It looks forlorn, the edges wrinkled. Alone. I want to find a stray Nerf football in the hallway, trip over a stuffed giraffe. See dirt-covered tennis shoes left by the doorway. Smell the eraser shavings and pencil lead left over after Jack tackles an extra-tough math set. Or inhale the scent of soap bubbles and baby powder after Sam's bath.

Until now, I haven't allowed the emptiness to touch me. The boys' rooms, beds unmade, covers rumpled, tricks me into thinking they'll be back in an instant, a minute, an hour. Now it just confirms they are gone.

A hysterical sob unleashes in the empty abyss of my living room. On the walls, family photos, carefully framed, bounce back the guttural sound coming from my throat. I spin and dissolve in my own grief, like sugar crystals poured into hot tea.

After what feels like several hours, I run freezing cold water, splash my face, and let the rivulets fall into the sink. The tiny drops echo in the stillness, urging me forward. Enough with the pity party.

Thirty minutes into staring at the Mac screen, my neck aches. Notebook to one side, pen in hand, I've googled Mitchell one hundred different ways. News stories pop up about Mitchell being named a VP of the college, his charity work for St. Jude's, special events.

Further back there are fewer photos, more articles. Graduation from the University of Alabama, then again with his PhD. The other pieces I find document his comet-fast rise in academia with stops all over the state: Gadsden State, University of Montevallo,

Huntingdon, and UAB — the University of Alabama at Birmingham.

Not a single out-of-the-ordinary notation. No arrests, no domestic violence, not even a traffic ticket. In fact, to the discriminating reader, Mitchell Carson is completely, nauseatingly normal. To the outside observer, borderline boring.

Maybe I haven't been completely, utterly fooled by the man I pledged my life to 'til death do us part. So much for Mitchell's end of the bargain. He's not here. He is somewhere with my children. With a gun. The thought makes me angry, fuels a fire in me and energizes me. Now, as Graham would say, *time to figure out what the hell happened.*

Then I notice a tiny, but distinct, delineating fact. In every picture, Mitchell is alone. No Karen, his then very-much-alive wife. No Jack. No family shots. Always Mitchell. *What about all of Jack's school activities, scouting, peewee soccer?* I click through more pages. Nothing. No Jack. Nothing but Mitchell.

Dozens of photos flash past, his dark hair the perfect foil for a set of brilliant white teeth. Each looks identical. The same shoulder to the camera, same slight tilt of his head. Posed, measured, frighteningly precise. If I Photoshopped his head from the page, I'm certain it would sit seamlessly on the next, and the next, and the next.

And sure, his tragic story of loss attracted me at first. Then the movie-star good looks, a jawline impossible to ignore. Now the frozen-plastic angle of his face seems more Stepford spouse than sweet husband. I click back further and further. Widen the search parameters. Include Jack's name. Nothing. Then Karen's. I hold my breath and tap the Enter key. I hit pay dirt.

"Local children's author and illustrator to launch book tour." Wow. The image of Karen captures a beaming, waif-like creature wrapped in a gauzy moss-green dress. Her long, straight brown hair hangs to her waist in a shiny waterfall. The photographer captured her laughing shyly at the camera, sharing the moment with a man identified as her agent.

It's clear the agent, Will Harris of Harris Talent of Mountain Brook, adores her. They're holding a children's book between them, a gray-silver mouse on the cover. And there's the title: *Beach Mouse Magic.* The very same book I bought for Sam. I scan the photo for clues and notice Will's eyes on Karen, not the camera lens. And Mitchell, for once, is nowhere to be found.

The author of the story praises Karen's work, mentions a three-book deal from a major publisher, and talks about the successful book signing held that morning. Evidently a *Beach Mouse Magic* craze hit Birmingham and every nearby city, with busloads of schoolchildren and their parents clamoring for signed first editions.

Karen was scheduled to leave on a ten-city book tour less than a week later. I check the date with the details about Karen's car crash and swallow hard. A mere three days after the event and photo ran in the paper. Officers ruled out weather and poor driving conditions. The police speculated Karen might have swerved to avoid an animal or object in the road. Nothing definitive. My unease ratchets up a few notches.

There's a story about Karen's obituary; next, her funeral, attended by dozens of people. Donations to the Alabama Art Commission in lieu of flowers. Mitchell and Jack are listed, as well as Mitchell's father, Frank, who died shortly after Karen's accident. No other family members are listed.

I weigh my discoveries. People don't just drive into cypress trees with perfectly functional cars. And why didn't Mitchell say anything about a book tour? In retrospect, I didn't ask much when Mitchell and I were dating. The past is the past. I always thought Mitchell just wanted to focus on the present. Our family. Not hurt my feelings by bringing up his former life.

But maybe Mitchell wasn't trying to protect me. With a click, I shut down my overworked Mac. In my brain, I reorganize the puzzle pieces, slide them around to find connections. Karen. Spotlight. Birmingham. Mitchell. Book tour launch. Ten cities.

In the time before the accident, Karen was leaving — albeit temporarily. Possibly with Will Harris. Or not.

It may be that I am totally overreacting and my imagination's gone berserk. But what's certain? It's obvious I didn't examine what lay behind my husband's shiny-clean exterior. And now I may end up paying an extraordinarily high price.

CHAPTER 26
GRAHAM

MONDAY, APRIL 12

"Graham, the thought occurs to me" — Marley Kennedy, proprietress of Miss Beulah's café, glances at me — "that it might be faster to hook you up to one of those IV drips every morning."

She's married to a town cop, Mike, and she's adorable and bohemian, a tiny gap between her two front teeth. Her hair is piled on top of her head, a scarf intricately woven into the layers of golden strands. Marley also has an incredible memory for names, favorite drinks, and preferred sweets. She hands over my travel mug, her bracelets jingling. "We can set it up over in the corner."

I hide a smirk. I've actually come to adore my morning harassment. As Marley moves to ring me up, the raw edges of her red tie-dyed dress sweep the wooden floor.

"Well, I'll take that under advisement.

After all, we attorneys are all about efficiency and productivity." I nod with mock courtroom seriousness. "However, it might scare the tea drinkers. I'll get back to you." I raise a hand to wave at Marley and push open the wooden door.

The humidity rises up and swirls around my legs as I stir up the morning-still air. It's no more than a hundred steps back to my office, and the streets are dead quiet. A dragonfly buzzes my head, wings beating silent against the fence post where it lands.

Ava is waiting on the steps, elbows on her knees. Her hair is tousled and shines red-gold in the early light.

"Hey, good morning," I call out when I come closer. Immediately, when I see her face, I want to take back the words. She's breathtakingly pretty without a bit of makeup, but her sea-green eyes are brimming with worry.

Be professional, Graham. Clearly, she hasn't slept. And she's here on business.

"Hey," she says, offering a weak smile.

"What brings you over here this morning?" I ask, raising an eyebrow.

"The workmen are at the house. Every day. They're making great progress, but the pounding and banging are getting to me." She looks down at the ground. "I thought maybe we could talk about the case." Gingerly, she stands up, reaches out a hand to steady herself on the railing.

"No problem. Want me to go back and grab you some coffee?" I hold up my cup. "Just takes a second to walk down there."

"Thanks, no." She presses a hand to her lower stomach and grins weakly. "Nerves."

We step inside; I push a pile of paper to the side of my desk. I am careful to sit across my desk from Ava and give her lots of space. It takes her less than five minutes to run down yesterday's events.

"I don't need to tell you this now, but I'm going to say it anyway," I lecture. "Your husband is a smart man. He has an agenda, which seems to involve getting you into as much trouble as possible."

Ava clasps her hands tightly.

"Stay away from him, Ava. I mean it. His truck, his apartment. Try not to talk to him on the phone. If you have to have a conversation, make it only about the kids. Got it?"

She nods.

After clearing my throat, I continue. "In the meantime, unless you disagree, I'm going to draw up a proposal, a parenting plan. It'd relieve Mitchell of all financial responsibility; give him liberal visitation, you physical custody. I'll fax it over to Douglas's office by lunchtime. How does that sound?"

"Will it work?" Ava lifts her chin, hopeful.

"No telling." I begin to jot down a preliminary outline. "It's worth a shot. If he says no, we haven't lost anything. We'll go forward with the mediation."

The fact is Mitchell is unlike anyone I've ever come across. Normally, most guys would cut and run with a deal like this. Free and clear, no child support. But this almost-ex-husband . . . no telling.

"If Mitchell goes for this . . ." Ava hesitates. "Graham?" She waves a hand in front of my face and snaps her fingers. "Are you okay?"

"Sorry. Just brainstorming." I run a hand through my hair. "Any luck finding out about the wife?"

She fills me in on the book, the tour, the article, and Will Harris in Birmingham.

"Remind me about your husband's family."

Ava swallows. "Mitchell's dad passed away right after Karen died. He had an awful time of it, losing both of them at once." Ava winces and closes her eyes. "His mother committed suicide when he was really young. Had to be terrible. I can't imagine."

"Convenient dead end. If it's all true, though, it's certainly enough drama to make anyone a little crazy." My fingers drum on the desk as I weigh our options.

Ava props her head against her fist, pressing the knuckles into her temple. "I can do some more research —"

"Look, I'm trained to be skeptical. And pessimistic. Forget the Internet."

Ava hesitates, puzzled. She cocks her head and purses her lips.

"Go to Birmingham." I make a pushing gesture toward the street. "What's stopping you?" I shrug my shoulders. "You can hire a PI, but that's some big bucks."

"I don't know," she says. "Where would I start?" Ava is hedging. I can't blame her. But it doesn't mean I'm going to give up on the idea.

I feel a little uneasy pressing her too much but shake off the worry. "Anywhere." She can do this. She's got to learn to trust herself.

Ava considers this. One finger runs down the table, stops, and taps. "With that Will Harris guy? Mitchell's old neighbors?"

"Yes," I urge. "What you find out could make all the difference."

CHAPTER 27
JACK

TUESDAY, APRIL 13

Mobile Prep's nearly deserted when I flop down on the school's front steps. I peel off my navy-blue backpack. The weight of it hits the cement with a thud. I pull at the neck of my uniform shirt, shading my eyes from the sun piercing through the oak leaves overhead. Afternoon heat rises from the circular driveway, paved smooth and black. Bees, fat with nectar, buzz around azalea blossoms so bright pink you have to squint.

Behind me, the glass door opens. "Jack," a voice asks. "Someone coming to get you?"

"My dad'll be right here." I twist my neck to look at my teacher.

"You're sure? I'm happy to drop you off somewhere. But I have to leave now. My daughter has a doctor's appointment at four thirty," she says.

"S'okay. Thank you," I reply, forcing my mouth into a big smile.

She pauses, nods with a frown, then disappears back inside.

I turn back to the street, pull up my knees, and lean back against the brick of the building. Yesterday, Mo's sister Molly took pity on me and dropped me by the apartment. Of course, Dad bawled me out for a half hour because he thought someone kidnapped me.

I close my eyes and imagine I'm not here at all. Different time, different place. Namely the Baxter Building, home of the Fantastic Four. Now my biggest issues would be foiling Doctor Doom or Silver Surfer when they try and stir up trouble. Sure, this superhero family argues with each other, holds some grudges here and there, but they always end up as a team. That's the kind of family I want.

Mr. Fantastic is a scientist and absolute genius, but stretching out my arms and legs in all directions isn't my idea of the best superpower ever. He's married to the Invisible Woman, who can shield everyone with force fields and disappear. Their friend, The Thing, crushes everything in his path and survives almost anything, but — like him — I'm not sure I'd be happy looking into the mirror at a stone face every day.

It's the Human Torch who's the coolest.

He's the Invisible Woman's brother. Johnny Storm can burst into flames, absorb fire, and control any nearby blaze by thinking about it hard enough. Best of all, he can fly away.

Which is what I'd do, if I could, when I see the Range Rover finally make its way to the empty car pool lane. Of course I can't, so I take my time getting up from the curb. My dad's on his cell phone and waves me into the truck. He's animated and relaxed, oblivious that I might be worried he's not coming at all. Dad's mood has been rock-paper-scissors every day this week. Monday — pretty mad; Tuesday — okay; Wednesday — not so great. You never know what you're gonna get.

"Hey, how was your day?" Dad hangs up, claps a hand on my shoulder and squeezes. "School good?" His fingers drum on the steering wheel.

Here's the truth: I'll probably survive third grade, but I hate geography, miss my brother during the day, and worry about Ava.

However, there's no sense ruining the ride home. "Fine."

My dad waits a beat. "I've been thinking. You must need some of your things, more of those comic books, your ball caps, the Demarini bat I bought — you know, from the house." He coughs. "Ava's house."

It's still my house too. Buildings race past, their doors and windows a blur of white and gray. Neighborhoods come next, and Dad slows down to make the turn. Older teenagers cut neat stripes of green on shiny riding lawn mowers. A few girls balance on training-wheel bikes. *How many of them have to divide stuff up between houses, deciding what stays and what goes?*

"Why don't you call her? I'm sure she'd be happy to drop off whatever you need." He wrinkles his forehead, expecting an answer.

"Um, sure." We pull up to the apartment. Dad keeps the engine running and doesn't apologize for dumping me off with the sitter. He hasn't made it home before dinnertime yet. "I have to get back to work. Use Isabel's phone. She won't care."

I heave my backpack onto the seat and start to slide out. "Okay."

My dad puts the truck in park. "Having your stuff here is important, don't you think? This is home now."

What he's saying — what he's trying to get across — is probably meant to help, but it only makes me feel like throwing up my lunch.

"You'll feel better," he says. "Really." Like

he's trying to convince me a big, fat tetanus shot won't hurt. It's moments like these, it's the flicker of worry on his face that gets me. Like the parents on the news whose kids are missing. *Sheesh.* Enough already with the guilt.

I slam the door and watch him pull away.

"Sure," I say and attempt a half hearted wave at the Range Rover's taillights.

"Hola, Señor Jack. ¿Cómo estás?" Isabel shouts above the music. She has the radio cranked to a Spanish-only station. It's loud enough that the neighbors might complain, but Sam seems to like it.

He's bouncing up and down in the kitchen in time to the beat. Isabel's juggling at least three frying pans full of smoky, savory food. She tosses chicken, peppers, and onions like an expert. Tortillas sizzle in another, refried beans in the third.

"Estoy bien," I reply, trying out some Spanish Isabel taught me. I hover over the sizzle and spit of the stove grease. "Who's coming to dinner?"

Usually I long for crispy fried chicken, buttered greens, and puffy yeast rolls, but whatever Isabel's making smells incredible.

"Señor." She swirls around and cups her thick hands on my cheeks. "We will have

fiesta. You and baby Sam are too skinny!" she declares, brandishing the spatula like a pirate. "No food in cupboards. No food in icebox. Isabel fix this." Hands on her hips, she sways in time to the song. Sam laughs.

For the first time in what seems like forever, I laugh too. For real. At a Mexican woman cooking us dinner, at my brother crazy-dancing to salsa music, me about to eat refried beans, which I surely would have gagged at a week ago. Over the din of Sam's clanging pots and mariachi trumpets, I manage to ask Isabel for her phone and tell her I have to call Ava. When Isabel turns the music down, I punch in her cell number, jiggling my leg impatiently.

"Can you bring my comics in the blue box and my Titans cap?" I picture my room. "Um, my soccer ball and cleats. My *Sports Illustrated,* if it came. Some books. My bat from Dad, the new silver one. Anything else you can think of."

I worry that I sound greedy, a spoiled kid at Christmas. Then I start to worry about something else. Something much bigger. *Dad. Ava. Here at the same time. Not good.*

"How long will it take you to get here?"

Ava promises less than ten minutes. *Phew.* I hand the phone back to Isabel and pace circles around Sam, who thinks it's a game.

He grabs at my legs, beats on my shin with one hand.

"What's going on, big guy?" I pick him up, carry him to the living room. Sam pokes at my nose and jabbers. We plop down near the television, which seems to play a continuous loop of muted Latino soap operas. Today a spandex-skirted heroine cries silently into her shiny red pillow. *Like we need more drama around here.* We watch for a while, and then I click it off with the remote.

I study my brother as we stack colored blocks. Green on yellow on orange. Another and another until the pile wobbles precariously and Sam whacks it down with a fist. He laughs and claps his hands at the mess, then blinks up at me.

"Do it again?" I ask and start over. I can't help but wonder if Sam knows what's going on with our family. Whether he understands any of it. I'm not even sure I do.

Ava's knocking. I spring to my feet, unlock the door and swing it open. She's balancing a box in one hand; several bags hang from the crook of her elbow.

"Ava!" I barrel into her chest and hug. Her hair's in a ponytail, but the wisps tickle my cheek. She smells like peach pie and vanilla ice cream. I untangle myself long enough to take the box from her arms. She puts down the bags and reaches for the Demarini bat and ball she laid on the porch.

"Thanks, sweetheart," she says and kneels down to grab Sam, who's in line for the next round of squeezes. When I step out of the way, I blink. Her ribs almost show through her white T-shirt.

Before I can think of anything to say, Isabel steps beside me. She makes clucking sounds with her lips, looks Ava up and down, and shakes her black curls. "Isabel," she announces, pressing a hand to her chest. "You the boys' mommy? Everyone too skinny," she scolds and gestures to the kitchen. "Come, come."

Ava hesitates at the doorway, wrapped around Sam like a blanket. "I can't," she says and frowns. "Really." She hugs Sam tighter. "I'd love to, thank you." Ava smiles at Isabel. "But it was nice to meet you. Dinner smells wonderful."

"Muchas gracias." Isabel glows and wipes at her forehead with the back of her hand. "Come," she says, then heads back to the kitchen.

"Just for a minute," I beg. "You need to see our room, Ava. Please?"

"It's not that I wouldn't love to. Jack, honey . . ." she protests and glances toward the street. I know she is looking for Dad.

"Never mind." My lip trembles. I try not to cry. My eyes sting. I hate this. I hate everything. I tear the bags out of her hands and stalk off to the bedroom. Stupid stuff. The bags hit the wall, and I throw myself on the bed, face first.

Of course, Ava's voice is already calling after me. "Jack?" She's in the hallway. I flop on my bed and stare hard at the ceiling.

Sam toddles over toward me and pats my leg. "Jaa." On one elbow, I prop myself up and squeeze his fingers.

"Here's your box." She sets it down on the floor. "I left you some cookies, too, in the other room. Your favorite." Ava sighs. "I'm sorry, Jack. This is hard on everyone. And I really, really want to be here and see your room and play with Sam and talk to Isabel, but I can't."

"Are you trying to fix it? You promised. You said you'd try."

She walks over, kisses me on the head. "I am. I have to leave, though." Sam clings to her, then screams bloody murder when she lets go. "Take care of him," she mouths and dabs at her eyes with the sleeve of her jacket.

Ava's bawling; Sam's a mess. I scoop him up close and rock him, not even realizing I'm crying until Isabel wipes my tears away.

CHAPTER 28
AVA

TUESDAY, APRIL 13

Full-fledged exhaustion slams me when I turn into the driveway. It's all I can do to steer the Jeep into the carport. My head throbs from the dagger-sharp pain of leaving Jack and Sam.

In my emotional delirium and recent acute insomnia, I think I hear a baby's cry. Deep, low, then caustic and biting. Added to the guilt, which grew wings and followed me home. I press my forehead against the steering wheel. But the noise bleats again.

It's inside the house.

I stumble from the Jeep, unsteady, throw my bag over one shoulder. My keys jangle against my leg. I reach for the knob but realize the door is already open. The air is stuffy, humid, stale.

"Did we blow a fuse?" I wonder out loud, and press my fingers to my head. "Was I in that much of a hurry?" My voice echoes in the empty house, then the alarm pierces the silence.

My purse makes a satisfying plunk on the ceramic tile. The oven light blinks at me, mocking my disbelief. "What in the world?" I press the digital display and shut off the oven, hot to the touch. "Come on. Am I losing it?"

Try as I might, there's no amount of effort that brings back any cogent memory. I am vigilant about locking the house, double-checking the oven light. And the air-conditioning. I take a few steps and glare at the defunct thermostat. Off. With the touch of a button, a blessedly cool breeze blows through the vents.

Gosh! What else?

Wine. I could use a glass of wine. I pull out the drawer, search for the corkscrew, which has likely gathered dust by now. There's every imaginable kitchen tool you can think of, except what I want. My lost vegetable peeler, a cheese slicer, and a Ginsu carving knife capable of cutting through a large tree branch. I set the shiny blade on the counter.

A heavy footstep nearly sends me into orbit. I whirl around. Mike Kennedy's familiar face peers back at me through the glass-framed back door. Hand shaking, I turn the lock and let him in.

"Mike, for the love of —" I clutch my throat in mock strangulation. "Are you trying to kill me? You scared me to death," I scold him and smile.

"Ava, I . . ." Mike struggles and swallows hard. "I need a favor."

"Sure. How long have we known each other? Anything for you." I grin. "As long as it doesn't involve a speeding ticket."

"It doesn't," he assures me, much too readily. "Not at all." He scratches his head and cracks his neck. "Damn, Ava. I hate to say this . . ."

I look where his eyes have landed, my hand with the corkscrew. The Ginsu knife. With its enormous silver blade glinting on the counter.

Laughing, I set down the corkscrew, fold my arms across my chest, and lean against the sink. "Now, really, what are you doing here?"

Mike clears his throat and adjusts his collar. "Can I take a peek around the place?" He shoots me a look. "It seems your husband thinks you might have a few things here that belong to him."

"Well, I have a lot of things that belong to him," I joke. "Half of this house. His clothes, his shoes."

Mike holds up an arm for me to stop. "He's serious. Did you go by his place earlier?"

"Sure I did." I hold my breath and count back from ten. "I dropped off some of Jack's things." Perfectly legitimate, since he called me and asked me for them. But I won't say the words. Swear to myself the kids won't be involved in whatever crazy scheme Mitchell has decided to cook up.

"That's trespassing," Mike informs me.

My brain rewinds. "What?"

"Trespassing," he repeats. "And he thinks you may have taken . . . I'm going to say 'accidentally borrowed' a few items." He checks his notepad. "He's willing not to press charges if you give them back." Mike wipes his brow with a white cloth pulled from his back pocket. "Of course he won't be so forgiving the next time."

Incredulous, I blink at the person I've known all my life. He's acting like a stranger. Have I fallen down the rabbit hole? I feel like I'm in some crack-addict version of *Alice in Wonderland*. Please! Anyone! Wake me up!

"Can I take a look around?" Mike asks. "Or do you want to hand them over now?"

"Hand what over?" I snap back. "I have no idea what you are talking about. This is insane."

He doesn't flinch at my outburst. "If you don't allow me to check the property, I'll have to get a search warrant." Mike stares back at me.

This is surreal. "Go ahead." I nod and step back to let him pass.

When he heads for the foyer, I follow. Under the glittering crystal chandelier sits our half-built heart pine staircase, with its grand, curved railing and hand-carved balusters.

"Renovations, eh?"

"Mitchell's idea. Not mine," I say, shaking my head. "Does this look like my kind of project?"

Mike rubs his chin. "Nah, not really."

We fall silent.

"Listen." His deep voice reverberates in the empty room. "So sorry to have to bother you with this. I really don't want to have to take you down to the station." He takes a half step toward the hallway, then straightens his shoulders. "It shouldn't take long and will save us both a heck of a lot of hassle."

I sink down on my heels against the wall. What. The. Hell? Doors open and close, drawers slide in and out. Curtains whisper as Mike moves them. I'm certain I hear him lift the rug.

Thorough as always, he inspects each bathroom from top to bottom. He pokes his head in the garage, glances in the trash, shuts the door. He spends what seems like an eternity combing through every inch of the house. In any other situation, I'd ask if he'd clean out the gutters while he's at it and then mow the front yard. Somehow, tonight, I'm sure he wouldn't find my attempt at humor funny.

And then Mike coughs. "Ava?" he calls out.

I stand up. "Where are you?"

"Master bedroom."

When I reach the sound of his voice, I can't make sense of what I see. Money, a roll of it. A wad. More than I'd ever keep. Mitchell's Alabama ring. And a piece of paper with the college insignia embossed at the top. Nicely, neatly placed in the top drawer of my nightstand.

Mike doesn't speak.

"Those are not mine."

"Not yours." His lips curl. He doesn't move from where his feet are planted.

I throw up my hands.

"It's . . . I've never . . . there's no way." In my haste to expel whatever voodoo black magic has leaked into my bedroom, I realize I am possibly incriminating myself in some way.

"Ava."

"There's no —" I stop myself.

Mike scoops up the cash, the ring, and the letter. "I'll just be going."

Scenes of the county jail flash in front of me. Bars slamming shut, the clanging of handcuffs. Feet leaden, I manage to escort him to the back door. "Good night, Mike."

"I'm awfully sorry to have bothered you, Ava." Mike shakes his head.

Not as sorry as I am. I close the door, double-check the lock, and move a chair to block the entrance. Nothing's safe anymore.

Nothing.

CHAPTER 29
JACK

TUESDAY, APRIL 13

The apartment's a total mess when Dad gets back. Soap bubbles float from the kitchen where Isabel's washing dishes. Except for the kitchen, the lights are all off, and I hear my dad cuss when he trips over the baseball bat propped by the front entrance.

I wince and grit my teeth, hoping the noise doesn't wake up Sam. But when I look, the red lights keep moving across the monitor screen. Back and forth. Back and forth.

"Oh, there you are." Dad darkens the doorway, holding something big and bulky. What he's carrying smells sweet, like saltwater taffy mixed with bubblegum.

I glance up from my Spiderman comic book. "Hey, Dad." I strain my neck to see what he's carrying.

When Isabel walks into the room, wiping

her hands on a kitchen towel, her tan hands still shiny and wet from the dishes, my father flicks on the light and holds out a humongous arrangement of fresh flowers. I squint hard at the brightness but peel one eye open enough to see white daisies, lacy purple lilies, and crinkly pink carnations.

"For you." He gives Isabel with a small bow, a knight's offering to his maiden.

Isabel gasps and clutches her chest, her crucifix. For a moment, I think she might be allergic or having a heart attack. Instead, she begins to cry.

I gulp. Dad waits. But then Isabel wipes her eyes on the towel and throws up her arms. *"Sí, sí."* She nods and reaches both hands for the bouquet. *"Gracias."* When Isabel buries her nose in the flowers, the petals seem to pat at her face, telling her everything will be okay.

I jump up and make a beeline for the other room. Even there, I can still see and hear them talking.

"My husband —" Isabel lifts her head and begins again. "What he always bring me," she explains. "He die last year. The pneumonia."

"I'm so sorry." My dad squeezes her free hand. "I just wanted to say thank you for all that you do for my family. *Muchas gracias.*"

Isabel flutters her eyelids and stands on tiptoe to kiss his cheek. The next instant she is back to Super Nanny status. She bustles away, grabs a potholder, opens the oven, shows my dad our dinner.

"Eat!" she dictates, and grabs her oversized gold purse from the counter. She hesitates before leaving. "Baby Sam misses his mama," she whispers and shakes her head.

Isabel's dark eyes, full of questions, search my dad's face. It's plain she doesn't understand what's going on. Then again, neither do I. She glances at my dad's hand, wedding ring still on. Her red lips part and close.

"Good night, Isabel. Thank you," he says firmly.

I come out of my bedroom and watch from the window as she makes her way down the sidewalk, past all of the houses, under the yellow glow of streetlights.

"Homework done?"

"Yes, sir," I reply.

"About time for bed, don't you think?"

I nod and hold the slick pages of my comic book close.

"Anything special happen today?" A dark cloud passes over his face.

"No, sir. Nothing."

Robot-like, he avoids my gaze. "So where'd you get the cookies?"

"Uh, Ava," I answer, feeling like I'm telling a secret no one should know.

"How long'd she stay?"

I listen for the anger building in his voice, the bubbling up of lava that bursts from the earth. But it's not there.

"Not long," I reply.

He actually smiles at his plate, but his eyes stay hard as the granite countertop, which makes me bite the inside of my cheek and wish I'd lied.

"How nice. So you gave her the tour?"

I hesitate, shuffle one step back from my father, my chin touching my chest.

"I'll take that as a yes." Dad turns. "Look at me, Jack."

I clutch the comic book tighter, until I can feel my rib cage. Then I raise my head.

Dad keeps his voice even and flat, but now he grips the table, making his knuckles bulge bone-white. "That woman is *never* to set foot inside this apartment again. Do I make myself clear?"

Heat rises in my chest, creeping up to my face. "But you told me —" I argue.

Dad brings a finger to his lips. "There's nothing more you need from that woman. She's trying to trick you. Get you to take her side." His jaw tenses.

I lift my foot.

"We're not done until I say so, got it? You're already in big trouble, mister. Do you want more?" My dad's breath comes fast and hard. A bead of sweat drips down the side of his cheek.

"Wake up, son," he hisses. "She doesn't love you." He stands up, strides over, and squeezes my shoulder. "It was all a trick, a game. She adopted you to make me think she was good, that she cared. And all the while —"

He grips tighter, until my skin folds. I wince at the pain and clench my teeth.

"Go on, son. Get some sleep." He pushes me toward my room. "I have work to do."

Once I'm inside the bedroom, I let my shoulders droop and grip my knees with both hands. The pounding in my head slacks off to a slow, steady beat. In the other room, my dad is calling someone and pacing the floor. I leave the door open just a crack, crouch down, and listen.

"Dispatch? This is Mitchell Carson at 88 South Davenport. Apartment A2. Could you send someone over please? Right away. I need to report a burglary."

Chapter 30
Jack

It's been the longest week. Sam crying all of the time. Isabel talking about her dead husband. Dad freaking out and calling the cops didn't help. And now, we're back in Dr. Bennett's office.

"Hey, Jack," she says, adjusting her red glasses. "How are you?" Her assistant, a small dark-haired girl with a long ponytail steps out from the office then, giving me a smile.

"Um, hey."

"Heather's going to play with Sam today, if that's all right."

I dart my eyes at Sam, who's carrying his fuzzy brown bear like an airplane, making buzzing sounds, and circling the room. I'm not sure he'll go, but Heather bends down and catches his attention with a bright new plastic corn popper, one that you have to push. She shows Sam how it works, making

212

the blue, red, and yellow balls go crazy when the wheels turn fast. He claps his hands and squeals, then trots after her down the hallway to the lobby for his turn.

Dr. Bennett smiles, sits down on the floor across from me, and takes a deck of cards. She cuts them, shuffles them with a flick of each wrist, making my eyes zigzag, and settles them back in place. "Want to play cards?"

I wrinkle my nose. "Cards? Like *Go Fish* or *Crazy Eights*?"

Dr. Bennett laughs. "No, this is my own game. It's kind of like War, but I call it 'Truth or Scare.' Want to hear about it?"

"Sure." I sit down across from her at the small round table.

She reaches into her pocket and pulls out a short silver tube with a plastic top. After setting it next to her hip, she starts to deal the cards.

"Okay. We each get half the deck," Dr. Bennett explains. "At the same time, we both flip over the top card. If yours is higher — like an ace beats a king, or a jack beats a nine — *you* get to ask a truth or a scare. Ask anything you want. If my card is higher, I get to ask. The only rule is that you have to be honest. Got it?"

"I think so." I peer down at the stack and

wish I had x-ray vision.

"Ready," she says and places her hand on the top card.

After a beat, I reach out my hand, touching it to the shiny deck.

"Go!"

I flip up an eight of spades. Dr. Bennett turns over a two of diamonds.

"Ha," I say, puffing up my chest. "Truth or scare?"

"Scare," she says and crosses her arms. "Go ahead."

I think about what I want to ask. I decide to see if there's anything she's scared of, like bugs or snakes or worms. I hunch my shoulders and tap my chin. "What's the one thing you're most scared of in the whole world?"

"Flying in an airplane. Terrifies me. I usually get sick." Dr. Bennett makes a sad face. "I'm kind of a chicken."

I can't keep from smiling. I didn't expect her to say that.

"Ready?" she prompts. We flip the next cards. "Ace of diamonds," Dr. Bennett says.

Mine is a three of clubs. I swallow.

"Gotcha." Dr. Bennett winks. "Truth or scare?"

"Truth," I say, holding up my chin.

"Okay. Tell me something special about

your dad," she asks.

I tilt my head and tug at my ear. It's a pretty easy question. "He was a really good football player in college. He played for Alabama. He has one of those big college rings." I hold out my hand, making a fist.

"Nice," she says. "Ready? Go." We flip again.

"I win," I gloat. "Truth or scare?"

"Truth."

"Hmm." I pretend to debate about my question. I actually could think of about twenty. It's kind of fun. "How about . . . why are you this kind of doctor? And do you have to have one of those?" I squint and point at the metal tube.

She glances down and laughs. "This is an inhaler," she explains. "It doesn't have anything to do with being a doctor, though I needed a doctor to get one." I nod for her to continue. "So it's called an inhaler, because when I have an asthma attack from too much exercise or too much dust or pollen, my airways sometimes close up." She makes a motion toward her neck. "I can't breathe."

I feel my eyes get big.

"I'm fine," she says, laughing a little bit. "I only need my inhaler in an emergency."

"Okay." I exhale, glad I don't need an inhaler.

She rubs her hands together. "So as for real life — and my job as a doctor — I like to help people. And solve problems." Dr. Bennett looks straight at me.

I stare back. "Do you?" I ask. "Solve problems, I mean."

"I've been told I'm pretty good at it." She grins. "You can let me know."

I like this. "All right. That's a deal. Ready, go!"

We flip over our cards, but she wins this round. I pick truth.

"Tell me something great about your mother." Dr. Bennett sits back in her chair and watches me.

I take my time answering. "My real mom or Ava, my mom?"

"Both."

"I don't remember much about my real mom. She was an artist." I hesitate, flustered. "Ava, she was my school counselor for a while, 'til she met my dad." I snap my fingers. "I've got it. Something about Ava. When we were on vacation in the Smoky Mountains, we stayed at this big resort. Some girl started choking in one of the restaurants. Everyone was screaming and yelling. The girl turned blue." I take a breath. "Ava jumped up, did the Heimlich, and this piece of broccoli popped right out."

"Wow! How'd that make you feel?"

"Good. Really good." I nod my head. "It was pretty cool."

We draw again and I come up with a three of clubs. Dr. Bennett's holding a nine of diamonds.

"Truth."

She taps her chin. "Okay, here's a tough one. With divorce in Alabama, anyone over fourteen can say which parent he or she wants to live with. I know you're only eight, but we can ask for the judge to listen. Who would you pick?"

That's easy. I turn my head toward Sam. "Anywhere with my brother. I think —"

A knock at the door interrupts. My head swivels around before I can stop it.

I jump when I feel Dr. Bennett touch my shoulder. "We'll finish this next time, Jack. Let's not rush it."

Another knock, louder.

"I'll bet I know who that is." Dr. Bennett raises her eyebrow and gets up to open the door. She calls for Heather, who brings a red-faced but happy Sam back into the playroom. He's still holding fuzzy bear and dragging the new toy, which explodes with a pop-pop with every step.

I sigh and take both hands, pushing the cards to the center of the table. I wanted to finish the game, but I grab my backpack and hover over Sam.

"Hey, sport." Dad steps inside and throws an arm around me, squeezing. "Ready to go?"

"Yes, sir," I say.

Dad reaches down to pick up Sam, who promptly begins yelling like someone's pinched his leg with a pair of pliers.

"Take this, please." He shoves the diaper bag at me, hard. My dad, jaw tight, bounces Sam around to try and quiet him down, but it just makes my brother more upset.

Sam starts shrieking and kicking his legs. *Mama! Mama!*

I cover my ears with my hands. Dr. Bennett grabs a little cylinder and shoots it into her mouth.

"Sorry," Dad says, raising his voice above Sam's cries. "Didn't mean to upset everybody. He never, ever does this. I can't imagine what could be wrong."

I don't say a word, but I know he's lying. Sam cries every day for Ava. I pinch my lips together and don't look at Dr. Bennett.

Dad pats Sam, shushing him on his way out the door. "Thank you so much, Dr. Bennett. See you next time."

"Next time," she agrees.

Sam's cries fade into the roar of the truck engine while I think about my last answer to the card game. I wanted to answer. I was ready. I love my dad. I really do.

But right now, I choose Ava.

CHAPTER 31
MITCHELL

FRIDAY, APRIL 16

My father, Frank, and I never agreed on much, but there's one philosophy of his I can live with. "There's no such thing as luck; sometimes fate needs a little push."

Today the push looks a lot like Jack's De-Marini baseball bat. I know football is not Jack's thing, but he's a natural athlete. I want him to widen his horizons past the soccer field, so we settled on the great American pastime. Signed him up for a clinic this summer at the Birmingham Baseball Training Academy. Then I bought him some gear.

After careful research, I chose this bat. Perfect name, Vendetta. The online write-up sold me. "The composite barrel and flexible inner core reduce vibration zones, increase the sweet spot and produce the ultimate bat speed." Too bad Jack won't have a chance to break it in at the plate.

Dad is taking the first swing.

Isabel stayed overnight, so I steal out of the house at 4:00 a.m., drive to campus, and park in a remote space behind the deserted college post office. The building is on a small corner of the grounds, far away from sleeping students in their residence halls.

I step out, gravel crunching beneath my shoes. It's warm, and the air is moist and heavy with the smell of a coming storm. As if they've anticipated my arrival, the crickets swell with music, the rubbing of gossamer wings filling my head. The gunmetal-gray barrel glints as I pull back and swing. My headlight splinters apart, sending plastic flying into the fresh-cut grass. Next, I smash the windshield edge. That blow sends a spiderweb of cracks radiating from the corner.

In the soft glow from a nearby streetlight, I catch a glimpse of myself in the side mirror and hesitate. For a moment, I see my father's face in the reflection. Angry, jaw twitching, beads of sweat gathering on his forehead. His voice resonates through the empty lot. *Mitchell.*

The shock forces me to look away, swipe a hand across my forehead. When I look again, my own face stares back. *Damn.*

Screw you, Dad. Screw you for leaving us. My kids will know their father. This'll make sure. I give the bat another go for good measure, this time against the driver's side door, leaving a dent the size of my fist. Nicely done, if I do say so myself.

Back inside the Range Rover, I take a cloth and scrub every inch of the bat clean. Satisfied, I drive the five miles back on empty streets to my house. Ava's Jeep sits on the edge of the driveway. I ease in, careful not to kick up gravel. Fortunately, the office air-conditioner provides enough white noise. I step next to the vehicle, unzip the ragtop, slide the bat inside.

Done.

Hours later, my assistant's silver Ford Fusion sits, perfectly parked, in her usual spot. She's on time every day, prompt, and chipper to a fault. My desk has never been cleaner, my calendar so well organized. Mary Grace actually anticipates my needs. A rare talent even the best-trained workers seem to miss.

As I open the door to the reception area outside my office, Mary Grace pounces to take my jacket. She smiles broadly, and as I ease out of my sport coat, I breathe in a hint of vanilla and warm undertones of caramel on her skin. It's pleasant and soothing, like the smell of pecan pie on Thanksgiving.

"Good morning, sir," she says. "Coffee, Dr. Carson?"

"Certainly." I smile.

"On your desk, sir."

"Any messages?" I ask and adjust my yellow tie in the mirror. "My appointments for today?"

Mary Grace rattles off a list of who's who, followed by a down-to-the-minute schedule. Ava's mother is last on the list. I've scheduled one last meeting to discuss the athletic center donation. Today I'm coming to her.

"Well now, that gives me about ten minutes to check e-mail and drink my delicious coffee."

She beams in delight. "Yes, sir. Anything else, sir?"

I step into my office and call back. "Repair shop number. Do you have one?"

"Sir?" Her face pales, making the sprinkle of freckles on her cheeks stand out.

As much as I hate to repeat myself, I need to be vague. "A body shop, really. That's the number I need."

Mary Grace draws herself up to her full height, all of five feet, three inches. "Are you all right? Was there an accident?"

I rub my chin thoughtfully. "You could say that."

She rushes to the window and peers out, a hand above her eyebrows. Mary Grace draws in a sharp breath when she sees the dents. Wide-eyed, she darts a glance at me, then back at the truck. "What in the world?" she murmurs. "Did a tree branch fall on your truck? Did a deer jump in front of you? Or a bear?"

I bite the inside of my cheek to keep from laughing, then remind myself I need the jump-to-your-death kind of loyalty Mary Grace offers. Her concern is awe-inspiring and deeper than I'd imagined.

With a soft touch, I take her elbow gently and lead her away from the window. "It seems someone is a bit upset with me."

Mary Grace whirls, mouth open, indignant. "Who would do such a thing?"

"It doesn't matter." I fold my arms across my chest. "Could you find the number, please?"

Flustered, her fingertips fly across the keyboard. "Of course, sir. It's just . . . I'm so . . . shocked." She produces several numbers and scribbles them down on an orange Post-it. "Would you like me to call?"

"Yes. Forgive me, I'm not thinking straight." I force a grateful nod of my head.

"Of course, please call. Then I can focus on my day."

"Have them come get your vehicle, sir?"

"That would be perfect." I drop the key into her waiting palm. "Just let me know what they say after they take a look."

"Will your wife be by to pick you up or will you need a rental?" Her pencil hovers in midair.

I squint my eyes, run a hand through my hair. "I'll need a rental." I pause. "Actually, on second thought, schedule everything for in the morning. I'll need the truck this afternoon."

"Very good." She hands back the key.

"And Mary Grace? About Ava. Do not let her in the building. If she calls, I'm not here or I'm in a meeting. If she comes to the office, call security. No. Better yet, call the police." I close the door firmly.

"Yes, sir." Her lower lips quivers. Slowly, she reaches for the phone.

CHAPTER 32
JACK

SATURDAY, APRIL 17

I haven't had the guts to ask what happened to Dad's truck. The broken headlight yawns open wide like a monster's mouth, yawning and bearing its jagged teeth. When Dad isn't looking, I brush the dent on the side with my fingers. The crater, rough and uneven, looks like it belongs on the moon. Missing paint chips show glints of silver underneath.

When we climb inside the Range Rover, I stare through the shattered windshield, the sunlight catching a million tiny corners. It's like seeing the world through a kaleidoscope, the diamonds and triangles piecing the trees and road together.

As we ride along, hitting the occasional bump, I grip the armrest and hold on. Dad drives fast, and when the accelerator hits 70, everything tingles, my hands, my ears, my feet.

If I had spider-sense, like Peter Parker,

and his other powers, I'd be a wall-crawling, web-shooting superhero. I'd be in the middle of battles with great foes like Doctor Octopus, the Sandman, and the Green Goblin. Homework, chores, and dealing with adults would be the least of my problems.

As Spiderman, I'd know trouble was coming and make a plan to deal with it. Learn to trust my instincts. Figure out who was evil and who was just plain weird. Creepy guys, like Grandma Ruth's husband. *George.* That's Ava's stepdad. He's about a hundred years old, yells when he talks, and smells like bug spray. He's hardly ever home, and that's a good thing. Otherwise you'd have to drag me to their house with my heels digging into the dirt.

Grandma Ruth's house rises out of the ground like a brick mountain, dark red with white pillars. The first time we visited with Ava, years ago, I half-expected to see a royal flag flying overhead or a knight atop a snorting silver steed — complete with moat and drawbridge.

"Yoo-hoo!" And there's Grandma Ruth, waving at the top of the winding driveway. I've always thought it would be so awesome to ride my skateboard all the way to the road, but Ava says I'd break my neck.

The look of happiness turns to surprise as she checks out the dents in Dad's truck.

"Mitchell, what in the name of the Lord happened?" She covers her mouth with short, white-tipped fingernails. "Something at the college? Or was it those hoodlums who stand around by the Winn-Dixie?"

"Now, Miss Ruth," Dad says. "Don't go getting all upset. It's a bit of a story. One we might want to discuss *inside*." He raises an eyebrow and glances down to make sure I'm not paying attention. On purpose, I've already turned my head and busied myself getting Sam from his car seat. But that doesn't mean I'm not listening.

"Jack darling." Grandma Ruth squashes me into an awkward hug. She smells like baby powder and flowery body spray. Ava says she goes through an entire bottle a week, which maybe explains why Grandma Ruth doesn't cook on the gas stove or get too close to the grill. Ava says it might set her on fire. No way if I was a girl would I ever use that stuff. Unless, of course, I wanted to blow something up.

"Oh," she exclaims and squeezes Sam's chubby leg. He shrinks into my shoulder. "You're so big! Mitchell, they're both so handsome." Grandma Ruth stretches her lips into a toothy smile, which must seem scary to Sam, because he starts to cry.

"Maybe he's hungry," I pipe up. There's always something sweet in the kitchen. If Maybelle, the cook, knows we're coming, she whips up the best Snickerdoodle cookies. Even Sam's big enough to have one now.

"Run along then, y'all." Grandma Ruth flashes her big diamond as she waves us toward the kitchen. "Wash your hands when you finish, now. Don't get everything all sticky."

"Yes, ma'am," I call and head for the stairs.

The kitchen's right off the porch, so I settle Sam close to the window to listen. He's on his second cookie by the time the conversation gets any good. I'll have to move on to Fritos and ice cream if this lasts too long.

First they start talking about the athletic center at the college, and it's so boring that I almost stop listening. Numbers, dates, names. Some big party. But Dad sounds happy, really happy, and I sit up straight and strain to hear.

"Glad to do it, Mitchell," Grandma Ruth is saying. "You're family."

Dad says something I can't hear. They're both murmuring then, and Grandma Ruth makes that sucking sound like someone slapped her. All I can catch is "college ring" and "money."

"I'm so sorry, Mitchell." The voice is Grandma Ruth's. "You're certain it was Ava?"

Ava?

"I'm afraid so," my dad answers. The chair creaks. "She's not been herself lately."

"How do you mean?"

Dad tells her about calling the police. The day Ava came over to drop off my stuff. The day I asked her to come, practically begged her to stay. I curl into a ball and hug my knees close. Grandma Ruth doesn't say much, just murmurs and clucks.

And then Dad again. "I suspect she's seeing someone."

I jerk apart, one leg shooting out like I can't control it. Sam reaches out a cookie-covered hand to touch my face. Grandma Ruth begins whispering. She does it anytime there's something important or upsetting to talk about. I lean closer to the open window, trembling.

"It's like she's back in high school. That summer she ran away with that hillbilly to Texas. They were going to get married. To think. Ava can be so foolish and headstrong. I was mortified," Grandma Ruth says. "I thought I'd have to resign my membership in the Junior League."

My dad mumbles something.

"No, she should be past this type of juvenile behavior," Grandma Ruth exclaims. Sam drops his cookie at the noise. *Shh!* I put my hand over his mouth and move him to the left. I crouch closer to the floor, just in case.

Dad clears his throat. "She may call and ask for money."

"Oh no." Grandma Ruth's voice becomes muffled.

I've let go of Sam, trying to listen. As fast as he can, Sam runs off toward the parlor. Crap! The absolute off-limits tower of porcelain dolls and expensive, breakable stuff. Before I can reach him, he's grabbed a figure by the neck. Sam cocks his arm like a baseball pitcher and lets her fly. I cry out, leap through the air, and manage to get under the statue.

Whew! It lands in my hand; I curl my fingers around it. Spiderman couldn't do better. Except . . . out of the corner of my eye, I see Sam attempt to scale the display in the corner. I scurry to grab my brother. A few clear glass vases and bowls, tinted yellow, rattle and tip. They'd be safer in an earthquake. Then the entire case tilts.

I snatch Sam from underneath the

furniture and roll with him across the wood floor. Crash! Shards of etched glass sail past my head. A thick candlestick lands next to my cheek. Shaken, I realize the force from the falling shelves, or a random shard of crystal could have really hurt Sam. Maybe even killed him.

I close my eyes and picture blood splatters and my brother lying still in the center of the room. Acid churns in my stomach. Sam whimpers while I hug him to my chest. Under my weight, his heart skips like a jump rope. *Whop, whop, whop.* Another plate crashes to the floor.

The noise sends Dad sprinting, with Grandma Ruth not far behind. When I estimate my father's feet are about an inch from my head, I open one eye and squint at his brown shoe leather. Sam grunts and wiggles, trying to wrestle his way out from underneath me.

"The Fostoria!" My grandmother clutches at her chest.

I'm not sure which is worse: the anticipation of my dad's punishment, or guilt over the absolute certainty of Grandma Ruth crying for days.

Dad yanks me up by the arm and shakes me. "Jack, what in God's name —" Sam sees this and wails like his feet are being held to a fire. He's so loud my grandmother claps her hands over her ears and starts to sob. I bend down to pick up my brother, but Dad pushes me out of the way, puts Sam on the sofa. "You've done enough, haven't you?" His face is purple. "You were supposed to be watching him."

"It was an accident, honest!" I exclaim. "Sam ran away from me. He grabbed one of those china things, then almost dropped it, but I caught it, then he tried to climb —" No one is listening, and I'm not sure my story's making much sense. Or matters. "Grandma Ruth, I am sorry."

My father slaps me across the face, hard. "You'll speak when spoken to."

My face stings, my arm's sore. Sam is still bawling. Dad points me to the truck. "Not another word, mister."

Grandma Ruth doesn't flinch or move, just stares at the broken pieces.

I've been banned. An outcast. Just like Peter Parker, who always tries to do the right thing, messes up, tries to fix it, then screws stuff up again. Mistakes make Peter Parker different from other superheroes. More human, like me. If it only took a spider bite, would I do it? Heck yeah! Regular kid one day, superhero the next. Crawling up buildings would be great, flying over cars, hanging by a thread, having superstrength. And, of course, spider-sense.

Anything I can do to avoid trouble sure would come in handy.

CHAPTER 33
AVA

SUNDAY, APRIL 18

The sun's barely up over the horizon. Sitting on the back porch steps, wrapped in a blanket with an untouched cup of hot tea in my hands, I stare aimlessly at the new swing set in front of me. Empty seats sway on long chains. The red slide, slick and sturdy, juts from a small lookout platform on one side. There are monkey bars, a rope to climb, and a sandbox.

It was my big surprise for Jack and Sam, despite Mitchell's complaining about the frame turning to rusty metal and the sight of it cluttering up our pristine yard. At the time, it sounded glorious and nostalgic. I'd scrimped and saved, squirreling away dollars for the last year and a half.

It arrived in the driveway last night on the back of a huge flatbed truck. In the chaos, I'd forgotten about it. I didn't have the heart to send it back. The workers took one look at me and asked for a mere twenty bucks to unload it and set it up. Deal. I threw in a few glasses of sweet tea for good measure.

Red streaks thread their way across the sky now, cutting through the morning's silvery mist. Miles from the porch steps, the whistle of a train echoes into Mobile Bay. A second blast, faster, longer, rushes past, carried by the breeze.

Graham's warning to make no contact with Jack and Sam hangs above me like a neon stop sign. Mitchell's staged "break-in" has me glancing over my shoulder on every corner, checking the backseat of the Jeep to make sure no one is waiting. Sure-fire scare tactics, I'll give him that. But my love for my children is stronger.

I see them everywhere, especially in their bedrooms on dark nights. I catch myself padding by Sam's crib so as not to wake him. I pass Jack's room, hoping to catch a glimpse of dark, tousled hair on his pillows.

In the folds of the blanket, I find my phone, pull it out, and stare at the blank screen. One call. It can't hurt. It's early, but the boys are up.

I press Mitchell's number. "It's Ava," I say when he answers, summoning strength at the sound of Jack's voice in the background. A door slams. "I'd like to say hello to the boys, please. It won't take but a minute."

The scuffing sound of a hand over the phone muffles any noise. Mitchell says Jack's name once, then again. I wait. Nothing. Mitchell seems to talk to someone. Again, no answer.

"It's not a good time."

I bite my lip and barter for time. "Um, are the boys okay? Are they sick?" I tread lightly, a gingerly placed footstep on ice.

"They're fine." Mitchell jumps on the defensive, volleys back. "I have everything they need right here."

Except a mother. "Tell me how they're doing, then —"

Mitchell interrupts. "Jack doesn't want to talk to you."

The phone goes dead. *He's hung up on me.* In my brain, I rewind and replay the conversation, trying to slow my racing heartbeat. My eyes sting and I rub them furiously while I head for the house.

Inside, I turn on the faucet, cup my hands, and drink. The water is so cool; I splash my cheeks, hoping for sudden reason or sense to take hold. Elbows on the counter, shoulders heaving, tears mix with the droplets falling from my face. My lips taste salty-wet. I could drown in my own grief.

In that moment, I understand desperation. Complete helplessness. How some parents kidnap their children. Run for Canada, Mexico. Disappear. My thoughts dart and hover like tropical fish trapped in an aquarium. Thick walls of glass, no way out.

I walk over to the fridge, trace my pink Valentine with a finger. As if someone was reading my deepest thoughts, the front door rattles with a hard knock.

What now? I tighten the blanket around me, find my phone, and dash to the bedroom. When I peer out the window, Mike Kennedy's patrol car is sitting in the driveway. My throat's as dry as parchment paper left in the sun.

With shaking hands, I punch Graham's number and pray that he's there. Voice mail. I hit redial. Voice mail. Deep breath. One more try. This time he picks up. The sound of spraying drowns out his voice.

"Sorry," Graham shouts over it. "Couldn't hear the phone. Someone's power washing his house on a Sunday morning. Are you okay?"

Finally, the noise stops. "Mike Kennedy. Outside my door," I manage to get out, jumping on one foot in the closet to pull up my yoga pants.

"Crap. That was fast." Graham curses a few more times. "Don't talk to him. Let me handle it. I'll explain later. Be right there."

I stall for time and hope Mike doesn't have a warrant, still hating the thought of him standing on the porch in the now-sticky morning air.

Good as gold, I hear the rumble of his Harley in less than five minutes. My heart lurches toward the sound. Acting like an intruder in my own home, I tiptoe around the corner and peek. Graham parks, ambles over toward Mike, and after five seconds, the two of them are having a heart-to-heart on the steps. I watch from the safety of my kitchen, my thoughts buzzing so loudly that Graham has to call my name twice to get my attention.

"Ava?" he says. "Ava? Can you come out here?"

On shaky legs I manage to walk to the door and open it. Graham lifts his chin and nods a hello as a blast of humidity hits me. "Can I borrow the keys to the Jeep?" he says in a loud voice. As he waits, he whispers under his breath. "Please tell me the Range Rover's in your name too?"

From the corner of my eye, I see Mike, leaning against his patrol car. He's waiting, watching. And none too happy with me for keeping him outside.

After a moment, he nods in my direction. Curt, polite. As if we're now strangers.

Why does that matter? I shake my head at Graham and give him a curious look. "It's unlocked."

"Stay here," he whispers.

I can't breathe. I don't move a muscle.

Without a word, they head back to the driveway. Mike, not Graham, opens the door, fishes around in the front, checks the backseat, then unzips the ragtop. He moves out of sight for a second or two, then pops back up with Jack's bat in hand. He holds it out under the spotlight, examines it. The once brand-new, shiny bat now looks like someone bashed a tree with it. The paint's chipped and peeling.

My skin prickles as Graham narrows his eyes and crosses the driveway. "Did he say when and where this allegedly happened?"

"Yesterday morning, before dawn." Mike shifts uncomfortably. He doesn't want to be here any more than I want him on my front lawn.

"Can someone please fill me in?"

Graham shakes his head at me. A warning to wait.

"Mitchell seems to think someone vandalized his truck." Mike looks at me. "He also said a very distinctive bat had been stolen. A Demarini Vendetta." He holds up Jack's bat. "One just like this."

I suck in air, gasping at the allegation. It's the bat I brought to the apartment.

"Any proof that it's my client? Any witnesses?" Graham frowns.

"Nope."

Graham, on the other hand, doesn't look a bit worried. "Ava, the truck's joint property, right? Both names on the registration and title?"

"Yes. Both vehicles."

He turns to Mike. "Then it's simple. Mr. Carson may have indicated that the vehicle is his alone, but that's clearly not the case."

Mike glances at me. "All right."

"Since the truck is joint marital property, the husband can accuse my client of vandalism all day, but the fact is she could burn down this property if she took the notion." Graham smiles. "Not that I'd recommend lighting any fires. Am I right, officer?"

"Fair enough." Mike sets his jaw and flips his notebook closed.

"Thanks." Graham shakes his hand like they're old high school buddies at a reunion. "I'll take that." He puts out a hand for the bat.

"Gladly. I've got plenty of work to do.

Sorry to bother you, Ava. Again." Mike hands it over and heads back to the squad car.

I motion furiously for Graham to come inside. "Can you please explain?"

"My pleasure." His silver-gray eyes twinkle at me and I have to look away to concentrate on what he's saying.

Once he's inside, I shut the door tight and lock it. "What is going on?" I ask. "The bat was at Mitchell's apartment because Jack called and asked for it — said he wanted some stuff from home. It was a gift from Mitchell, a big deal. I was trying to be nice, so I brought it to him. How did it get in the Jeep?"

"How do you think?" Graham says slowly, shooting me an incredulous look. "Ava, really. Come on. Get real."

"Mitchell?" My breath comes hard and fast. I am furious and in disbelief.

"I have proof. I actually may have a witness." Graham says.

"What? Who?"

"Ava, it doesn't matter. Just like you . . . he can do what he wants to his own truck."

"Yes, it does," I argue back. "Mitchell is trying to set me up. Make it look like I'm some crazy person who's going around bashing in trucks for fun."

"Of course. But since the Range Rover's in both your names, the police can't charge you with anything. It's joint property."

What Graham is telling me finally sinks in.

"Don't get me wrong, I don't like the appearance of it. We don't need to give him any opportunities like this again." Graham taps his fingers on the counter. "I assume you're going to keep the house, since he moved out. So get an alarm system. Change the locks. You might want to get an alarm on the Jeep. That might scare him away if he tries to mess with it. Park in public places. Stay around crowded areas. Don't ever be alone with him. I'm serious."

"All right."

"Get a new phone number while you're at it." Graham nods at Sam and Jack's photo on the fridge. "And a cell phone for the kids. Program in your new number. No harm in that. Then you can talk when you like — or at least while Mitchell's at work. And Jack can call you."

Graham crosses his arms and looks at the bat.

"Especially if there's an emergency."

"All right."

"And the important thing right now is to stay calm. Don't let on to your husband or anyone else that we know — or think — he's done anything. Mitchell's attorney has our settlement offer, and there's a small chance that they might take it." Graham gives me a stern look. "We have mediation tomorrow. I need you to be tough. Keep it together, okay?"

"Okay," I say.

"Good." Graham nods. "We have to figure out how to beat Mitchell at his own game." He pauses. "How are you holding up?"

I purse my lips, trying to stay strong. It doesn't help. My eyes fill with tears anyway. They're spilling over faster than I can wipe them away.

Graham grabs for a tissue and catches my elbow to steady me. "Ava —" But he doesn't finish his thought. Instead, very carefully, he presses the cloth to my right cheek.

My pulse slows a little. I watch Graham's hand as he folds the tissue in half and dabs awkwardly at the left side of my face.

"I'm so sorry," he murmurs. "You don't deserve this."

We stand there in silence, Graham drying my tears, until I've cried all that I can for the moment. When I can breathe again, I inhale deeply, inches from his chest, almost absorbing his outdoorsy scent of leather, fresh air, and gravel dust.

From deep within me, I feel a surge of emotion. A mix of longing for human touch and a jolt of shame that I'm having those feelings at all. I am still married, after all. Graham is my attorney. My adviser. A professional. Nothing else. I won't be — I can't be — the kind of woman Mitchell is painting me for the court.

I step back, shake my head. "Thank you," I say. "I'm fine now. Really."

Graham nods and frowns as his eyes meet mine. "Of course, Ava. The last thing I want to do is upset you any more."

I shake my head. "You didn't. Thank you for coming. I think — I just need to be alone right now."

"Of course." Graham says a quiet good-bye, opens the front door, and walks back to the Harley. I watch him from the porch, my hands clinging to my shirtsleeves.

Halfway to the bike, he pauses, looks back at me, and flashes his signature grin. "By the way, nice swing set. The kids will love it."

That makes me smile. "Thank you."

"Get some rest," Graham reminds me. "We've got a big day tomorrow."

CHAPTER 34
MITCHELL

MONDAY, APRIL 19

The term *mediation* — on the surface — means that two parties should work together to find a mutually acceptable resolution. Play nice. Get along.

What a joke. Here's why: the court can order a couple to try and resolve their issues, but no one can force you to reach an agreement. There is the fact that you have to show up. And your attorney will nag you to make a good faith effort and work toward whatever is in the best interest of the children. So fine. Let's get it over with.

Douglas stands at the door of the arbitrator's office, adjusting his bright red tie. "Dr. Carson," he says, beaming. He holds out an arm to show me the way to our cubbyhole closet, which connects to a joint conference area.

I walk past his Brooks Brothers suit and ignore his syrupy-sweet salutation. The room screams claustrophobia. It's stuffy and hot, poorly lit, and smells of dusty citrus potpourri. I want air-conditioning, a cold drink, and closure.

"Ava's on the other side of the building," Douglas informs me. He's holding a copy of some official legal-looking letterhead. "They sent over a settlement offer this morning," he explains and hands it over. He peers at me from above his glasses, which have slid down his nose, no doubt from the humidity. "It's pretty damn generous."

I stifle a laugh.

From my initial scan of the document, I see Ava is going for broke. No child support, no payments of any kind. Just the children. Sole custody. Her attorney makes reference to visitation whenever I "desire."

Under the table, I curl and uncurl my fists. Fury burns in my veins. The proposal is a joke, an insult at best.

A knock at the door interrupts. Douglas jumps up. "It's time."

The conference room, despite the palpable tension, is admittedly twenty degrees cooler.

Ava is already seated behind the expansive oak table. In her gauzy yellow sheath, hair pulled back, sans makeup, she looks young. Innocent. Every bit the victim. I grit my teeth. How appearances hide the truth.

When she bends her head to confer with her attorney, I study Graham Thomas, royal-blue tie slightly askew, shirtsleeves rolled up, and his longish hair in need of a trim. His leather jacket hangs from his chair, motorcycle helmet on the floor behind him.

I turn away when I notice the arbitrator stand. "Thank you for coming today. Let's get started." He's thin, in his midsixties, and graying at the temples. After introducing himself, he goes through the ground rules and asks for questions. Douglas looks at me and raises an eyebrow.

"I don't have a question," I begin. "But I have two comments."

"Certainly." The mediator smiles expectantly.

Pressing my hands flat on the table, I stand and hover over the small group. "First," I pull out Ava's proposal and toss it down. It skids across the table like a sled on a snowdrift. Ava watches but doesn't make eye contact. "We won't be needing this." I narrow my eyes at her attorney. "Don't send me anything that insults my intelligence. I know what you're after."

Douglas whispers for me to calm down. I ignore his pleas.

"Second" — I stand up straight and point

a finger at Ava — "stay the hell away from my truck, my apartment, and my children."

To my surprise, Ava shoots back. "They're *our* children Mitchell. Jack and Sam. Sit down." Her lawyer glances nervously at the mediator and touches her arm. Ava clears her throat. "Please sit down, Mitchell."

"I will not take directions from you or anyone," I shout and point a finger in Ava's face. "You've been lying to me since day one. I never should have believed a word you said."

The mediator begins to get up and wave his arms as if he's directing air traffic on a runway. "Come now —"

I slam my fist on the table, shaking the ice in our water glasses. "She's dangerous and out of control! I have my rights!"

Douglas gets ahold of my elbow. "Excuse us," he apologizes and drags me out the door.

Once outside, he explodes. "What in the hell do you think you're doing?" He blows out a breath of air and runs a hand through his hair. "Do you want them to think we're the crazy ones?"

"She's trying to ruin my life," I retort. "I want a restraining order against that woman. Right now."

"I'll work on it. But I can't promise."

Douglas folds his arms. Beads of sweat appear on his forehead. "I am going to ask you, though, to get ahold of yourself and get back in that room."

My cell rings. I take it out and pretend to glance at the screen. An hour ago, I instructed Mary Grace to call in case there was no other escape route from this God-forsaken joke of a meeting.

I straighten my tie and smooth my sport coat. "You forget who's paying whom. I call the shots. Not you." I narrow my eyes. "Am I clear?" I jab at his shoulder for effect. A tap to let him know who's in charge.

Douglas reels back, off-balance. His glasses tilt. Douglas pushes them back on his nose with one finger. "Um, clear." He begrudges me even that one word.

I walk away. And smile.

"I'm needed at the college," I snap over my shoulder at Douglas. "Get me the order. Today."

CHAPTER 35
JACK

TUESDAY, APRIL 20

I want to escape, crawl into a secret place and close the door. Not hang out in Dr. Bennett's office.

Today I feel like Bruce Wayne, minus the zillion-dollar mansion and butler, Alfred. As Batman, he hides in the shadows, takes cover in the Batcave, and feels at home in the dark. He's a loner, an outlaw, but eventually takes on a sidekick, Robin. Together they outsmart the bad guys, take the law into their own hands, and trust no one. They can never reveal their true identities. If they did, *Game Over.*

So, like Bruce Wayne, I act normal, keep my guard up. Inside I'm Batman — watching, waiting, looking for clues. Trying to decide who's good or bad, who to believe. I have to look out for me and Sam. I'm not sure anyone else will or can.

Like Ava. Can she really fix anything? She

only sees us once a week. This afternoon it's her time. One whole hour. I should be happy, like Sam, but my insides spin like someone's put me inside a smoothie machine.

"Hi, Jack," she says, her whole face a smile once she sees us. She's wearing a dress, blue like the Caribbean Ocean I've seen on postcards, and a white bracelet Sam and I gave her last Christmas. My eyes sting when I see it, and I whisper hello back. I make my eyes read words on the page, but they start to twist and dance. All I can see is that morning, seeing stacks of presents, the sound of red and green wrapping paper crinkling. The smell of eggs and brown sugar coffee cake is like heaven. In that moment. Ava's hand brushes my head. My dad laughs at Sam.

I choke. My throat goes dry, like I've swallowed dust. I shield my face with the comic book until Ava picks up my brother. After a half hour, I am still reading the same words. My back hurts from sitting still. One leg's asleep. I lower the book an inch and I peek at Ava. Like always, Sam clings to her side like Velcro, crumbled cookie in one hand. She starts reading, and I pretend not to listen, but Ava does the best silly voices when she reads from *Moo, Baa, La, La, La!*

After *The Very Hungry Caterpillar* and *Green Eggs and Ham,* I look at the clock. It's already time for Ava to leave. She gets to her knees and unwraps Sam, who starts to whine. Ava murmurs to him, stacking blocks and arranging toys around his feet.

"Can you play with him?" Ava asks, blinking up at me, patting the rug, and rubbing the back of Sam's little overalls. She glances around the room. "Have you seen his fuzzy bear?"

I nod, put down the comic book, and drop to the floor. It takes me a few minutes, but I find Sam's favorite toy next to the bookcase where he left it. Handing it to him helps a little, but he's locked on Ava, red-faced, looking like he'll never see her again.

Ava opens her mouth, but nothing comes out. She shakes her head, smiles a little, and moves her hand to her heart instead. She kisses Sam on the head, does the same to me, then slides something small and smooth into my hand. She takes a quick breath and whispers in my ear.

All of a sudden, my heart screeches to a stop. I'm mad at my *dad.* This isn't Ava's fault. She couldn't do anything. I reach for the blue of her dress but only catch air. She's already gone. The door clicks shut.

Sam cries harder and louder now, his

yowls like an abandoned kitten. Hands trembling, I slide Ava's gift into my pocket, lift him into my lap, and wrap my arms around him. He hiccups, and his tears wet my shirt, making a dark puddle. As I rock him back and forth, the first tear falls on my cheek.

And I finally realize what Ava said. "I love you. No matter what."

Chapter 36
Lucy

TUESDAY, APRIL 20

The door creaks a little as I open it. On purpose, I've given the children time to breathe. If anything it's a small way to dignify and honor their private pain.

When I step into the room, Jack's head snaps up. His eyes, rimmed with red, meet mine. Sam, holding a fistful of his brother's shirt, breathes heavily, an occasional hiccup shaking his small body. I try to smile, but it falters.

It's a battle I fight daily, as I am only human. The emotional side of me, the mothering side, aches to fix the children's pain and lost hope. Yet my objective, clinical side must observe, filter facts, judge, and make recommendations. In the best interest of the children. A heavy burden. Almost too much to carry. Weighted by the responsibility, I settle the latter over my heart. I bend down, putting myself at eye-

255

level with the boys.

"May I?" I glance from Jack to Sam.

Jack nods his permission for me to take his brother. I want him to feel in control, like he's making decisions, protecting his brother in some small way. Sam snuggles into my shoulder, sticky-sweet and chubby. One arm wraps around my neck as he begins to relax. I sit in the small chair across from Jack, pull the seat closer. After a few pats on the back, Sam is able to relax. Worn out from excitement, confusion, all of the tension and emotion. His first bear cub snore makes Jack smile.

"Babies are funny, aren't they?"

Jack's happy look vanishes like vapor in the atmosphere. He fiddles with his fingers, unsure of what to say. Finally, "Yes, ma'am."

"How's this week been? Everything okay at school?"

"Sure," he answers with a quick duck of his chin.

"Don't worry, I won't interrogate you." I lean to the side and feel for my bag.

Jack watches. "Are we going to play that card game again?" He furrows his brow.

Sam stretches and readjusts in my arms. He yawns and turns his head. Gone again.

"Not today. Maybe next time." I fish out a few sheets of paper, then a marker or two. I plop them on the table casually and push them across to Jack.

"If it's okay, I'd like you to do a few drawings," I explain. "How about your house — where you live. And your family." I reach down into my bag and pull out a few more markers, lay them flat in front of him. "Do you like to draw, Jack?"

He chooses a gray marker. "Sure, sometimes. I mostly like comic books, graphic novels, anything with a lot of action."

"Great! A future book illustrator in our midst."

Jack uncaps the marker. "Like my mom. That's what she did." He stares at the paper intently. Thinking. After the invisible wall he seemed to build when Ava was in the room, the personal admission both startles and pleases me.

I jump ahead with my question before thinking it through. "What kind of art did she do?"

He looks up and blinks, eyes sad and empty. "I don't remember all of it. I guess she was good at drawing animals and kids." Jack swallows hard. "She died, you know."

The hurt must eat at his very soul. Instinctively, I reach for his hand but stop myself. If he were mine, I'd fold him in my arms and try my best to hug the pain away.

I remind myself of my role and tread lightly. "I know. I'm so sorry."

Jack averts his gaze. "Don't be. It's okay."

The brush-off is quick and deliberate. Practiced. Learned. He hunches over the paper and begins to make lines. His arm moves smoothly across the table, fingers guiding the picture-in-process. In minutes, in immaculate detail, a large bungalow-style house appears, a driveway, swing set. Distinctive black gum trees with red-dark leaves surround the home. He pauses, surveys his work, then adds a man's torso, legs, arms, an unsmiling, dark head. A woman with long brown hair next, then a small boy, which I take to be Jack. *The first family. Mitchell, Karen, Jack.*

Before I can interject, he grabs a second piece of paper. There, four people come to life. Again, a man I presume to be Mitchell, whom he places on one side of the page. On the opposite, a strawberry-blond woman, a chubby baby on her hip. A sullen-faced boy is sketched out, his foot on a soccer ball. In the middle of the paper, Jack outlines a house in the background, larger, more regal and foreboding.

It's here. In Mobile. The drawings are amazing. Jack's talent is obvious. The intensity on his face pours into the page. Jack caps a green marker, lays it on the table. He spreads out his two creations side by side, then selects a red pen. With a deft motion, Jack puts a hard-lined X through the woman on the first page.

Shock value or true emotion? Whatever the reason for this "message," he's chosen to share it with me. A huge step for an eight-year-old.

Jack tips back on his chair and sets his jaw, studying the drawings. If I had to guess, I'd take a stab at intense anger and justifiable confusion in equal amounts.

I decide to ignore the red X for now. "Which one is your dad's new place?"

"Neither." Surprised at the question, Jack brings all four-chair legs back to the carpet.

"Why not?"

"My things aren't there. My bed. Most of my stuff, my books. You know."

"Okay. Fair enough." I examine the first picture. "Tell me about this one."

Jack wrinkles his forehead. "It's the old house. My real mom, Karen, my dad. Me."

"What was the best thing?"

He closes his eyes for a moment. "The swing set." He actually smiles and his face goes soft and dreamy. "I used to pretend I was Superman on the swing. I'd lie down on my belly and get a running start then just let go. Stick my arms in front of me, one fist out, like Superman does. My mom — Karen — I think she used to clap for me when I did it. It felt like flying." He stops abruptly. A cloud steals the air between us.

He thinks he's said too much.

"Thanks for telling me that. That's special." I lean forward and rebalance Sam. "So tell me about the second picture you did. Who are those people?"

"My dad. Ava. Sam, of course. And me."

"The house in this picture is a lot bigger. And no swing set," I comment. "What do you think about that?"

"It's a mansion, I guess." Jack rolls his eyes. "Even Ava said it was too big when they got married, but my dad said he had to have it."

My neck tingles. "Wow."

"So, anyway, my dad wouldn't let me get another swing set. He said it would just rust in the rain. And we'd look like trailer park people." Jack rubs the knees of his pants. "I just wanted it for Sam, you know."

I smile. "And then what happened?"

"Ava said she'd work on dad to get a swing set, but I don't know if she tried. Too late now," Jack says. He tips back on his chair again, looks past me to the wall.

I take the pictures and push them toward Jack. With my index finger I tap the red X on Jack's biological mother, Karen. "Is that why she gets crossed off? Because she's . . . gone?" I remind myself that Jack can't answer one hundred questions at once. I'm a psychologist, not a detective. And I need to listen.

"She was leaving us anyway," he snaps. "For her boyfriend, some guy she worked with."

Who told this child that? Did he overhear an argument? See something or someone?

"And you know this for sure?"

Jack hesitates. He rubs his temples. "My dad told me. Why would he lie?"

I don't answer, move my finger to the other drawing, point to Ava. I raise an eyebrow.

"Ava was going to leave too." Jack crosses his arms, defensive.

"Did you ask her, Jack?"

"I just know." He shrinks back in his seat. "It's what my real mom did."

"You might want to give Ava a chance. Talk to her."

"What for?" He's being cavalier on purpose, testing me. "Why should I?"

Fine. We can play it this way. My serve.

"Think about it this way. If you were ac-

261

cused of, say — robbing a bank — wouldn't you want someone to listen to your side of the story before they threw you in jail?"

Jack is silent. Then he volleys back. "Why wouldn't she just tell me herself?"

Match point.

"I don't know," I answer. "Sometimes adults don't think they need to. Or maybe she can't find the right words to explain just yet. You'll have to ask her." He keeps his chin down. "While we're on the subject, can I ask what Ava gave you today?"

Jack twists to the side, reaches into his pocket. He holds up gum, black package with an artsy, glowing green 5 on it. "Want a piece?" He turns the box and looks at it. "We had this deal going. Whenever I'd get mad or upset, she'd give me a stick of gum instead of a lecture. Like, to say, instead of freaking out, wait five minutes, think about things. Whatever's wrong might not seem so bad then. She was there to talk to if I needed it, but she never pushed me."

Smart. Very smart.

A knock at the door startles both of us. "I think that's your dad. Time to go." I slide the pictures in a folder, out of sight. "And Jack? Thanks for the tip," I say. "I think everyone could use some of that gum."

CHAPTER 37
AVA

The mediation debacle and Mitchell's crazy behavior propel me to work harder on my plan of attack. I pace back and forth in front of Graham's beat-up wooden desk, one hand locked on my hip, the wide planks of the hardwood floor protesting under my heels.

It's a gorgeous April day. Outside the window, azaleas bloom in pink and purple glory, raising their faces to soak up the bright sun and azure sky.

Adjusting the sunglasses on my head, I check the GPS on my phone one last time. "I'm going to find Will Harris, Karen's literary agent," I say, announcing my plan to Graham as though I'm embarking on an archaeological dig. "I called yesterday to check his schedule. His assistant said he's in most of today and tomorrow."

Graham leans back in his chair, propping

263

his legs on the desk. "I like it. Not making an appointment is a risk, but you don't want to scare him off on the phone. If he'll talk, get some insight into Mitchell and Karen's relationship, their marriage."

I shiver and hug my arms close. "All right."

"I know it'll be weird for you." Graham looks down and taps his pen on a notepad. "But it could make all the difference in getting your kids back."

"If Harris isn't there, I can go talk to neighbors." I run a finger along my lip, trying to imagine Mitchell's former world.

"Definitely. Mitchell and Karen had to have some social life. They didn't live in a bubble." He cups his chin in one hand. "You'd be surprised how much people love to gossip. Remember — Karen was big news, even though it's been a few years. And if anyone's going to get people to talk, it's going to be you, not me."

My heartbeat quickens. "Thanks."

He gestures to a stack of paper on his desk. "I've got lots of work to do while you're gone. Mitchell's attorney's lighting fires faster than I can put them out. We have to turn that around. Put them on the defensive for a change."

"Definitely," I agree.

Point made, Graham grabs his mug, takes a drink, and makes a sour face. "Ava, now my coffee's cold."

"Sorry." I smile and gather my bag.

"Get out of here," Graham barks, feigning annoyance. "I've got at least one other client who needs me." He pauses. "And for the love of God, find something."

The roads are clear and dry, so I make it to the outskirts of Birmingham in just over three hours. As I navigate along I-65, I click on the radio — no Baroque — and admire the long, green mountain ridges rising on either side of the blacktop.

Birmingham itself sits in the Jones Valley, just over the prominent ridge of Red Mountain, named for the ribbons of iron ore discovered on the layers of shale and sandstone. At the highest point, the sprawl of the cityscape comes into view, a stretch of tall, mirrored buildings rising in unison to greet the midday sunlight.

I exit the interstate, taking Palisades Drive to Oxmoor Road, where I pass the bricked edges of the Homewood Library, nestled in a grove of thick pines and towering magnolias. Several miles later, I reach my destination and park on the street near Will Harris's office. At the curb, I cut the Jeep's engine, confirm the address, and sit for a moment, summoning the courage to feign nonchalance with his office staff.

The area is clean and well-landscaped, with careful signage to blend in with the white lace of flowering dogwoods, the deep greenery of southern sugar maples, and budding camellias.

The building itself is funky, dressed in rustic clapboard siding. There's a Caribbean restaurant downstairs, accounting for the Bermuda-blue shutters and yellow door. Bougainvillea, lipstick-pink, spills from hanging baskets. Below them, jaunty daisies beckon from ivy-filled window boxes. Upstairs, two wrought-iron chairs and a patio table rest up against a small balcony outside the office doors.

I take the stairs to the second floor, where I'm greeted by a young, freckled reception-ist. She checks her computer screen, purses her lips, and adjusts her glasses. "Do you have an appointment?"

"No." I smile. "I'm just a friend, hoping to see Will. Is he around?"

This story seems to satisfy her. "Ah, Mr. Harris stepped out for lunch. You may want to check downstairs."

I thank her and head back outside, then realize I've only seen a black-and-white photo of Harris, taken several years ago. How will I know what he looks like now?

The restaurant downstairs bustles with customers. I scan the faces as Bob Marley's voice floats from the speakers and a bamboo wind chime clinks happily in the breeze. A cute couple, arm-in-arm, steps away from one of the few empty tables. I claim one and sit down before I can change my mind. The air smells heavenly, warm and spicy sweet. In a flash, a smiling waiter with spiky dark hair grabs the empty dishes, greets me, wipes down the table, and slides a menu under my nose.

"Can I suggest the jerk-chicken wrap with mango chutney on the side?" he asks.

"Sounds great." I agree. "And sweet tea?"

"Perfect," the server praises and jots down my choices. "Anyone else joining you?" He sticks his pen behind his ear, reaches back to grab a pitcher.

I shake my head. "No. I was actually hoping to run into someone."

"Been here ten years." My waiter fills my glass, the ice tumbling and clinking from the container. "I know everyone. Hit me."

"Shouldn't be too hard. He works upstairs." I raise my glass and take a sip of sweet tea. "Will Harris?"

"Sure." The server's eyes sweep the room.

"But nope. Not today."

Under the table, my hands shake. My palms are damp with sweat. "Did you happen to know Karen Carson?"

His face clouds up and he scrunches his nose. "That was tragic. She did something with Will. Kids' books, right?"

A shout comes from the kitchen. *Order up!*

He jabs a thumb toward the window. "Be right back."

Someone else entirely brings my lunch plate. I take a small bite and revel in the taste, tropical, a bit of tang and sweetness.

"Good?" he asks when he comes by my table.

"Delicious." I pry a little more. "So Karen and Will came in here a lot?"

The server hesitates, tapping his bottom lip with the cap of his pen. "Are you with *E! News* or something? *USA Today?*" He puts a hand on his hip.

"Gosh, no. Nothing like that." I widen my eyes and smile. "It's a long story. The dad and son moved to the school district where I work. I'm a school counselor." *Was a school counselor?* "Just trying to get some background. To help the family."

The waiter leans on the table and lowers

his voice. "Well, you've met the kid's dad, then."

A chill threads up the side of my neck, where Mitchell used to touch me. "Of course." I nod and inch closer.

"I only met the guy once." He pauses and rolls his eyes. "That was enough. Believe me."

I swallow hard and fight a wave of nausea. "So that said . . ." I struggle to force the words out. "Any chance she had a boyfriend?"

The server's mouth twists to one side. "Karen? Nah." He shakes his head. "Her husband might have been a jerk, but she wasn't the type."

The waiter lays my bill on the table and squints, looking past my shoulder. "You can ask Will. He's right there." He nods at the space behind me.

I whirl around. Through the open window, I catch a glimpse of someone in khakis, a lemon-yellow shirt, and a navy sport coat. Keys in hand, he walks with purpose to a white BMW convertible, where another man is waiting in the passenger's seat. Harris checks his watch and tosses his briefcase into the backseat.

He's leaving! My brain screams at me to run. I throw down a twenty, bound out of my seat, dart around tables, and push past the hostess. Once out the door, I dash helter-skelter in my heels across the parking lot and skid to a stop between the BMW's headlights.

The two men, both immaculately dressed, stare at me through their Ray-Ban Aviators. Neither smiles.

Will Harris finally pulls down his sunglasses. His pale blue eyes are chilly and flat. "Please tell me you're not a budding author in desperate need of an agent because you're the next female James Patterson?"

I finally catch my breath. "No."

"Good." He sighs. "I get lots of that." He glances at me up and down. "So you are . . . ?"

"Ava Carson. I'm married to Mitchell Carson. And I need help."

He puts the car in reverse and begins to inch away.

"Mr. Harris, please," I plead and restrain myself from lying on the hood. "I have two young boys. Mitchell filed for custody of my children and got it. I didn't even know he'd done it until it was over."

Harris's eyes drop away from mine.

I suck in a breath, stringing the facts together before I lose him. "Now I have supervised visitation. I see my children one hour a week. *One hour.* I don't have a job, Mitchell's bad-mouthed me to the entire community, turned my family against me —"

The other man heaves a dramatic sigh. "Soap opera . . ." he drawls.

"Look, my dear." Harris lifts his chin. "Sorry. I'm a literary agent, not an attorney," he snaps. "And we're late for a meeting."

My heart thumps. "It's just a few questions about Karen," I persist, raising my voice. "What her relationship was like. Her state of mind. Before the accident."

When I don't budge from the bumper, Harris puts the car in park.

"I know I must sound crazy. And paranoid. But please . . ." I yank the purse off my shoulder, dig through my bag, and pull out a picture of me, Jack, and Sam. Last Christmas, in front of our tree. I jut out my arm, ramrod straight, holding the photograph.

He frowns, purses his lips, and rests his fingers on the steering wheel. "Two minutes."

"Thank you," I breathe.

Harris presses his fingers to his temples, rubbing at the skin. He motions me closer.

My heels crunch on the uneven gravel. When I stop next to the driver's side door, Harris turns his head.

"Mitchell would drive by the office." He lowers his voice. "He'd call Karen a dozen times a day. Follow her sometimes." He shakes his head. "Karen was a mess, but she did a good job hiding it." Harris splays his fingers, pressing them to his chest. "I was sure Mitchell was just going through a phase."

I bite my lip.

Harris adjusts his sunglasses. "Any of that sound familiar, dear?"

"Yes." My brain spins in circles.

"I wanted to tell Karen to see someone, a shrink or a lawyer, but in the end, I stayed out of it. It was her life, after all . . ." He flicks his wrist. Despite Will Harris's annoyed attitude and ruffled demeanor, it's clear he cared about Karen. But it's also obvious I've overstayed my welcome. The man next to Harris checks his manicured fingernails.

I scribble down my address and number, hold it out. "Would you call in case you remember anything else?"

Harris frowns and wrinkles his nose. A doubtful look crosses his face. He hesitates, then takes the paper gingerly with two fingers.

"Look, dear," he says and cocks his head. "Why don't you just talk to Frank? He always seemed like a good guy. Frank was close to Karen. They adored each other."

"Frank?"

Harris shoots me a funny look. "You know. Mitchell's father."

Open-mouthed, I step away from the BMW.

I thought he was dead.

CHAPTER 38
JACK

"Psst. Jack-ass."

I ignore my new nickname. Hilarious. The school bully, Taylor, dreamed it up in his massive spare time. Somehow, he's decided I'm his next target. And it's obvious he's spent every waking minute designing ultimate ways to drive me crazy. Five minutes, I remind myself. Take five minutes. Calm down.

"Jack-ass," I hear again.

I wait for the right moment. Just like Wolverine would do. As leader of the X-Men, a band of mutants, Wolverine's trained in martial arts, so he's a super-fighter. His claws, which come out of his hands, cut through metal, stone, and wood. He's strong and has the power to heal in minutes from about any cut, wound, or disease.

"Baby."

274

Eyes forward on the board, I don't move a muscle. Just like Wolverine. In control, deciding on his options. He hides it at first, but then you can tell he's about to explode. His muscles start to bulge, and he goes into these all-out rages. When that happens, the claws come out, and look out bad guys. Villains try to blow him up, poison him, and shoot him. He's unstoppable because he can heal himself; even bullet holes disappear on his body. Everyone's afraid of him. And they should be.

Taylor's right behind me, so I jerk back hard and sudden, sending his desk into his fat gut.

"Hey, ugh, you idiot. Why'd you do that?" Taylor yells at the top of his lungs. He's the tallest, biggest kid in the class, but the first to act like he's being murdered when he stubs a toe. To make matters worse, his mom works at the college for my dad. Taylor dropped that bomb the other day. He says she's in charge of a lot of stuff.

Our teacher spins around, pushes her glasses up her nose, and stares at Taylor, then me. We are clearly on her last nerve, and she's not about to take any crap from anyone.

"Jack did it," Taylor bellows like a water buffalo. "He pushed his desk back on purpose. Ow, my stomach. It hurts."

"Taylor, that's enough. Jack?" She clearly doesn't believe I did anything.

"It was an accident," I plead, wide-eyed at the lie I am telling. "I was stretching."

"Don't let it happen again." She narrows her eyes and turns back to the board.

"Yes, ma'am," I reply.

"Loser."

I heave a sigh.

"Jack-ass."

A spit-wad splats the back of my head. Gross. Ugh. I want to puke.

"Faggot."

A finger finds my back and pokes hard. Again.

"Hands off," I hiss.

"Make me."

Another poke. Another spitball, this time behind the ear. It's drippy wet. The paper slides to my shoulder where it sits like a target.

The class titters. Our teacher glares.

The clock creeps forward another minute. Not nearly fast enough. Taylor reaches his foot forward and snags my backpack with the toe of his tennis shoe. I watch from the corner of my eye as the navy sack slides farther away. Jerk.

"I wonder what's in here." Taylor starts

on the zipper.

"Leave it," I murmur under my breath.

"Oh, lookee here, a baby bottle. Some diapers."

Everyone around me erupts into a volcano of laughter. The sound singes my pride, burns at my brain. The noise sears my skull. My blood pumps like crazy.

"Class," the teacher yells. "Quiet, please!"

"Oh, and here's a photo of your mom kissing her new boyfriend." Taylor chortles.

I am out of my seat then and launch myself on top of Taylor. He's surprised at first and doesn't fight back. Chairs fly; desks overturn. We're a mass of flailing legs and arms. Taylor struggles, but my fists pummel his face until a geyser of blood spurts from his nose. He's crying, for real this time with snot and tears mixed into the bright red.

Everyone is screaming. My teacher's in shock, mouth covered with manicured fingernails. The guys don't know who to cheer for, because they're not used to anyone standing up to Taylor. A few people pull me off him, drag me across the room and into the hallway. It takes three kids in the classroom to hold him down from coming after me. From five feet away, through the glass, Taylor looks like a jungle warrior — face bruised and purple, black eye, chest heaving.

When the door opens, the bell rings and drowns out the noise from inside the room. "Both of you, principal's office. Now," our teacher shouts over the din.

Taylor bursts into the hallway and nearly runs down Mo. But my best friend, dressed in his hoodie and plaid uniform pants, stands his ground. He's almost eye-level with my enemy and pats him on the head like a puppy.

"Easy dude. Watch where you're going, little guy." Mo smiles. They had their "come to Jesus" meeting last summer. Mo painted Taylor's bike hot pink after Taylor made the huge mistake of stealing Mo's skateboard. Oh, and Mo disconnected the bike's brakes. Needless to say, Taylor doesn't mess with Mo. Ever.

Taylor steps aside, breathing hard and glaring at me. Muttering, he throws his backpack over one shoulder and lumbers down the hall.

When he turns the corner, Mo flips me a quiet high five. "You mess him up?" he hisses, glancing both ways to make sure we're not heard.

"Yup, but didn't start it," I say back in a whisper.

"Nice, dude." Mo nudges me.

My shoulders droop in spite of my victory. "My dad's going to lose it."

Mo nods. "That he will."

I groan. "See ya." I start walking past the lockers, letting my fingers brush the cool, smooth metal. My loafers scuff the tiled floor. My knee starts to ache, and with each step, my legs feel heavier.

Outside the glass windows of the administrative office, I pause and listen. Phones ring, copy machines whirr, and there's a rush of muffled chatter. When I turn the knob and open the door, I can smell pencil shavings.

Taylor's already in his conference with the principal, so I take my place at the end of a row of padded red metal chairs. It squishes when I plop down. When I glance down at my hands, I draw a sharp breath.

In my lap, my knuckles are raw and bloody. My shirt's torn at one of the buttonholes and my pants are dirt streaked. I lean to my right, catching my reflection in the big mirror behind the counter. It doesn't show much better. A fat lip, red cheeks, and a sweaty face.

"Jack?"

I jump and look up.

"Head on in there." One of the ladies points me toward Mr. McReed's office, our assistant principal. He's much younger, new to the school this year, and I've heard he's a lot nicer to first-timers in detention.

When I limp in, he puts down his Coke and settles his round belly behind his desk with a sigh. He rubs his red face with his chubby hand, as if trying to rid it of the stress of the day.

"Jack."

"Sir?"

"Looks like you're in some trouble."

"Yes, sir."

"We need to talk about this. And just so you know, I've called your dad."

I was afraid of that.

CHAPTER 39
GRAHAM

FRIDAY, APRIL 23

"It's an emergency," my brother's wife pleads. "It would be a huge, huge favor. And I wouldn't ask if it wasn't life or death."

I swivel back and forth in my office chair, listening. As it turns out, the crisis involves my nephew, a book report on *The Red Kayak,* and a deadline by the end of school today. Thanks to a sprained ankle, my sister-in-law can't drive; my brother's out of town. So that leaves me. The lovable family degenerate who will seize any opportunity to redeem himself.

"He's going to fail if he doesn't turn it in. He'll get a zero, and then he'll have to go to summer school, and then —"

Did I mention my sister-in-law is a bit of a drama queen?

"Whoa!" I stop her, stand up, and peer out the window. It's a gray day, unusually cool, and wet. I grab my jacket and keys.

281

"Done. It's done. I'm leaving now. Walking out the door. Be there in five minutes."

Behind me, the fax machine beeps to life. I stop and backtrack. After thirty seconds of whirring, a single page appears. When I flip it over, my stomach drops.

A restraining order. Signed by the judge. Sworn out by Mitchell Carson, signed by Evan K. Douglas, that rotten excuse for a lawyer. Breaking and entering, missing cash, vandalism of his truck, blah, blah, blah. Damn. Add a black mask and hatchet and I might be known as Ava's executioner. But first things first.

Perched at her door on crutches, my grateful sister-in-law hands off the paper with a quick hug and a Post-it note with instructions to Mobile Prep.

My arrival garners some attention: local attorney, clad in a black leather jacket and boots, riding up to the school on his Harley. I cut quite the figure, I imagine, among the rows of gleaming BMWs, sleek Mercedes, and new Volvos. Once I switch off the engine, two of the younger boys run up to check out the bike.

"So awesome," one says, his blue eyes wide behind his round glasses.

Oh man." His friend admires the chrome trim and tires. He's four feet tall with a ball cap and freckles. "How fast does she go?"

"Fast enough to make mamas cry and the police want to give me a ticket." I grin and pull off my helmet, then wave over the teacher.

She gives me a hesitant smile but doesn't come any closer.

"I'm Graham Thomas, ma'am." I amble over and greet the teacher. "Here to drop something off for my nephew." I rattle off his name, birthday, and classroom number. "I'm on the official list."

"Right this way." The teacher nods primly, shoos the kids away from me, and leads me up the front steps. After she punches a code to allow me in, there's a loud click and a sharp buzz.

"Thank you," I say, pushing open the door.

"The office is just inside," she replies.

The atrium is sparkling clean and smells of Windex. Overhead, huge skylights brighten the shined floor. To the right, tall, lush green plants frame a wall lined with plaques, trophies, and awards. To my left, there's a huge saltwater tank filled with angelfish the color of sunflowers, bright blue chromis and a handful of orange clown fish. I pause and watch the sea life bubble and swim around the coral and vegetation.

Straight ahead is the administration's office, double doors propped open. I'm about to stroll in when I hear a distinct voice.

Mitchell Carson.

I duck behind the tank, watch, and listen.

An office worker with a close-cropped cap of gray hair hovers closer to the counter. "Thank you for coming, Dr. Carson. We've been concerned." She glances toward the assistant principal's office, leans toward him, and cups a hand around her mouth. "Our Jack just seems out of sorts these days. This fight is so out of character."

Mitchell steps into view. He slides a hand across the counter and pats her fingertips. "He's had some trials lately. Some challenges."

She leans closer and whispers. I strain to hear.

"I'll let Ava know," Mitchell promises. "Right away. There's no need for you to notify her."

I ball my fists and grit my teeth.

"Of course," the woman agrees. "Jack should be out in just a few minutes."

She turns and stands at the copy machine while it staples and spits papers in a steady rhythm. She holds a clipboard on her hip and marks boxes with a pencil. Another office worker joins her.

"My, you ladies here must keep the whole school running," he says. "I'm just in awe. I don't suppose I could steal you away to the college, now could I?"

"No, sir." The second office worker giggles like a schoolgirl. "I retire this summer after twenty years."

"Gosh." Mitchell clasps a hand to his heart and feigns shock. "You're much too young."

Please change the subject before I get sick.

"How is Ava?" she asks.

This perks my attention.

"I'm sure you've heard that we're separated." Mitchell lowers his voice. "Now this is just between us, but Ava's had a breakdown. I had to move out with my boys. Get an apartment. She's violent . . . took Jack's bat to my truck, stole money from me." He squeezes his eyes shut. "The judge himself has decided she can't see the children without being supervised."

This gets a gasp from the woman, who steadies her balance with one hand on the copy machine.

"I do have help. A marvelous housekeeper named Isabel. She's teaching the boys Spanish. I don't know what I'd do without her."

"Oh," she breathes.

"Of course, I take the boys to see their

grandmother," he continues. "Despite all that's happened, Ruth adores those boys. They desperately need attention from family members with a proper moral compass."

He doesn't stop there. I wonder if he thinks the twelve disciples are listening from their graves.

"But the worst of all of it . . . word is . . . Ava has a . . . 'friend.' "

"No," the woman gasps.

I'm on my feet, incensed. Just as I start to storm into the office and set the record straight, the phone starts ringing. The worker collects herself and picks up the call. She murmurs into the receiver, makes a few notes, and hangs up.

"Is there no end to the injustice in this world? Lord Jesus, help us."

Mitchell smiles. "We'll be all right. He will provide and show us the correct path. I pray for Ava to get well. To get help. And I hope you will too."

She bobs her head. "Amen." The woman takes a deep breath. "May I have the ladies group at church pray for your family, Dr. Carson?" She blinks her eyes wide, hopeful.

"Of course." He squeezes her hand. "That'd be awfully sweet of you."

I can't stand another minute.

"Hi there." I bound in and greet the office

lady, flash my best jury-winning smile, and plop the paper down in front of her. "I'm delivering this for my nephew. It's very important. Due today. I'd appreciate it if you could get this to his teacher right away."

"Of course, Mr. —"

"Graham Thomas." I stick my hand out to shake hers. "Nice to meet you. I'm his wife's attorney, by the way." I wave at Mitchell, who's purple-faced. "Hi there. Did you practice a script for that or make it up on the fly?" I tap my temple. "I'm thinking the latter."

The office worker is struck dumb. I take full advantage.

"While I have your attention, please pass this along to the ladies." I cock my head and grin. "One, don't believe everything you hear. Two, Ms. Carson doesn't have a boyfriend. And three, the person who needs praying for is right over there."

I point at Mitchell. "He's the one who's made a deal with the devil."

I turn without another word and leave.

CHAPTER 40
JACK

FRIDAY, APRIL 23

Mr. McReed escorts me like a prisoner. I want to wriggle at the firm pressure of his fingertips digging into my arm and guiding the center of my back. But I keep still, duck my chin, and shuffle along the tile floor. The cleaning people must have come through with their mops and pails, because everything's wiped down and smells like lemons.

When I glance up, only halfway, I see that Dad's waiting for us. He's stiff and straight-backed, arms crossed, like his entire body's been carved out of a huge chunk of pine.

Mr. McReed stops and clears his throat. "I think we've gotten to the bottom of this. Call me directly if you have any questions."

Breaking from his wooden mold, coming to life again, Dad reaches over and shakes Mr. McReed's thick hand. "Thanks. And I'll speak to his mother. No need for you to call her."

Mr. McReed nods and smooths his tie over the generous swell of his belly. "Very good."

"We'll get this taken care of, man-to-man, right, Jack?" Dad turns to me and smiles. It's not a real smile, though. It's hard and solid, like Doctor Doom's metal mask. Even though the only part of his face you can see are his eyes, the archenemy of the Fantastic Four is one scary dude. Dark, strong, and smart.

Before I can check behind Dad for a flowing green cape, he grabs my neck and steers me toward the door.

"Thank you, Dr. Carson." Mr. McReed turns and plods back to his office.

The double doors close behind us, and we step out into the swelter of the afternoon. Overhead, angry storm clouds gather in clusters of steel gray and charcoal. The wind howls, long and low, like a wolf separated from the pack. The force of it, sharp and biting, whips at the edges of my shirt, pulling me toward the parking lot. Dad walks faster, with long, smooth strides, and I have to sprint to keep up. He doesn't look at me until we're safely inside the truck. That's when it all falls apart.

I spy a comic book on the front dash and

read aloud: *"Metamorpho: The Element Man."* It's old, but the colors are still bright behind the clear plastic bag, backed by a piece of cardboard so it doesn't wrinkle.

My jaw drops. "Ah, cool, Dad. This is vintage. 1975. It must be worth . . . what . . . thirty dollars?"

"Let's see." He does some calculations in his head. "Oh yeah, DC Comics, first issue special. Thirty-nine bucks plus shipping."

I hold it up and squint, admiring the artwork, the light blue color. Dad starts the Range Rover and I buckle up. A few fat drops of rain hit the windshield and spatter. We ease out of the parking lot as I open the plastic wrap gingerly, pull the book out, and turn each page like I'm reading the original Ten Commandments written and delivered by Moses himself — if they had paper back then.

I pause and look up. "It's in really, really good shape. Oh my gosh. This is . . . I'm so pumped up! I love it."

"I thought you would." Dad keeps his eyes forward, both hands on the wheel. When the rain starts pattering harder, fingertips on the windshield, then drums, he turns on the wipers. The thin black arms click into place, sweeping back and forth over the broad sheet of glass. I watch the back-and-forth motion. *Swish, slosh. Swish, slosh.*

I go back to the smooth, shiny pages, absorbing the colorful artwork and story line. We bump along for at least another few miles when I realize Dad's not talking. Not a word. He usually peppers me with questions about my day, asks about homework, or wants to know about tests this week. This afternoon, though, nothing.

Suddenly the silence curdles inside my belly like rotten milk.

I cough. "Dad, I know Mr. McReed talked to you. But . . . don't you want to hear what happened from me? My side of it?"

He doesn't answer. We bump over a few potholes.

"Dad?" My voice strains over the rain and road.

At a stoplight, he finally shifts his gaze. "Yes, son?"

I choke. Now the expression on his face reminds me of a cross between the Green Goblin and Doc Ock, Spiderman's worst enemies. Slowly, hand trembling, I put the comic book in the center console.

"What's the matter?" he asks.

I move the comic book farther away. "I don't deserve it. The present."

"And why not?"

My heart hammers fast. He wants me to

say it out loud.

"Because of the fight at school. And detention." I sniff and wipe at my nose, look away.

"Yes? What else, Jack?"

I swallow. "I hit him because he was talking bad about Ava. That she has a boyfriend."

"Do you know she doesn't?" His face turns dark and angry.

This time, I don't answer.

Dad pulls to the side of the road, gravel crunching under the tires. The engine rumbles, soft and smooth, while he watches me. Dad takes the comic book and holds it up.

"This was a reward. For my wonderful son who does just what he's asked. Every time." He tilts the comic book back and forth. "Do you deserve this today, Jack?"

"No, sir."

His icy voice lowers to a growl. "That's what I thought."

With a fluid, deft movement, Dad rips the comic book in half, then in half again.

In horror, I reach my hand out to stop him, then yank it back as if it's covered with hot grease.

He shreds each page, faster now, pulling apart words and pictures. The tearing sound fills my ears. I can hardly watch as the book's pages fall into jagged triangles, odd-shaped squares, and long, pale ribbons.

I shrink back further, pressing my head against the cold window. My fingers find the door handle and I hang on, the metal cutting into my skin. Chest heaving, sweat on his forehead, my father lets the last piece drop into the pile between us.

"Fair?" He raises an eyebrow and dares me to challenge him.

"Yes, sir," I croak, holding back tears. It's then that I notice that the rain has stopped.

"That's right." Dad answers, rolls down the window, scoops up the mess, and lets the tattered remains of *Element Man* fall from his fingers like confetti. A few strips catch in the breeze and sail away. Others tumble to the ground. One thin scrap sticks to the side mirror, and Dad flicks it off like trash.

He turns to me again. "Follow the rules, get rewards. Break the rules, suffer the consequences." Dad starts the engine and pulls back onto the road.

As we drive away, I watch in the rearview mirror as the pieces float and fly in wild, looping circles. A few bits float to the side of the road and balance on blades of grass. Most flutter to the pavement, finding their places among the dirt and gravel, waving good-bye.

Chapter 41
Ava

FRIDAY, APRIL 23

The house smells of lacquer, acrid, with an undertone of golden honey. I've flung open every window and door as the workmen begin painting the second coat on the new staircase. As the air, blessedly cool for an Alabama morning, filters into the house, ruffling papers on my desk, I inhale, filling my lungs. Anything to slow the breakneck pace of my pulse.

I watch the dogwood blossoms sway, dipping and clapping together in the breeze. Beside them, camellias, adorned with candy-pink blossoms rustle their forest-green leaves. The ferns, in hanging baskets on the front porch, twirl like dancers on a stage, fringed skirts spinning.

The scent of my tea floats in steamy wisps toward the ceiling, carrying hints of nutmeg and cloves. When I exhale, I practice slow, steady patience. One sip. One breath.

Repeat. I haven't been able to wrap my brain around the idea that Mitchell's father is still alive.

Does Mitchell have his eyes, coal black, edged with granite? Does he drink his coffee black and strong? Will I know his voice, the deep, resonating sound, before he speaks?

My phone rings, a sharp, blaring notice, and I jump at the sound.

Dr. Bennett's name flashes up on the screen.

"Good morning, Ava," she says. "Hope it's not too early. Can we schedule your home visit?"

"Sure." I pull a stray curl behind one ear, shuffle to find my calendar, and check my empty schedule. The days yawn forward for weeks, empty. "Would Wednesday or Friday work?"

"Friday looks good to me," she replies. There's a pause. "I also need Mitchell's permission to pick up the children and drive them to your house. Unless there's a sitter or a grandparent who could do it?"

Immediately, I shake the vision of my mother. Her high brow and fine cheekbones. Her perfectly articulated disapproval. Her thin lips, curling down. We've not spoken. And I won't step a toe in a lioness's den only to be rejected.

"I'm sure —" I hesitate. "Well, I think he'll be fine with it."

"Okay, I'll take care of it." She clears her throat. "So the other reason I needed to talk is this. When I called Mitchell to confirm his home visit on Monday, he informed me he'd have to change the time until later that afternoon because Jack has detention."

I choke. "Detention?"

"There was an incident at school around two o'clock this afternoon. Apparently, Jack was involved in some sort of fight. A scuffle, Mitchell said."

"Scuffle?" I repeat, rushing back to the window, as if I might find my son standing in the yard, a sling over one shoulder. When I look, the only sign of life is a tiny sparrow pecking between blades of grass. "Is Jack all right?"

"Mitchell didn't tell you?"

"No," I say, trying to keep my voice steady.

"From what I understand, Jack's a little banged up. It sounds like he'll be fine." Dr. Bennett clears her throat.

My throat closes. I'm dizzy with worry.

"I didn't want it to shock you," she continues. "If you happen to run into Mitchell and the boys in town — before your next visit."

"Thank you," I reply, sitting down heavily. "Jack's not one to make trouble." I suck in a breath. "Did Mitchell say what happened? Is the other student okay? I assume it was another child, not a teacher?"

"Someone in Jack's class. He's okay, too." She pauses. "I'm not certain what the disagreement was about, although I plan to try and find out more Monday. I believe he'll have detention for a few days."

Biting my lip, I glance at the clock. It's past five thirty. Too late on a Friday to get in touch with anyone. "I'll talk to the school. It'll have to be next week."

"Of course," she agrees. "I'm sorry I wasn't able to reach you sooner. I've been with clients all day."

The moment I hang up, my phone buzzes with a call from Graham.

"Hello?" I answer quickly.

He's breathing fast, and his words come out clipped. "They got their restraining order," Graham says flatly. "In Alabama, it's called a Protection from Abuse Order, or PFA. You can't contact him or go near him."

I open my mouth to protest, but Graham keeps talking. "There's more. I just ran into Mitchell. Did you hear about Jack?"

"Yes, Dr. Bennett . . ." My chin falls, and I press my fingers to my forehead, squinting at my shoes. Then I stop, realizing what he'd said. "Wait, did Mitchell tell you?"

"Are you kidding?" Graham asks. "I was delivering homework for my nephew. I heard Mitchell talking, so I hid behind that huge saltwater tank in the lobby." He punctuates the story with a few gory details of the run-in.

"Now I've heard everything." I groan.

"Hey," Graham exclaims. "I defended your honor. Told those women in the office not to believe everything they heard."

My chest warms with a twinge of satisfaction. "Must have been quite the speech."

"Ha. Mitchell made it clear *he* was going to call you about Jack. I heard him say it. That the secretaries shouldn't bother trying to reach you."

"He had no intention of telling me." Of course.

"Nope."

I close my eyes and hold my breath. Getting angry won't do any good. I focus on what I have to tell him. "Graham?"

"Yep?"

"Mitchell's father is alive."

"I'll be dammed!" He exclaims.

"Thursday afternoon I found Will Harris, who, by the way, was not that thrilled to see me. But he told me to talk to Frank Carson." I pause and shake my head. "I'm still in shock."

Graham laughs. "Ah! Our golden boy is beginning to look more like Pinocchio. Good work."

I flush with pleasure. "Mitchell's dad is living in Moulton, just north of Cullman. To think, after all these years . . ."

"Just a few hours away," Graham finishes my thought.

As I stare out the window, my thoughts turn. They're already on the winding stretch between here and there.

"I'm going to go find him."

CHAPTER 42
AVA

SATURDAY, APRIL 24

As I pass through Cullman and travel northwest, the Jeep rattles, making my water bottle jump and slosh. The scent of burned wood permeates the air, and the occasional jet screams overhead, leaving contrail wisps in the painted-blue sky.

Moulton itself is tiny and well cared for, population just over three thousand. There are stately brick churches, newer homes with landscaped lots, and a plethora of fast-food restaurants. As I pass through and turn off onto a small street on the outskirts of the city, I enter a strikingly different world.

This neighborhood contains small one-story homes, front porches decorated with sagging flowered sofas, broken bicycles, and rusted soda cans. An occasional resident of the community stares, sleepy-eyed, suspicious. Mangy dogs glare at empty water bowls; skeleton-thin, skittish cats hide in

301

tall grass. I double-check my GPS and turn right.

The house sits close to the road. The roof appears relatively new; the yard is cut short, and an American flag flutters in a gust of warm air. While not pristine, the home is obviously in better shape than the rest on the street. This alone makes me feel slightly better, though I'd feel safer with a canister of Mace.

The mailbox, dented silver, bears no markings, no name. A late-model turquoise Buick spans the entire driveway. Long and sleek, fins, whitewall tires. *Stop admiring and procrastinating. You won't find anything sitting inside the Jeep.* I silence the lecture in my head and step out into a blanket of humidity. Rusted hinges protest with a loud squawk as I push open the gate. Next door, a barely bathrobed woman in pink curlers blows gray puffs of cigarette smoke. I wave, but she sits, her dark arm moving to her full lips, then away, watching.

Fine. I knock twice with my knuckles, firm. Nothing. Again, harder. I peer through the glass, but it's covered with curtains.

"Mr. Carson," I finally call out, my mouth inches from the door.

A rough voice answers. "I don't want any. Go away or I'll call the cops."

Okay. At least I've got the right place.

"Mr. Carson, please. I'm not selling anything." A trickle of sweat runs down the small of my back. April is not supposed to be this hot. If I stand here much longer, I'll faint or melt away, and he won't have to face me. Maybe that's his plan.

"Don't you understand English? Get out of here." A gruff command. A soldier's order.

"Sir, I just need a moment." I rack my brain, rub at the beads of perspiration on my neck.

Silence. "It's about Jack," I finally say. "And your son, Mitchell."

Another few minutes tick by. I walk away from the door, check my cell phone, and pace across the wooden planks. The lady next door hasn't moved.

But then, something or someone rolls near the front door. I hear a lock click, and the door swings open a few inches. A thick-linked chain snaps tight. I turn and step toward the door. The end of a pistol stares back at me.

"Wait, hold on," I exclaim and hold up my hands, fingers spread.

"Name," he barks.

"Ava. Ava Carson. I'm married to your son." For good measure, I give him

Mitchell's birth date. I rattle off our home address. "And Jack's middle name is Franklin."

This seems to convince him I'm not on his doorstep to rob him blind or steal his TV. He studies me like a scientist, as if I'm a bloodstain under a microscope.

"We're . . . we're having some problems. I was hoping you might —"

"First of all, get in here." He reaches a gnarled hand and unlatches the chain. "Standing out there on my porch isn't the best idea."

I step inside the dark room and let my eyes adjust to the light. It's thirty degrees cooler, the air-conditioner hums in the corner. The place, sparsely furnished, is neat and clean. No photos. A few books, magazines. *The Cullman Times* lies open on the table.

Mitchell's father stares back at me from his wheelchair. "I'd offer you a cold drink, but all I have is tap water. Don't get out much."

"I'll take some."

He doesn't move. "Help yourself, young lady. The kitchen's that way."

"Thank you." It's four steps to the sink. I find a clean glass, gulp greedily.

When I turn, he's behind me. I jump.

"Sorry," he says. "I tend to move quietly, even in this old thing." He gestures to the wheels. "So, you're a ways from home, I take it?"

I nod. "Four hours. We're in Mobile. It's quiet. Relatively safe." I glance down at the pistol in his hand.

It occurs to me that Mitchell has one just like it. I look closer. Exactly like it. My stomach flip-flops.

Frank puts the gun away. "It's for protection. Neighborhood's gone downhill. Used to be nice, back in the day. Real fine." He glances wistfully away from me. "After 'Nam, everything changed."

"Yes, sir," I agree. "I'm sure a lot's changed."

"Have a seat." He gestures to a chair. "Tell me why you've come all this way to see an old man. Something wrong with my son? He sick?"

"Mr. Carson, when was the last time you saw Mitchell?"

He rubs his head. His gray hair is cut military style, high and tight. "Nearly five years ago, I reckon." He adjusts his wheelchair. "Not since the accident. I take it you know about Karen."

"A little bit."

"She was a good girl. Quiet. Didn't

305

deserve to have those seizures."

Everything stops. I hold up a hand and stop Frank. "Wait. Seizures? As in epilepsy?"

Seizures. Epilepsy. The accident?

Frank shakes his head. "When they lived close or she'd visit, I'd remind her to take her medicine. She'd hassle me about taking mine. Damned blood pressure. It was our running joke for years. Both of us with our little yellow pills. We laughed about that." He chuckles.

"Was she very ill?"

"Not until the last few weeks before her book tour. She was tired. Working a lot. It was like her body wouldn't cooperate."

"And then she had the accident?"

Frank nods. "Police never did really figure out what happened. We had a real nice service for Karen. Then, six months later, Mitchell dropped out of sight. Like damn Charlie." He heaves a sigh. "I called; he changed his number. A buddy drove me up to his house. It was sold. No forwarding address, no nothing."

"And you haven't tried to get in touch since? Find him?"

"I'm thinking he doesn't want to be found. My vision's crap, especially at night. Can't hit the broad side of a barn, even with my .45. A few friends who used to stop over

306

and pick me up, they've died off. The rest of the folks in these parts, well, they're not so friendly. No one wants to adopt an old white guy, if you know what I mean." He grimaces and taps his leg. "Damn thing. Spent thirty years in the service — most of it across the pond — and get hit by a drunk driver less than a mile from home."

I take another sip of water. "I'm sorry. So, why? Why would Mitchell disappear?" The question escapes before I can stop myself.

Frank tugs his ear. "Don't know for sure. Folks got curious, asked a lot of questions about Karen. Wanted to know what happened. Told him how sorry they were. They were just being kind. But all of the attention made Mitchell really uncomfortable and jumpy. Nervous all of the time. Even *I* asked him why he was acting so strange."

"Did he tell you?"

He grimaces. "Nah, wouldn't talk about it. So he took off with Jack. I guess he thought . . . other people left him . . . why shouldn't he leave?"

"Do you mean when you deployed? Changed duty stations?"

"Sure, that was part of it when he was younger. We traveled some. But once I came home from 'Nam in '72, I struck a deal with the wife."

"Which was?"

"She and Mitchell stayed put. We stayed married. I went where the army told me to go. Lasted about five years."

"When his mother . . ." I can't make myself say suicide.

Frank nodded. "She'd finally had enough. Of me being gone. Of the army. Of life. He'd already run away once or twice." Frank sighed. "I think to get his mother's attention, which didn't work. She began drinking. In secret, of course. Mitchell never said a word. She sure didn't tell me. And I'd come home and collapse for a few days, run around, see buddies, play a few rounds of golf. Then the army'd send me somewhere else."

I ran a finger around my glass, listening.

"Depression, that's what it was with my wife. I found out later from the neighbors that she wouldn't leave the house, wouldn't see friends, refused to answer the damn phone. But back then, no one talked about it. You sucked it up, did your job. The separation was part of it. The army wives had each other, or so I thought." He rolls over to the edge of the counter, pulls out a small photo album, flips to the front page. In black-and-white, there's Mitchell as a child, his mother, serious and serene, and

Frank. "She left us in '77. Killed herself on Christmas Eve."

My heart twists.

"That's when Mitchell ran away again. For a good long time. Finally found him in Phoenix, Arizona, of all places. He was just a kid, tall for his age. Talked some lady into buying him a Greyhound bus ticket. I brought him home after three weeks of searching. He was never the same."

"Was he the one . . . Did he find his mother?"

Frank nods and frowns. He makes the shape of a gun with his thumb and forefinger and places it under his chin.

"We never talked about it. Not once. Mitchell went off to Alabama, made perfect grades. Met Karen, moved up the ladder fast at these schools where he worked. Karen was good for him. And I thought Mitchell was even better when Jack came along. I miss that boy so much. I bet he's huge. Do you have a photo?"

"In the Jeep. I'll grab it before I leave." That seems to satisfy him. I hesitate to press too much, but he seems to like the company. "Were they having any problems?"

Frank brushes a piece of lint off his pant leg. "Not according to my son. He wasn't one to admit defeat of any kind. But to answer your question, the usual, I guess. Karen never talked about it much."

"She was pretty. I saw a picture."

"Must have been a book signing, or some announcement. She never mentioned it unless someone asked," Frank muses. "I do know all of her success seemed to bother Mitchell a bit."

"Because . . . ?"

Frank chuckles. "Mitchell always had to be top dog. He was the head of this and that, on such and such committee, awarded some thing or the other. He didn't share the spotlight well. And he was jealous. Imagined things more than once. I guess you might know a little about that."

"A little," I agree. The doorbell rings. My chest tightens. *I need more time.*

"Um, Mitchell . . . was he involved with Jack's activities? After school —"

Ring! Ring! The person at the door isn't very patient.

Frank smiles, checks his watch. "Ah, right on time. My dear old ball and chain." He wheels to the front of the house and opens the lock. "Where've you been all my life, darling?"

A stocky young woman stands in the doorway. "Don't give me no lip, Mr. Frank." She wears purple nursing scrubs, an ID

310

from a home-health agency, and carries a huge canvas bag. "How's your sugar? You takin' your blood pressure pills?"

"Why don't you come here and find out?" Franks scoots his wheelchair back and winks.

"You no account dirty dog. I'll string you up with my hand tied behind my back if you don't —" One hand on her hip, the woman steps into the living room and almost faints when she sees me. "Oh! Mr. Frank, why didn't you tell me you had company?"

I stand up. "Daughter-in-law." I shake hands.

"Evangeline." She sizes me up. "Didn't know Frank had family 'round here. I come to check on his diabetes, his blood pressure, and to see whether he's taking the rest of his medicine." She shoots him an evil look, then grins.

"I'm Ava. Nice to meet you."

"Same here. We are going to be awhile," she says pointedly, glancing down at her watch and back up at me.

I swallow, digest this, and give Evangeline a small smile. "Oh, I was just leaving." Reluctantly, I kiss Frank's rough cheek and whisper in his ear. "If you think of anything else, here's how you can reach me." I dash

311

off my cell number on a scrap of paper. "Can I have yours?"

Frank nods and lists off the number.

When I finish writing, my father-in-law is still studying me. "Say hello to Jack, would you?" he asks. "It's been forever. Bring him next time?"

"I'll sure try."

There's no good way to explain — in front of his nurse — why I don't have his number. Or that I didn't even know he was alive until a few days ago.

"Bye now, honey. Drive safe," Evangeline says and busies herself around Frank, clucking and talking under her breath. "Got to get to work here."

My hand on the doorknob, I hesitate. *I didn't have a chance to tell him about Sam.* It'll have to wait. Along with so many questions. So many things I want to ask. With a deep breath, I look at Frank one last time, wave, and close the door behind me.

Before I head for Mobile, I dig through my bag, find Jack's most recent school picture.

For good measure, I scribble my cell phone number on the back and tuck the photo inside the screen door where Evangeline is sure to find it.

See you soon. I promise.

Chapter 43
Jack

SUNDAY, APRIL 25

The cinnamon roll scent wafts out of Miss Beulah's, sweet enough to bring the Incredible Hulk to his knees. I float in, stomach grumbling, in a frosting-filled haze. Dad's dreamed up this idea of guys' Sunday brunch. I think everyone in Mobile has the same plan. There's barely room to sit down.

We need to "bond," he explains. Except I'm too hungry to care, and Sam won't keep still. As Dad goes to order, I settle my brother the best I can in the coffee shop's wooden high chair. When I push him close to the table, he grabs at forks, spoons, and napkins, knocking them to the ground. The silverware hits the floor, clattering and clanging, bouncing in every direction. Head down, I pick up every piece and place them out of reach.

Sam screws up his face, his pouty bottom lip sticking out an inch. His small fists find

313

both eyes, digging and twisting, and he lets out a huge yawn. I want to remind Dad that he's been up for hours, since before dawn, and will only get crankier if he doesn't get a nap.

I dig in the diaper bag, searching for a book, a toy, or his fuzzy brown bear that he loves so much. But there's nothing. A few diapers. Wipes. A tube of tacky white rash cream that smells like cod-liver oil. I wrinkle my nose.

When I sit up, empty-handed, Sam's slapping at the table, content for the moment because he's flirting with one of the baristas. While she plays peekaboo, Dad comes back, and I excuse myself to go to the bathroom. Even though I don't have to go, getting up may help the pain in my gut disappear. So I make a beeline for the back, keep my head down.

The owner, Mo's mom, with her twisted-up blonde hair and swingy silver earrings, almost runs me over. She balances a tray of something sweet and gooey above my head.

"Hey, Jack," she laughs. "Watch out. You'll be wearing this next time."

"Sorry," I say. "Is Mo around?"

She shakes her head. "Still sleeping, hon."

"Okay," I mumble and squeeze by as best I can.

I can only imagine what Dad would do to me if I came back covered with white icing. Guaranteed way to get in trouble, whether or not it was my fault.

Safe inside the confines of the men's room, I wash my hands, dry them, and stare into the mirror. My reflection stares back, but I imagine I'm Dr. Bruce Banner, one of the smartest people on earth. Banner is Hulk's real identity. He's a total brainiac, PhD in nuclear physics, expert in biology, chemistry, and engineering. Calm, cool, collected. Until a gamma bomb he invented explodes. If he just wasn't quite so curious . . .

A shrill cry interrupts my daydream. It's Sam, I'm sure.

Back at the table, my brother's twisted himself into a total meltdown. Red-faced, crying, he's yelling "Mama!" as loud as anyone I've ever heard.

"Where have you been?" My father snaps. He's dialing the phone with one hand, patting Sam's back with the other.

I can't form the words over the screams. Or tell my dad what to do. He won't want to hear about fuzzy bear or taking a nap. Or that he really needs Ava. I clamp my mouth

315

shut and try desperately to distract Sam with funny faces.

"Where's Isabel?" Dad mutters, redialing.

Mo's mom attempts to distract Sam with a muffin. He knocks it to the floor and bangs on the table. Tears stream down his cheeks. "Mama! Mama!"

My father finally gives up. He hangs up, hoists my baby brother to his shoulder, and throws a twenty on the table.

Then I see the reason why Sam's freaking out. In the corner, a woman with her back to us looks amazingly like Ava. It's not her. I can tell. But to Sam, there's no difference.

"He thinks she's Ava." I point and try to tell Dad.

He frowns and scans the room.

"Sam thinks that's his mom," I repeat.

All of a sudden, it's Dad, not me, that turns into the Incredible Hulk. There's no stepping into a phone booth like Superman or fast costume changes in the Bat Cave. His skin doesn't turn green. But somehow my dad has turned into a monster.

He puts a hand on my neck. We storm through Miss Beulah's and burst to the outside. So much for male bonding. Dad's got us buckled in and gone before the next traffic light change. Jaw set, he calls Isabel again. This time she picks up. By the time we reach the apartment, Sam's still red-faced but ten times calmer after we've bumped along in the Range Rover for a few minutes. Live oak trees, with their curling arms full of green leaves, wave as we roll by. The sunlight winks through the branches.

I take off my brother's shoes and rub his feet, which he seems to like. After another mile, Dad clicks the radio on. Soft melody, just instruments, no singing, floats into the backseat. Sam kicks his legs, toes wiggling with the notes. Phew. Music.

I fall back against the seat, exhausted. My head pounds. But Sam's okay. And my dad's turned back into a human being again. Like the Hulk, deep inside, maybe he wants to be normal. He just can't figure out how.

CHAPTER 44
MITCHELL

SUNDAY, APRIL 25

I'm looking at the staircase in my house. It's everything I imagined, stately, imposing, with wide, smooth planks of dark wood with even grain. I run a hand over the glossy finish, and my palm races down the railing.

The warm, raw scent of sawdust lingers, mingling with the smell of dinner — freshly cracked pepper, earthy beef juices, and sweet caramelized onions. I hear her chopping vegetables in the kitchen, picture the knife blade slicing through crisp orange carrots, dicing firm Yukon gold potatoes. She'll add tender peas that burst in your mouth and tangy sweet creamed corn.

Earlier I'd parked on the road, behind a grove of trees. And waited. When I was ready, I walked, picking my way over branches, pushing aside brush. I'd slid my key into the lock and turned. The locks hadn't been changed, almost if Ava was expecting me to come home.

My hands run along bookshelves, caress the walls, and finger the matching satin shades topping each lamp. I pluck a pillow from the sofa and bring it to my nose, deeply inhaling. Everything reminds me of Ava.

My shelves. My space. My house. Pausing, I close my eyes and picture my fingers around her slender, white neck. Squeezing the tendons, crushing tender vocal cords. Stopping the blood from pumping.

I step into the kitchen. "Hello, Ava."

She whirls around and drops a carton of eggs. *Ker-plunk!* Cracked white half-shells roll every which way. Yellow goo seeps into cracks in the ceramic tile. Her lips part into a small oval.

"Where have you been?" I challenge her.

She swallows and grips the counter, balancing there as if the slab of granite is all that will keep her from falling.

"You can't be here," Ava says, lifting her chin. The voice she summons is strong and defiant.

I ignore her question and step closer, enjoying that despite the attempt at bravado, her body begins to quake. "Where were you?"

Ava makes a sweeping motion at the yolky

mess on the ground. "It's no secret, Mitchell. The grocery store. And now I'll have to go back."

"Don't play games," I snap. "I'm talking about yesterday. You were gone all day."

My wife shakes her head. "That's none of your business, Mitchell."

Rage boils in my chest. "It's always my business. This" — I point at the wall — "is my house. This" — I stab a finger toward the ground — "is my property."

Her eyes dart toward her iPhone, near the sink. We both spring, but I jump farther and faster. Our bodies collide, a tangle of flesh and clothing, of breathing. I snatch the case, triumphant, and lock it in my hand. Ava shakes her head, a strand of hair coming loose from where it's gathered behind her head. Her lips part.

Before she can speak, I splay the air with my arm, cutting across the space from wall to wall. "I'll tell everyone you're following me," I threaten. "Stalking me. And you'll lose your measly hour of visitation a week and everything else."

"How are you going to prove this?" she demands in a hushed voice. "I'm in my own house. Minding my own business."

I don't reply. Instead, I dial my own number and press speakerphone. On command, Ava's iPhone emits a mechanical dial. And repeats. Inside my breast pocket of my sport coat, my cell bleats a response. My wife's face drains of color. I grin, hang up, and call my phone a second time. And a third.

"You should have thought of all of this before you began calling me, Ava." I laugh, stilted and halting. "You should have thought of this before you went off and found a boyfriend."

Evidence in place, I stalk to the kitchen sink, grab a hand towel, and wipe the cell clean of any marks. My breath comes now in short bursts. Ava closes her eyes. There is only silence and the pulse of my blood.

"I wonder if you planned this from the start," she finally murmurs. "You had everyone fooled. Especially me."

She leaves the room, chin held high. Chasing is futile. She's already lost. I strain to hear her bare feet. On the staircase. In the hallway overhead. In our bedroom.

In the silence, upstairs, I hear a lock click into place.

Chapter 45
Graham

MONDAY, APRIL 26

When I open my door Monday morning, the paper is open on the front porch, edges damp. I blink twice, making sure I'm not still in a dream state. Delicate fingers touch the ink on the page. A watch face catches the sunlight. My gaze travels from the wrist to arm, then shoulder. Ava looks up at me, forehead creased, green eyes pale and pained. God, she is beautiful. *Get ahold of yourself, counselor,* I remind myself.

"Hey," I manage, after I've caught my breath. "I take it this isn't a social call?"

Ava glances behind her, then pops to her feet, looping her bag over one shoulder. "Mitchell was in the house last night."

My heart lurches. "What?" I open the door and pull her inside. "Let's go back to my office."

Ava collapses into a wide, stuffed chair in the corner. She tucks her legs close, making herself small and compact. "I'm so stupid. I was unloading groceries. I haven't gotten the locks changed yet." She pauses and runs two fingers across her lips. "Showed up in the kitchen. Demanded to know where I've been."

"Damn." My chest contracts.

"I know." Ava shivers. "When I told him he couldn't be in the house, he freaked." She pauses. "He grabbed *my* phone and called his cell. Over and over."

"Like you'd been the one . . ."

"Like I wanted him there," she agrees, sweeping at the air for emphasis. She lets her fingers fall, coming to rest on her bent knees.

"What the hell?" I rake a hand through my hair. "How can you be so calm? Why didn't you call me?" I raise my voice an octave and pace in front of her.

Ava dips her chin and shrugs. "I didn't do anything. I let him win. I left the room, went upstairs, and locked myself in the bedroom. After a few minutes, he left."

Slowly, I stop walking. *Damn.* It's brilliant. Correction: she's brilliant. "No kidding?"

Ava grins a little. "No kidding." She looks past me. "Of course, I set the house alarm. With a new code. And sat up all night."

"I'm getting a patrol to go by your house.

Every few hours. Maybe every hour, if I can talk them into it."

Her eyes flutter to mine. "Thank you. That means a lot."

We both know even that might not dissuade him. My mind swirls. "Can you go somewhere else? Should we get you a safe house? An apartment?"

"I don't know, Graham." Her voice chokes on my name.

"There's got to be a way to protect you," I say, rubbing the stubble on my chin. "Let me think on it."

She nods.

"Let's get to the rest of your weekend. The trip. Tell me what you found out."

Ava rubs her temples, remembering. "It was one heck of a meeting, once I convinced Frank to open the door and put down his gun."

I raise an eyebrow.

"Once a soldier . . . always a soldier," she says.

"And?"

"Karen had epilepsy."

I straighten and wrinkle my forehead. "No kidding? Is that how she died?"

"Newspaper didn't say that," Ava replies. "But Frank told me."

I make coffee as she fills me in on

Mitchell's father, back from the dead. The pistol, Frank's military background and deployments, Mitchell running away. That he tended to be jealous of the success of others — no big surprise there. Ava wrapped up Frank's account of Mitchell moving away and not telling anyone after Karen's death.

"Whew!" I make some notes and wipe at my brow in mock relief. "Is that all? I thought you said something actually happened."

"I started to ask more, but his home-health nurse arrived. Frank has some medical issues. I didn't think I could quiz him while she was there. I left my number," Ava adds.

"That's all crucial to know," I say. "His behavior with Karen sounds suspicious. And disappearing after his wife dies? Not telling his own father? Then pretending his dad is dead? That's beyond weird."

Ava rubs her forehead. "I should have known. Why didn't I see this? He was so charming, so convincing."

"Sociopaths usually are," I snap. "They only show what they want to." I think about Ted Bundy and Ted Kaczynski. "If you cross them, upset their perfect fantasy world, they strike back."

She reels back a little at the statement, then runs a finger along her lip.

"What is it?"

"Something I asked Mitchell once. About dating after Karen died."

I raise an eyebrow. "And?"

"When he went out with people," Ava continues. "He said something about breaking it off before ever getting to date three or four." She locks eyes with me. "But he'd never tell me anything else. Why. What they did."

My hands turn clammy and cold. *Mitchell is terrified of rejection.* "Female staff?" I ask.

Ava shakes her head. "Not many equals." She presses her fingertips together. "I'm beginning to think he doesn't actually like women."

"Starting with his own mother," I say ruefully. "All the pieces of the puzzle are starting to come together, giving us a clearer picture of what Mitchell Carson is all about. It'll come in handy, I promise you. But, right now —" I pull a paper from the top of a stack next to my elbow.

Ava watches, her brow clenched tight.

"We have to deal with this." I hold up a sheet. "It came in late last night. Mitchell must be paying this guy a fortune to be at his beck and call. He's calling the shots, not his lawyer."

"What does it say?" Ava makes a face.

"It's a stalking accusation. Some not-so-veiled threats." I scan the fax. "They aren't going to press charges now out of the goodness of their hearts and all of that garbage." I shuffle through the stack. "This worries me more." I pass the page across the desk. "It's a new motion. Asking for emergency child support."

"What?" Her face falls.

"Ava, listen." I try to boil it down. "He can ask. He can also ask for you to shine his shoes and give out hula-hoops. It doesn't mean he's going to get it. In this situation, the judge will look at your past earnings. Had you been married say, ten years, and stayed home the entire time, this wouldn't be an issue."

"My earnings — when I did work — were nothing compared to his."

"Obviously, I'll be sure to point that out at the hearing. He's trying to hurt you. Wear you down. Get you to back off and scare you. We'll counter file, which should help."

Ava swipes a tissue from the box and dabs at her eyes. "Graham, I can't handle this."

"Yes. You. Can." I lean across the desk and point, trying to swing a balance between firm and semi-playful.

I'm rewarded with a half smile. She raises her hands in defense. "Okay, okay."

"But on the off chance they get somewhere with this crazy motion," I add, "put some feelers out for a job, even something part-time. You still have connections at the school?"

Ava nods. "It's about time I talk to them. I could use the work. Plus, I'd be close to Jack. The school's asked me to come back several times. Just last month Miss Anne mentioned it."

"Good. It's time you pay her a visit." I pause and get up out of my seat. I wince a little. My leg is killing me.

I stop when I notice Ava's expression of horror.

"Your knee!" she exclaims and sits straight up. "Yikes."

I reach down and probe with my thumb and index finger. Great. Swollen at least three times the normal size. "So much for the marathon." I stand up. "I'll have to withdraw from Boston."

Ava hugs her arms to her chest and gives me a curious look.

"Darn motocross accident back in high school." I pretend to twist handlebars on a dirt bike. "That last berm cost me the race."

"I thought —" She stops and shakes her

head. "Never mind."

"Listen," I say. "Don't worry about me. You get ready to do some damage control. Remember, Mitchell's doing his best to slaughter your reputation."

Ava slings her bag over one shoulder and shakes her head. "I'm not going to let him."

CHAPTER 46
JACK

MONDAY, APRIL 26

Dr. Bennett's outside Dad's apartment. I know, because as soon as the doorbell rings, I peek out the window. Her red glasses are the first thing I see. She's dressed up today, in a navy-blue skirt and jacket. Her hair is pinned back.

Isabel's in the back, doing laundry. The washer's on spin cycle, churning and bumping, and I know she can't hear anything. Other than the noise, I like wash days. The apartment always smells fresh and clean, like outside after the rain. Dr. Bennett frowns, rings the bell, and knocks again.

As I watch her, my hands get tacky and wet, and I rub them on my jeans. Because of detention, I'm not supposed to go out of my room. Dad lectured me, just before he dropped me off and headed back to the college. But now Dr. Bennett's cheeks are pink. And she's fanning herself with her hands. I can't let her stand out there waiting. I run to the back of the apartment.

"Someone's here," I say, tugging on Isabel's shirt. Sam and I follow her as she pads cautiously toward the front door.

Isabel leaves the chain in place as she opens the door a crack. Warm, damp air trickles into the apartment, making me shiver in the air-conditioned room. Dr. Bennett smiles and wipes her forehead with her fingertips.

"Hi there. I'm Dr. Bennett, here for my appointment." She smiles and waggles her fingers at baby Sam, who coos and sticks a finger in his mouth. "Hi, Jack."

I wave hello.

Isabel looks puzzled. "Doctor Carson, he no here right now." She smiles and attempts to shut the door. "Come back later, no?"

"No," Dr. Bennett says, frowning, "not come back later. I have an appointment now." She twists her wrist and points at her watch. "Can you call him, please? Tell him I'm here?"

The suggestion doesn't go over well. Isabel purses her lips.

"I'll wait right here. Maybe he forgot." Dr. Bennett smiles and backs away. "How about that?"

Isabel picks up Sam, puts him on her hip,

and shakes her head. "You no wait. You come back. So sorry."

"How long will you be here tonight?" Dr. Bennett asks Isabel. She's still smiling, but a tiny trickle of sweat rolls down one cheek.

I hold out my hand, wanting to tap Isabel's arm and interrupt.

"What time do you go home?" Dr. Bennett tries to change the question. "What time are you finished watching the children today?"

"Sometime six o'clock. Most night, finish seven. But Friday night, Bingo!" This makes Isabel light up. She loves Bingo.

Dr. Bennett's eyes meet mine. I try to smile, but my stomach feels heavy like I've swallowed rocks.

"You come back?" Isabel asks again.

"No, I'm —"

"Uno momento." Isabel closes the door on Dr. Bennett. After the lock clicks into place, she bends down and looks down at me. She's so close I can see gold flecks in her dark eyes. "You know thees lady?" she asks me softly.

"Yes," I answer. "She's nice. We go to her office once a week. She knows my dad. He takes us there."

Isabel hugs Sam close, bouncing him up and down. Knowing my babysitter, she can't stand having someone waiting outside. "She supposed to come?"

I shrug. "I don't know. Dad didn't tell me."

Isabel shakes her head and clucks her tongue. "Five minute," she mutters. "Five minute." When she opens the door again, Dr. Bennett's still standing there. Isabel watches her with a wary eye.

"Hey, Dr. Bennett. Isabel says you can come in," I say. "Dad's not here. And I don't think Isabel wants to call him. She says you can stay five minutes."

Dr. Bennett smiles and steps in. "Thank you," she says to Isabel and shakes her hand. "I'm Jack and Sam's doctor."

"Sí," Isabel says and closes the door behind her, shutting out the heat.

Dr. Bennett fans herself again, and this time I can smell the lotion on her skin, like tangerine and grapefruit.

She pats my arm. "Jack, can you give me the grand tour? I had an appointment with your dad and was supposed to meet him here at the house, but I guess he got caught at work."

"That happens a lot," I say.

The dryer chimes, signaling the load is done, and Isabel excuses herself to go check it. She hands me Sam, who wriggles out of my arms and runs to the sofa to bury his head. I guess she's decided Dr. Bennett isn't a mass murderer or robber.

When we walk through the rest of the house, Dr. Bennett looks up at the high ceilings and the fancy molding around the windows. The carpet, creamy white, makes her ankles wobble because it's so thick. Dr. Bennett purses her lips when we get to my bedroom. I feel my face get hot. It's empty, except for a small table, my backpack, my comic books, and my bed.

"Dad doesn't want the place all cluttered up," I say, repeating what I've heard since we moved in. "Want to see the kitchen?"

Sam wants to be carried then, and plays with Dr. Bennett's dangly earring. When we get to the kitchen, Dr. Bennett asks for a glass of water. Sam sits on her lap.

"Sure," I say and get a cup from the cabinet.

I open the freezer, which is bare except for ice, grab a handful, and plunk it in the plastic container. When I open the fridge and reach for the bottled water, it hits me how every shelf is empty. There's an apple, a leftover soft drink, half full, and a jug of sweet tea. I catch Dr. Bennett looking, but she doesn't say a word. She drinks the water and sets the cup in the sink.

"Well, Jack, I'll be sure to tell your dad that you were an excellent host. It was great to meet Isabel. Does she do a lot of cooking? I suppose she's not much into country fried steak, meat loaf, and ribs." Dr. Bennett grins.

I laugh. "She's the best," I say. "Tamales, enchiladas, tacos." I rub my belly in anticipation of tonight's supper.

"That's great," Dr. Bennett replies and reaches over to rub my head. Sam's cuddled into her shoulder, fingers in his mouth.

I point to the square cooler with the shoulder strap in the corner. "She brings us dinner every day and takes the leftovers home at night, unless Dad wants them."

"Wow, you're lucky to have Isabel. I'm glad you have her around." She sets Sam on the floor and calls good-bye to Isabel.

I walk with her to the door. "Bye," I tell her.

"Thanks, Jack. See you soon."

I close the door and lock it behind her, then wait to hear footsteps. Her heels clicking down the steps. But there's nothing. I hold my breath and listen. There's a murmur, Dr. Bennett talking on the phone to someone.

I strain to hear, scrunching up as close as I can to the crack in the door. "This is Dr.

Lucy Bennett. I'm about to leave Mitchell Carson's place of residence. His home visit with the children was scheduled for this afternoon."

My heart lurches. "Mr. Carson didn't find time to meet with me, unfortunately. I did speak to the sitter and his son, Jack. Because of my extraordinary patience, I gave your client an extra twenty minutes to remember our meeting. However, he's still not here. I can't overlook this."

The words burn a hole into my chest. What does this mean for me? For Sam?

Dr. Bennett starts to walk away. "I'll notify Judge Crane first thing tomorrow," she says.

I swallow hard. My dad's definitely in trouble.

CHAPTER 47
AVA

TUESDAY, APRIL 27

I've made a special trip to Miss Beulah's, and my Jeep is filled with the buttery scent of still-warm blueberry scones. I park in front of Mobile Prep and balance the box of pastries and carafe of Columbian coffee on my way into the main office.

"Hey, everyone," I say with a big smile and set my surprises on the counter. "I brought everyone some treats this morning! Just a little thank you for all of the hard work you do."

A startling round of nothing greets me. Blank faces. Stone smiles. Mechanical gestures, like puppets on a string. My mouth goes dry, but I single out the person I know best. Her gray hair is shorn close to her head.

"Miss Anne," I say. "It's so good to see you."

"Thank you." Her voice is shaky.

337

My heart drops as she turns away. I watch her hands quiver as she feeds the copy machine. One finger presses a green button and the huge gray box whirs to life. The copy light flashes across the width of her belly, back and forth. Paper spits out with the beat of my pulse, one-two, one-two. She holds up her index finger and moves her mouth, counting. Another employee walks by and ignores me.

Swallowing my hurt, I press on anyway. "Miss Anne, I know you're busy, but I was hoping to speak to Mr. McReed." I raise my voice above the clatter of the copy machine. I shift my briefcase on my shoulder and interlace my fingers.

She pauses and glances back at me, "I'm sorry, Ava, he's not in right now."

A few students wander in, sign a sheet, look me up and down. They whisper and erupt into a fit of giggles. Another teenager makes an announcement over the loudspeaker about yearbooks. The UPS man stops in, grabs a signature. At least he nods hello. I'm invisible to everyone else.

My feet begin to ache. I'm tired of smiling. I feel foolish and desperate. By this time, I've leafed through the school newspaper and read every single announcement tacked up on the bulletin board. The copy machine finally stops. Anne takes her sweet time collating and stapling. When she turns, I lean forward to catch her.

"Please, I realize that perhaps I should have called first. Can you spare just a minute?"

Anne shifts her gaze to the floor then back to me. "What can I do for you?"

I practically melt in relief. Finally. I move closer to the counter and speak softly. "I was hoping to talk to someone about coming back."

"Back?" Her body jolts as if an electric shock has run through it.

"Yes." I try not to frown at her reaction. "Everyone's always talked about me coming back. There being space here at the school whenever I decided I was ready. Don't you remember?"

Anne's painted-on eyebrows almost jump.

"Um, I'm so sorry, dear." She clenches her stack of papers. "And there are no openings at the school. None. Budget cuts and all. However, if there's something else we can do for you, let us know." Her chest flushes and blotches. She's perspiring, for goodness sake.

My throat chokes with anxiety. "Perhaps I misunderstood." I slip a hand into my briefcase and pull out the résumé and cover letter I've prepared for Mr. McReed. "Could you make sure the assistant principal gets this anyway?"

Anne holds out her palm as if I'm going to bite her fingers off. Even she's not sure what or whom she should believe anymore.

I whisper, "Please. I'm not trying to put you on the spot. Would you just ask Mr. McReed to hang on to this in case something opens up?"

She takes the envelope with two fingers. Nods. And waits for me to leave.

I raise my voice several octaves, force a cheery wave. "Well, thanks so much. Take care." My face stings bright red with embarrassment. I can't help but think I'm in the midst of a nightmare I can't wake up from. I practically slink away, a garter snake weaving deep into the sawgrass. And then it hits me when I start to open the door.

There's no need to tiptoe or apologize. I'm Jack's mother. I used to work here — and when I did, I had a backbone. I stomp back to the double-glass doors. Inside the office ladies are engaged in the gabfest of the century, like flapping and pecking pigeons. The lone holdout, Miss Anne, stacks papers on the periphery. The gossip halts when I reappear.

"Pardon me. I forgot to ask," I say, fold-ing my arms. "Which one of you ladies called Mitchell to come get Jack on Friday? After the disagreement he had with another student?"

The office workers exchange uneasy glances. From the corner of my eye, I watch Anne swallow. Maybe she wasn't here. But she knows.

I muster up my sweetest, most concerned voice. "The handbook says the parents are to be notified," I say. "Both parents."

I allow this to sink in.

"While I'm sure your oversight was unintended, other parents may have cause for concern if you continue to neglect communicating in a timely way."

This time I get a murmur of support. Better than nothing.

If using kindness in the face of adversity is the type of damage control Graham is talking about, at least I'll leave the building with my dignity intact. I walk back toward the parking lot, shoulders back, head held high. If Mitchell wants to take me down, he's not going to win without a fight. And I'm just getting started.

CHAPTER 48
JACK

TUESDAY, APRIL 27

Balancing the novel on my knees, I start to read chapter one. It's pouring rain outside, my tennis shoes and socks are soaked, and my shirt's damp and clammy against my skin. I shiver. I don't feel like talking or playing games or doing anything other than getting lost somewhere else. Anywhere else but Mobile, Alabama. Or Dr. Bennett's office.

I concentrate on the words, the heavy feel of the book in my hands, and breathe in the sharp, woodsy smell of brand-new pages and fresh ink. Ava mailed it to me, and thankfully, Isabel found it and slipped it into my room before Dad saw it. There's no telling where it might have ended up otherwise. When Dr. Bennett comes in the room, I put the book down beside me.

"I'm going to let my assistant hold Sam for a while so that we can do an activity,"

342

she says. "Would that be all right, Jack?"

I don't think I have much of a choice, but I need to be polite. I glance up. "I guess so."

"Reading anything good?" she asks and motions to the novel now on the floor.

"Yup. Rick Riordan."

"He's great," she agrees and walks to the corner. She has something under a big blue tarp. It's heavy, and she strains, the wheels creaking, as she pushes it to the center of the room.

"A sandbox?" I'm surprised when she pulls off the cover. "Isn't that for little kids?"

"Sure," Dr. Bennett answers. "But sometimes it's fun to do this kind of stuff when you're a teenager or adult, right?" She continues, "Like mud pies in the rain, playing charades, hide-and-seek."

"Um, okay." I guess I never thought about it.

"And you've got a great imagination," Dr. Bennett says, probably to encourage me. "I thought you could just relax and spend some time messing around with this. Better than just letting me sit here and ask you questions all day while we stare at each other, right?"

I lift my shoulders an inch and let them fall. "Right."

"So" — Dr. Bennett produces a bag and holds it up — "here are some things to get you started. Just do whatever you want with them." She pauses. "Within reason. And in the sand."

"In the sand," I repeat and reach my finger toward the box. I draw a long, deep squiggle, feeling the sand push against my skin.

"Want a soda? I'm thirsty. Sprite?"

I nod, brush the grains off my hand, and take the bag. When I look inside, it's full of superhero figures like Spiderman, Batman, Black Canary, Green Lantern. There are a few creepy guys: Frankenstein, a zombie, a pirate, wild animals, a dragon. And some normal, everyday humans, including a miniature baby with reddish-blond hair like Sam's.

Dr. Bennett comes back, sets down the soda, but keeps her distance. I draw three distinct areas and put Frankenstein inside the first one. A small boy and a baby sit nearby. Black Canary's by herself on top of a mound of sand on the opposite part of the tray. Dead center, I set up a few lines of smaller figures, almost in classroom style. I draw a long rectangle around this group.

I take the boy from the square and put him in the center. I bring several same-sized figures to confront him. They fight and argue. I pause the action and swoop my arm, holding Batman. I make him pick up the boy and drop him with Frankenstein. The boy takes the baby to the corner of the square. Black Canary comes down from the hill and stands on the edge.

"You can't come in," I make Frankenstein growl.

I bury Black Canary in the sand behind the hill. I hesitate, then make Frankenstein burst through an invisible door and wrestle with the boy.

"Don't ever do that again," I yell, leaning Frankenstein over the boy. "You'll be sorry."

I grab Green Lantern and fly him straight into Frankenstein, who flips off the sand tray. Spiderman web-slings in and grabs the baby.

"Who are you?" I have the boy ask Spiderman. "Are you good or bad?"

I look up at Dr. Bennett. She's watching.

"I can't tell anymore." My eyes fill with tears. I throw the figurines across the table. They land and stick out at weird angles.

We both stare at the sand table.

"Anything you want to talk about?" Dr. Bennett finally asks. "I hear you had a rough week."

I sniff. "Some people at school said crappy

things about Ava on Friday. So I punched one of them because he wouldn't stop. Then my dad got me this great Element Man comic book but ripped it up after he found out about detention. I can't do anything right."

Dr. Bennett just listens.

"And Sam and I broke some stuff by accident at Grandma Ruth's. I got in big trouble over that. Everybody's mad."

"I'm not upset." Dr. Bennett tilts her head. "I know your brother loves you."

I wipe my eyes with the back of my sleeve.

"What about Ava?" Dr. Bennett says. "Do you think she cares about you?"

"She spends all her time with Sam," I choke out.

"Do you talk to her when she's here?" she asks gently.

"Not too much . . ." I jerk to attention. "How do you know? Did she tell you that?"

Dr. Bennett shakes her head. "No. I have to keep an eye on things. Just in case. The judge asked me to." She points to the mirror. "I'm just on the other side of that."

I sink my chin into my chest. Another tear leaks down my cheek. "I wish I could rewind the clock. Or turn into Superman and spin the earth in the other direction."

"Turn back time?"

I wrap my arms around my knees. "Yeah. Then I could fix things. Maybe then Dad and Ava wouldn't have had that big fight. Dad wouldn't have gotten mad and left."

"Where were you and Sam?"

My belly clenches tight. "When Dad left we were still with Ava in the house. Then later he kind of tricked her."

"What do you mean?" Dr. Bennett sits back.

The clock ticks a steady beat, and I check the time. Dad's late. Again.

"Ava let him come get us. He said he wanted to see us for a couple of hours at his new apartment. He was supposed to bring us back that night. Then he wouldn't let us go. Ava called. I heard them on the phone."

"I see." Dr. Bennett leans toward me and looks me in the eye. "There'll always be things we wish we could do over. But you didn't cause this. It's not your fault. Do you understand me, Jack?"

I lick my lips. "I guess so."

"Jack, I'm going to tell you something I tell every parent. I'm not on the mom's side. I'm not on the dad's side." She clasps her hands together. "I'm on your side. Sam's side. Period."

"So you decide what's going to happen

with us? Who we'll live with?"

"Well, partly." Dr. Bennett pauses. "I help the judge because he doesn't have time to get to know everyone like I do. He relies on me to give him good advice. He might not always agree, but I have a lot of experience doing this."

"Are you ever wrong?"

Dr. Bennett thinks about this. She takes her time answering. "About my job? What I recommend? Not usually."

I think about this, hard. "That's good."

Dr. Bennett steals a glance at the wall. The clock above her head says five twenty. Still no Dad.

"Let me check on something." She gets to her feet. "Can you wait here, Jack?"

My shoulders relax. "Sure." I stretch my arms over my head, crack my knuckles, and pick up my book, glad for the break. "No problem."

Dr. Bennett walks out and leaves the door open. I can hear her talking to her assistant. Sam's babbling.

"Any sign of their dad?" she asks.

"Nope," the girl answers. "You've got about ten phone calls to return. One cancellation Thursday afternoon. And the dentist called to confirm your appointment Monday."

"Great —"

Dad bursts through the door. He's breathing hard, and his hair is wet from the rain. "Hey. Where's Jack?"

"Dr. Carson, you're late." Dr. Bennett replies. "I have a schedule to keep."

"Big meeting," Dad says. "Couldn't miss it. Budgets, deadlines." He turns and puts his back to her.

"You missed your home visit yesterday," she reminds him.

I gulp. Dad stops and jerks his head back to look at her. "Oh, that."

If Dr. Bennett can tell Dad's upset, she doesn't show it. Her face is perfectly normal. She must be used to adults who aren't on time and blow off appointments.

"Come on, Jack. Time to go," Dad says.

"Wait just a moment?" Dr. Bennett asks. "I have one more thing," Dr. Bennett says. She turns on her heel and picks up a folder on the table. She flicks it open and holds it out to Dad. "I need you to sign a release."

Dad sets his jaw and raises an eyebrow.

"It gives me permission to drive the children to see their mother for her home visit Friday."

A surge of happiness rushes through me. Ava. At our old house. I'll see my room and my toys. Then I dig my nails into my palm.

I can't smile. Dad might see me. Dr. Bennett hands Dad the paper. He hesitates, then frowns and scribbles his name.

"Great. Thank you." Dr. Bennett slides the paper back inside the chart. "Oh, and about the home visit?"

My dad's face goes dark, and he waves a hand in my direction. "Get your brother. We have to go." His voice growls, the way it gets when someone really makes him mad. Then Dad's eyes slice at Dr. Bennett. "I'll have someone call you to reschedule."

CHAPTER 49
JACK

The Flash thinks, moves, and reacts at superhuman speeds. Handy for answering questions, getting to class on time, and avoiding food fights. If I forgot my lunch card or a homework assignment, I could run home. With the ability to speed-read, I could go through all of my textbooks and notes twice in record time. And, using vibration, Flash can walk through walls. That could come in handy if I get in trouble at school or with my dad.

While the rest of the class plays chase, swings from monkey bars, and generally torments the teachers, Mo and I hang out under the grove of trees near the soccer field. It's been raining buckets until this morning, and the sky's still clouded steel gray. A gentle wind rustles the oak branches, sending droplets of water down on our heads. I jump when a drop hits my cheek,

351

cold and wet.

"Wanna go over to 99 Issues later? Supposed to be getting a new shipment in." Mo kicks at a stone near the wrought iron fence. "Dude said he might be getting in some vintage Silver Surfer."

"Nice!" I get a temporary lift thinking about paging through a stack of old comic books. I even love the musty garage-sale smell when the sales guys pull them out of the crates. "What time?"

"Right after you get done with detention. My sister can take us."

"It's all right. We can walk."

I nod then think about my almost-empty wallet in my back pocket. "I'm not sure I have any cash, Mo."

"Spot you a few bucks, dude." He elbows me in the ribs. "Or you could just ask Ava." He points to the other side of the fence.

My breath catches. I turn and Ava waves, sticks her hand back in her pocket, and waits. Despite the dark afternoon, she's wearing sunglasses, a ball cap, some yoga-looking clothes. Sort of incognito, though her reddish ponytail gives her away if you look closely enough.

"Jack, hey. I'm so glad I caught you." She grins as I get closer.

I duck my head. "Uh, should you be

352

here?" I glance around, watching for my dad or the principal to jump out from behind the bushes.

"I'm on public property. And I only need a minute." She takes off her sunglasses and looks straight at me. "I want to clear some things up. First, I love you and your brother. This situation is not at all what I want, for everyone to be split up. Cross my heart."

My brain nudges me. "Do you have a boyfriend?"

Her mouth drops an inch or two. She takes a step closer and grips the fence. "Absolutely not. If anyone told you that, you have been seriously misinformed. Got it?"

I nod.

"Yes, ma'am."

"Now people talk and say ugly things, but that doesn't mean you have to believe them," Ava adds.

A pang of guilt hits me in my rib cage. I look down and press my loafer into the dirt, make a perfect imprint of my shoe.

"Jack, what is it?" she asks.

My mouth is suddenly parched. "Why can't you . . ." I stop and think. "Why don't you get back together?" As soon as I say the words, though, I think of how my dad has acted. Moving out of the house. Calling the police on Ava. Ripping up my comic book.

Ava presses her lips together. "I've tried to talk to your dad about it, honey. He won't listen. I've been to his office, I've tried talking to him on the phone, and we've had a meeting." She sighs. "But it is not your job to fix it. Okay? This is an adult thing."

My eyes start to sting. I fight back tears. "Yes, ma'am."

Ava reaches into her backpack and hands me a small, rectangular box.

I take it and my eyes get wide. It's a brand-new cell phone.

"This is for you. You can tell your dad you have it, if you like. That's up to you. I'm not trying to hide anything. I just want you to be able to call me. The numbers are programmed in."

My breath quickens. I nod and think about where I can hide it. Under my pillow? Under my bed?

"Use it if you need or want to," Ava says. She lowers her voice. "Anytime night or day. I mean it."

My jaw quivers. "What's going to happen? To me and Sam?"

"Jack honey, that's what we're all trying to work out," she says and puts a hand on her own chest. "What's best for you and your brother. I want you and Sam with me every minute of every day, do you understand that? But I have to share you. With your dad."

"Uh-huh."

"I know it's important you spend time with both of us. Your dad always talks about the good times you had at Cub Scouts and peewee soccer."

I wrinkle my nose. "Uh . . ."

"What is it?" Ava asks.

"Well, I always wanted my dad there, but my mom took me to all that stuff. He was always too busy. He'd promise to come, then wouldn't show up."

Ava's face looks a little funny. Like she's tasted something really awful like cockroach guts. She swallows hard and smiles quickly. "Okay. Well. So I'm sure he'll want to now, right?"

I scuff the dirt. "Yeah. Sure."

"So the psychologist, Dr. Bennett, explained that she is going to help the judge decide how much time you'll get to spend with both me and your dad?"

I kick a pebble with the toe of my tennis shoe. "Yeah. That sucks."

Ava smiles. "It kinda does, though I'd prefer you use another word."

"Stinks, smells rotten, bad, awful."

She laughs. "Better. Thanks, smarty pants."

Then the bell rings, jarring me back into reality. Behind me I can hear the shouts and laughter of my classmates as they trudge back toward the school.

Ava reaches through the fence and squeezes my hand. I cling to her, letting the warmth of her touch wash over me. Right now I feel safe. And I don't want to let go.

Mo calls my name. We're going to be late.

I drop Ava's hand and take a step back. It's just a few inches farther away, but now it seems like a thousand miles.

CHAPTER 50
AVA

THURSDAY, APRIL 29

I call Frank this morning, hoping to wrangle an invitation, but I don't get past the first word.

"I've found something," he says. It's important. A piece of paper, one he won't risk mailing. There's a package for Jack, too, a birthday gift. "Karen gave it to me for safekeeping," he tells me. "By the time I remembered I had it — months after the funeral — Mitchell and Jack were gone."

Less than an hour later, I'm on the road, heading for Moulton. The top's down, letting the Alabama sun warm my shoulders. The sky, strikingly blue, bears a line of contrails, perfectly spaced, underscoring the beauty of the day. The air, fragrant with pine fronds, caresses my cheeks and blows through my hair.

The highway's anonymity, one single red Jeep among hundreds of tan trucks, silver trailers, and black SUVs, relieves the stress of being on display in Mobile. The constant tension. The need to always look over my shoulder.

I rub at my neck, missing the casual fried oyster dinners at Wintzell's, listening to live music at the Blue Gill, catching a movie at the Crescent Theater downtown. I even miss popping open a great bottle of wine at home before watching the Crimson Tide.

Did I imagine all of those things? Did I dream that I had a husband who adored me? A man with whom I shared my bed and heart? I bite my lip. In my rush to love and be loved, I allowed myself to overlook everything that seems so glaringly obvious now in the daylight.

Willing fortitude, I push the thoughts from my head. One by one I heave and send them tumbling, end over end. Boulders crashing and breaking at the water's rocky edge. Instead, I think about Frank, replaying our conversation. He sounded fragile, worried, and told me to be careful. At least Frank, this time, won't meet me with a .45.

It's progress. And seeing Jack yesterday bolstered my confidence. Some bittersweet truths to swallow and digest. Difficult ideas to accept. I ache to fix it all, which is why I'm on the road. But no matter what I find out today, it won't repair everything. Jack's scars will be there. As will mine. Two things I have to accept.

I glance in the rearview mirror at the cooler sitting in the back. I've packed chicken salad sandwiches, crunchy raw vegetables, and a fresh-baked loaf of whole-grain wheat bread. A jug of unsweet tea with plenty of fresh lemons in a Ziploc. I wonder about the last time Frank ate a home-cooked meal.

When I pull up and jump out, I run a hand through my hair and take in the neighborhood. The house looks the same. The sidewalk, the driveway. At this point in my life, the same is really good. I knock on the door, and this time it swings open wide. Frank is ready and waiting. Hungry too. I dish out our picnic lunch, and we settle in.

Frank sighs. "It's such a treat to have a fine meal brought to me."

I pour tea into two clear tumblers and squeeze the lemon slices, releasing the pulp and juice. The scent of citrus fills the air, tickling my nose. Frank raises his glass and takes a long drink.

"Ah, delicious, Ava."

Seeing him so content makes me happy. Though I'm impatient to find out what he's discovered, I wait for Frank to tell me. I want him to enjoy the meal and the attention, two things I'm certain he doesn't get enough of.

I grin. "Glad to do it. As long as your nurse won't chase me down for putting the tiniest bit of mayonnaise in the chicken salad."

"I won't tell." He winks and takes another bite. After he swallows, he adjusts his wheelchair, leans over the table, and picks up an envelope. He holds it up. It's yellowed and bent.

"This took some doing. I searched for hours." He turns over the envelope in his hands. "I found it in my Bible, of all places. No wonder I hadn't seen it in a while — Big Guy's probably trying to tell me something," Frank jokes and points at the ceiling.

His face gets flat and serious then. "I think this might give some solid answers. You know, about Karen and Mitchell. How their relationship was at the end."

"Really?" I unfold the papers inside. It's a travel itinerary. Airline tickets, a hotel, rental car. I look up at Frank.

"The Bahamas. I remembered about the trip a few days after you left. It was for their anniversary, but Karen had planned on bringing Jack too." Frank puts his elbows on his knees, leans forward. "So there you have it. Luckily I don't throw much out."

My pulse quickens. I look at the dates of the trip, check my calendar, and do the math. "The trip was scheduled for after the book tour ended. She had the whole thing planned."

She wasn't leaving him.

Frank replies, "She left the itinerary here because it was supposed to be a surprise. She knew Mitchell would find it at the house. There were no secrets there, as you could guess. He'd go through drawers, open all of the mail, any packages. Karen knew he'd come across it, one way or another."

The numbers and words blur. "Mitchell told me, and Jack — everyone — that Karen left him." My hand shakes. "This proves . . . this means . . . he wasn't honest with me. With us."

"I'm sorry, sweetheart." Frank heaves a sigh. "In his defense, Mitchell might have actually talked himself into believing it. He's always had an overactive imagination, jumping to this conclusion or that." He rubs the back of his neck.

I stare at Frank, still clutching the itinerary. I smooth it out, study it again. "Do you remember how she was . . . when she dropped this off?"

"She was always cheerful, but Karen was tired then. She had a lot on her mind." Frank rubs his forehead. "Getting ready to start the book tour. She wasn't happy about being away from Jack, I know that much."

Pain pierces my heart. "Of course," I whisper.

We sit in silence, both absorbed in thought.

Finally, Frank clears his throat. "After Karen was gone, I always hoped they'd come visit. That Mitchell'd have a change of heart once he had time to heal. An epiphany about needing the only family he's got. Or I figured Jack would call and get someone to drive him down. He'd show up on my doorstep, like you did."

Frank wheels over to the bureau. He picks up a small, rectangular package and clutches it to his chest with one hand. "This was Karen's birthday gift to Jack. She brought it over before the accident, said it was a big surprise. I never opened it. Maybe I should have, but it didn't feel right."

Frank stretches an arm out so that I can reach Jack's gift.

"I'll make sure he gets it," I promise, taking the package and easing it into my bag. "He's a special, special boy. You know, I adopted him."

"Then you *can* bring Jack here." Frank smiles broadly and slaps his thigh. "Great! I'm sure he's so grown up."

"He's taller than me. And I'd love to bring him here, Frank," I answer and try to choose my words carefully. "But it's complicated with Mitchell right now. And Jack."

"How complicated?"

"Very. There's no good way to say this." I take a deep breath. "Jack thinks you've . . . passed away."

Frank's smile collapses. "What?"

I wince, furious at Mitchell for the hurt he's causing his father. "Jack doesn't know a thing about you living here. I'm certain."

Frank tugs out a white handkerchief and wipes his forehead. "Why? What did I do to deserve being cut off from my own grand-child?" He crumples up the cloth in his wrinkled hands. "I asked a few questions. Mitchell didn't like it."

"You did nothing wrong," I say, move closer, and touch his shoulder, the flannel shirt soft under my fingertips.

"I pressed him so hard because I wanted him to get some help after Karen died," Frank insists. "I drove him away."

"No. Mitchell chose to leave and take Jack. Now he's done the same to me."

Frank's head jerks up. "What did you say?"

"He left. He filed for divorce without me knowing. He wants full custody of the boys and is doing everything in his power to get it."

"Ava!" Frank rubs his temples, distraught.

I cross my arms, clenching my elbows tight. "I'm worried, Frank," I tell him. "If he finds out I'm here, I don't know how he'll react. He's been irrational. So angry. I don't want anyone else to get hurt."

"Don't worry about a thing." Frank tips his head toward his gun case, tries to look offended. "I'm a lot tougher than I look."

We share a smile. "Good," I say. "Maybe what you found, the itinerary, will help convince Mitchell about Karen. It's a start. We're working with a psychologist. She's seeing me and the boys —"

Frank holds up a shaking hand to stop me. "Ava . . . did you say . . . boys?"

Heart in my throat, I reach into my bag and pull out a photo. The one of Jack and baby Sam. He examines the picture.

"I did, Frank. This is your new grandson."

CHAPTER 51
MITCHELL

THURSDAY, APRIL 29

Isabel dresses me down in Spanish the second I walk into the apartment. She's made one of my favorite dishes — roasted Poblano peppers battered with her airy egg coating — but tonight I've kept her waiting.

"Chile rellenos will be cold." She urges me toward the kitchen. "Eat!"

Dutifully, and only for Isabel, I oblige, taking a forkful of the dish, smothered in her spicy roasted tomato salsa. The flavors burst in my mouth — lime, cracked pepper, and garlic. The fried coating is toasted to golden perfection, matched only by the smooth melted Monterey Jack cheese.

"Mmm." I widen my eyes as she hovers close. "Isabel, you've outdone yourself this time."

She beams with pride and clucks a few more times, pointing at the clock. Nodding and smiling, I guide her toward the front door, anxious to shoo her home.

"Yes, *sí, sí.*" I promise to be home on time for tomorrow's Bingo game, offer my best smile, and slip her an extra hundred-dollar bill. "*Gracias,* Isabel."

As I pat the small bulge in my jacket and smooth the lapel, I look around the kitchen, searching for a hiding place.

"Dad?" Jack's hushed voice floats from the bedroom into the hallway.

I stiffen, my eyes darting from the shelves to the cabinets and back again. I pinch the bridge of my nose, exhale, and duck my head into the boys' room.

Sam is snoring on his back, arms above his head. The moonlight finds a path to his chest, rising and falling with each breath. Jack is next to him, flipping through channels, the light from the small television flashing and dancing off the walls.

"Yes?" I ask, not stepping inside.

"Sam had a bad day," Jack says, almost to himself. He doesn't look up.

A flash of annoyance stabs at me. "What'd you do to fix it, son?" The gun pokes at my rib cage. It was my intention to hide it first thing. But Isabel, the chile rellenos, and my kids have made that impossible.

He rolls on his back. "I tried a bunch of stuff. He didn't want to play," Jack mumbles and turns away, clutching a pillow.

I grit my teeth. "Well, I guess everyone has a bad day, even babies. He seems fine now. I'm going to grab a glass of water, son. Be right back."

In the kitchen, I rummage on the top shelf, far out of Isabel's reach. After sliding the weapon between firm sacks of flour and sugar, I pat the thick bags back in place. *There.*

As I move away from the shelves, something glints. A silver rectangle wedged behind a pasta holder. I resist the urge to flick on the lights, rub my tired eyes. *Forget it. Get some sleep.* It's probably a toy, almost drained of batteries, or a kitchen appliance in need of resetting. It blinks again. *Argh. The last thing I need is a timer going off at midnight.* I push the container to one side and snatch up the object.

At first my mind refuses to comprehend it. I know what it is. It's the why that bothers me more. Why is a brand-new cell phone hidden in my kitchen? One I've never seen before. Isabel's? I turn it over in my hand and shake my head. Isabel's is several generations old and small, a dinosaur. As I power on the screen and stare at the lock code, I clench my jaw. *Might as well have Ava written all over it.* Slowly, deliberately, I walk back to Jack's room. This time I lean against the door frame, keeping my stance open and casual.

"What'cha watching?" Inside, my ribs contract with fury. My blood is on fire, ready to spew.

He barely glances back. *Super Friends. Justice League of America.* Jack turns down the volume a notch. "Season 1, Episode 7: 'The Giants of Doom.' "

"Really?" I say the word carefully, as if it has to be measured. My body tightens, but I gaze at Jack with forced calm.

This time he looks up. " 'The Final Challenge' is on next."

How appropriate.

"Want to watch it with me?" he asks, unable to muster an ounce of enthusiasm.

This is the thanks I get.

"Actually, we need to have a talk."

Jack's expression sours. "But, Dad," he complains and points at the television. "It's almost over."

I step in front of the screen and click off the program. "It's over now. And we'll talk when I say so." The cell phone is in my back pocket. "Has Ava tried to get in touch with you?"

Jack squirms in his seat, pokes out his bottom lip.

"Have you talked to her? I need an answer." The air-conditioner kicks on, drowning out his reply. "I can't hear you."

There's a struggle going on behind the invisible wall he's building up. I have to break through before the last stone is in place.

"Don't make me." Jack's eyes fill with tears. "It's not fair." He tucks his legs under his body and shrinks down farther.

I kneel down and grab his shirt. "You need to answer the question."

"No," Jack says, struggling. "I'm not taking sides. You can't make me choose."

He wants to leave too.

"Choose?" I clench my teeth and pull at the material, balling it in my fist. "There is no choice. You don't get to choose. Family sticks with family. Blood with blood. It's you and me. And Sam. Forever."

Jack rears back, closes his eyes, and clamps his mouth shut.

I will not be ignored. With both hands I yank Jack to his feet, digging my fingers into the flesh and bone. I stick the cell phone in front of his face. "She gave this to you, didn't she?" I squeeze tighter and shake him until his head bounces like an arcade pinball, then toss him back into the chair.

Jack falls, arms and legs askew. "Y-yes,

369

sir." Then he raises his chin, a flash of defiance in his dark eyes. "But listen —"

Rage builds in my throat, then, bubbling up and bursting out of every pore. "Don't you dare talk back to me!" I raise my hand back and slap his face hard. A whip-crack sound. My fingers leave a perfect imprint on my son's cheek. At the corner of his mouth, a tiny bead of blood pricks to the surface, dark on his fair skin.

Jack grabs his face. Reddish-purple blotches appear on his arms where I shook him. His shirt collar is torn. His breath, ragged, heaves with the rise and fall of his chest. Most surprisingly, his cheeks stay dry. *It's Ava. She's turned him against me. Brainwashed my child. Told him lies.*

"Son." I cup his chin and turn his head as if I'm handling the tips of butterfly wings. "I'm sorry. I need to make sure you hear me and pay attention. Your mother — sneaking around like she does — slipping you cell phones and God knows what else . . . that's what caused all of this. She made me lose my head, just for a minute." I step away and tap my temple. "We just have to forget about her. Stick together — you, Sam, and me. We're a team."

Jack, wide-eyed, manages a slight nod. *Poor kid. He's just worn out. All of this stress from Ava.*

A surge of excitement rushes through me. "Listen, buddy, I have a great idea. Let's just get away. The three of us. We'll go somewhere, kick back, take a little vacation. Who knows, Disney World, Universal, one of those theme parks? What do you say? It'll be fun. We'll leave tomorrow night!" I say with a flourish and rub my hands together in anticipation.

A flicker appears in Jack's eyes.

"Sure, Dad."

"Good, son," I say. "That's the right answer."

When I pull him close, Jack's body stiffens. Finally, one thin arm reaches around my waist. The other follows. It's then that I release him.

Without another word, Jack shuffles toward the bathroom. He shuts the door behind him, a soft click. *Tomorrow. A fresh start. And everything will be different. I promise.*

CHAPTER 52
JACK

FRIDAY, APRIL 30

We're on the way to Ava's. Our old house. I want to tell Sam — he'd be so excited if he knew. I watch out the window for a while, especially when we pass the country club. Men in bright pink and blue shirts cluster together, all holding silver clubs. The greens, rolling and smooth, are movie-perfect, the Crayola colors of shamrock and mountain meadow.

When we pass the last hole, and rows of white carts, I glance over at Dr. Bennett. She sure uses her inhaler a lot. I think she's kind of worried about having Sam in the car. It took her twenty minutes to wrestle him into his car seat. She checks on him every five seconds in the rearview mirror.

I run a hand over the door trim. The car looks brand-new and smells expensive, like leather. There's no dirt on the carpeting, not even a speck, and the seats are so clean

372

and slippery that my pants slide when we go around a corner. My stomach pitches back and forth, and I tighten my seat belt. I hope Ava doesn't ask about the cell phone. I can't tell her what really happened, but I don't want to lie either.

Dr. Bennett takes another puff from her inhaler. This time nothing comes out. She shakes it, holds it up to her mouth, presses it again. Still nothing.

"Are you all right, Dr. Bennett?"

She erases the worried look from her face.

"Jack, honey, I just need to get a refill for my medicine." She glances back at Sam. "I'll take care of it later."

Sam kicks and gurgles at the signs whizzing by.

"What medicine?" I press. "We can stop and get it." A pharmacy sign zooms past the car. "Look. See, right there." I shoot her a look and point out the window. "See?"

"Darlin', I'll be just fine." She checks her watch, then studies the GPS. "Hmm, should be here, just about a mile on the left."

I gesture to my own personal landmark. "Turn past that butterfly tree. See the flowers? Ava planted those. I helped."

Dr. Bennett makes the turn. "I'll bet you did. Thank you, Jack."

Sure enough, more foliage, bursting with

purple blossoms, appears. The paved driveway arches back and up, leading to the house, set back from the road. I sneak a peek at Sam. Even he seems to know he's near our real house. He babbles happily at my grin. We park next to Ava's Jeep.

Dr. Bennett unstraps Sam and gathers him in her arms. I bolt from the car and run to the steps. I take them two at a time.

Ava opens the door, exclaiming about how big I am and running her hand along my shoulder. At first it hurts when she touches my arms, drawing me close, but I can't say anything about the bruises or my dad. I can't believe the slap mark faded. I just lock that out of my head.

So when she finally folds me to her like a snug down coat on a cold Alabama night, I relax. I press my cheek against her body, inhaling cinnamon and vanilla. Ava smells like Christmas.

"Mama." Sam tries to wrestle away from Dr. Bennett. "Mama, Mama."

Ava releases me with a smile, then kneels down and scoops Sam to her chest, hugging him as if it's her last moment on the planet.

Ava wipes at her eyes and smiles at Dr. Bennett. "Coffee?" She lifts up a mug. "Have a cookie before Jack and Sam make them disappear."

In the kitchen I grab two cookies and hand a small one to my brother. The treats are warm with a bit of a crispy, golden edge. When I break one in half, the chocolate chips stretch and bend upside down into mini jump ropes. I catch a drip with my tongue, letting the sweet, smooth goodness slide down my throat and into my waiting belly.

"Yum," I declare, rubbing my stomach and making Sam giggle. My brother's already smeared chocolate across his cheek and is crumbing bits of cookie all over the floor. Ava laughs and chases him with a washcloth to wipe his face.

Dr. Bennett sits down at the breakfast bar and looks around, checking out the house and the kitchen. "Everything's so neat."

"Oh, I have plenty of time to cook and clean up." Ava lays the washcloth into the sink and swipes at an imaginary speck on the tabletop. "No one here to mess it up but me."

The coffeepot gurgles as we all stand there, awkward, waiting. Sam and I inch toward the playroom. Ava doesn't move. We're all just waiting for Dr. Bennett to give the okay.

"Oh my goodness. Go! All of you," she finally says, realizing it. "Please, spend time together. I'll entertain myself just fine right here."

Ava practically melts with relief. "Take a look in the back, guys."

I squeal when I see what's behind the house. Sam jumps up and down, clapping. There's a huge playground set and a sandbox. The breeze catches an empty swing and pushes it.

"You remembered!" I call out.

Ava spends the next hour playing with us. Sliding and racing and pushing. We laugh a lot and roll around in the yard. I laugh extra hard when I see Sam's hair sticking to his head in curls. My arms ache, and I've got stains on the knees of my pants, and there's grass in my hair. I'm hot, sweaty, and thirsty, but happy. Everything smells like sunshine.

When Dr. Bennett gives us the signal that it's almost time to go. I want time to stop.

I lock in place, burrowing deep into the dirt, like the roots of an oak tree. It takes Ava ruffling my hair to unbend my body, straighten my arms and legs. We shuffle toward the house, bone-tired.

"Give me just a minute," Ava whispers to Dr. Bennett but loud enough for me to hear. "I need to grab something." Then to me, "You and your brother need to get some water. Can you help him, please?"

I oblige and fill a sippy cup for Sam. "Yes, ma'am."

"Having a good time?" Dr. Bennett asks while Ava's out of the room.

"Yes, ma'am," I answer between gulps and snatch another cookie.

"What was the best part?"

My throat gets scratchy. I pretend to pay attention to my cookie, break it in half, and play with the crumbs on my plate. I think about my answer.

"It's home. All of our stuff is here," I mumble. "Now the swing set."

"So the swing set makes it better?" Dr. Bennett tosses out the question. "Or is it more space, a bigger place?"

"No, not really." I pull at the collar of my shirt. "I'd share a room here if I had to. Um . . . Ava has more time for us. She plays with us —"

"Play!" Sam bangs his cup on the ceramic tile.

Ava walks back into the room. "I know it's time to go." She holds out a package. "This is something from your mother."

I draw back. But when I blink again, and really look, it's just a box, plain, four corners, tied with a limp ribbon. Gingerly, I take it with both hands. "My mom? You mean Karen? What is it?" I examine the bottom, tip it to one side.

"We don't know for sure." Ava looks at Dr. Bennett, then puts a hand on my arm. "Your grandfather gave it to me."

I open my mouth but can't make words come out right. "M-my . . ."

"Your grandfather," Ava repeats.

Anger wells up in my chest. "You're not telling me the truth," I spout. "My grandfather is dead. Dad said so. He told me." I spit out the words like poison and toss the package on the table.

"No. That is absolutely not true." Ava flushes, puts both hands on the edge of the gift. "I met him. Your dad's father."

Sam stomps around underneath our feet. "Dad-dad-dad-dad."

"Stop it, Sam," I yell and cover my ears. "Quit it! Right now." Sam starts to cry.

Ava picks him up, hugs him close, and shoots Dr. Bennett an apologetic grimace. "Bad timing," she mouths. "I'm sorry."

I push the chair back so hard it crashes to the floor. "And I don't want any stupid present. Not from you or anyone." I run from the room, pass the new staircase, and out the front door. The door slams behind me. The windows rattle.

"She didn't care. She had a boyfriend," I say to myself. "She left."

CHAPTER 53
AVA

FRIDAY, APRIL 30

I sit at the window forever, replaying the last few minutes with the boys. The surprise on Jack's face, then anger. Jack tossing the box. Sam wailing. His tear-streaked face. Dr. Bennett patting my hand. It had been a perfect afternoon. Until . . . I press my forehead on the glass and run a finger down the pane, streaking it.

The house feels so hollow without the boys; the emptiness reverberates. I don't have the heart to sweep up the bits of dirt and grass, the crumble of cookies on the counter. I want to encase them in glass. Bottle the baby shampoo smell of Sam's hair, capture the brilliance of Jack's smile, uncorking it only to remember.

If I could, I'd photograph every sign that the boys were here. The forgotten fleece jacket in the corner, the footprints in the sandbox, and the damp white washcloth I used to wipe Sam's face. I'd line the hallways with pictures, framed neatly in rows, and memorize the images, imprinting them on my soul.

This would make it real, if only to me. It would serve as proof. Evidence that I am a flesh-and-blood mother for more than one hour a week. I let my eyelids fall shut and summon strength from the deepest crevices of my heart. Today I have to fight harder than ever against the negativity spinning in my head. Jack's reaction, after all, was normal. He will work through it.

I stand up, open the back door, and walk outside, determined to recall Dr. Bennett's advice about this afternoon. After buckling the boys into the car, she'd walked over and gripped my hand.

"Look at it like this," she said, her voice low. "Everyone has a center of gravity. Every family too. It's the intangible things that make us feel grounded and whole. And it's different for everyone — a good job, a strong marriage, or a close friendship."

I nodded.

"Often when that center of gravity tilts with trouble or disappointment, everything becomes a little unstable, a bit rocky," Dr. Bennett continued. "When you have a greater rift, like a divorce, it's more like an earthquake. And it takes time and work to achieve that equilibrium and peace again."

She hugged me then, and I clung to her, holding back tears. As I waved good-bye, watching the car until it disappeared, I thought of the one thing Dr. Bennett hadn't addressed. Would life ever get back to normal? If so, what would that normal look like?

CHAPTER 54
JACK

FRIDAY, APRIL 30

Dr. Bennett's driving us back to her office to meet Dad. Sam's asleep and I'm staring out the window at nothing, listening to the wheels roll underneath us, carrying us away from Ava. Dr. Bennett coughs. She doesn't look so hot, and asks me to check the glove compartment.

"Do you see an extra inhaler?" she asks and keeps her eyes on the road. "Maybe hidden under those papers?"

"No, ma'am," I reply. "Just a few maps, some gum." I rustle around, move things.

We pull up to the office. Dr. Bennett unbuckles Sam from his seat, hoists him onto her hip, and dials her phone. She tells me to get the car seat out and leave it by the steps for my dad. I think she wants to distract me, so I do as I'm told, but I can still hear her talking.

"Hi, Dr. Lucy Bennett here. I need a refill

on my Albuterol." Another cough. "I know this is last minute. I'm so sorry. How late are you open tonight?"

She waits and rocks Sam.

"Yes, thanks. Twenty minutes is super. Could you leave it in a bag outside the door? I'm still with clients."

The person she's talking to checks on this.

"Fabulous. That's great." Dr. Bennett gasps in relief. "Charge it to my account, will you please?"

She hands me the key, gestures for me to unlock the door and go inside.

"Thank you." Dr. Bennett hangs up the phone. She hands me Sam and tells me she'll be right with us; she has to check her messages. I duck into the tiny kitchen, swipe a Sprite from her mini-fridge, and open it.

In the two minutes it takes Dr. Bennett to go to her office, I flick on the lights, dump out the huge bucket of stuffed animals, and decide to turn the playroom into a WWE smack down, complete with body slams, flying sidekicks, and paw punches. Sam watches, finger in his mouth, while I pummel each toy in turn. Sam laughs as I leapfrog the rabbit with his duck.

"Hold it right there, mister," Dr. Bennett says. I didn't even know she was standing there. "This is not ultimate fighting."

I don't look at her face. Instead, I take a swig of Sprite and act mad that she's spoiled our fun. Dr. Bennett reaches for the yellow boa constrictor in my other hand. She pulls it away and the soda splashes my legs, my shirt, and most ends up on the carpet. The spray misses Sam, who — of course — now crawls directly toward the spill.

"Whoa, cowboy," Dr. Bennett exclaims and picks him up. "The office has paper towels. A few clean shirts. Why don't you check in my office — bottom drawer on the right?"

I dig through her drawer of Salvation Army finds and come up with a faded Grateful Dead T-shirt circa 1973. Cool. I grab it and pull my wet shirt over my head.

Dr. Bennett pokes her head in to see if I've found anything. "Jack, how's it coming —" She stops short and sucks in a lot of air.

I know what she's looking at. My arm and an ugly tattoo of purplish-red and yellow blotches.

"Wait," she says.

I hastily pull on the skeleton-adorned top.

"What in the world? What happened to you?" Dr. Bennett looks pissed. And like she might cry. "Let's go back to the playroom. We can talk there."

It's not a question. It's an order. I clamp

my mouth shut while we walk and promise myself I won't squeal on Dad. He'll kill me if I tell. Sam wrestles himself to the floor, eager to toss the stuffed animals around. He lets a giraffe fly a few inches off the ground as Dr. Bennett and I do a stare down.

"Um. I fell. The other day." I smooth the shirt, peer at the wall, at nothing.

"Jack. Come on. Did someone at school do that?"

I shake my head.

"Someone at the apartment complex? A neighbor?"

Another no.

"Jack, did your father do this?" Dr. Bennett tries to look at my face and sinks to her knees. "The shape of the bruises, those are fingermarks."

Now I'm angry. I want her to stop, so I raise my voice loud. "I told you I fell." Even Sam stops moving. I swallow and nod, push myself into a chair.

Dr. Bennett watches me. "Say I believe you, Jack. That what you're telling me is the truth."

My insides somersault. I can't look up. "Yeah."

"Can I ask you something else? If I believe you about falling?" She waits a beat. "It's not about you."

I exhale a little and shift my gaze to a spot on the floor. I stare at the piece of carpeting until it looks bleary and fuzzy. "Uh, okay."

"Did Ava, or your mom, Karen, ever hurt themselves?"

My face twists. I don't want it to. I try to make it stop. Then squeeze my eyes tight to block out the sound of her voice. I don't want to remember. But the words push out, almost like I can't stop them.

"Karen. Sh-she tripped down a flight of stairs. Dad caught her, kind of."

Dr. Bennett sits back on her heels. She glances at my brother, who's dragging a stuffed giraffe around by the leg. Its head bounces off the floor. *Bump. Bump. Bump.*

"Sam, c'mere." Dr. Bennett beckons him over.

He trots to her, only too happy. His curls stick up on one side, and he pushes the giraffe in her face.

"Well, hello," she says, grasping at the animal and turning him upright. "Can you find me the rhino, Sam? And we'll play?"

While my brother trots off, Dr. Bennett pulls a card from her pocket and scribbles something on the back. "Here's my number and home address. In case you want to talk. Anytime. For any reason."

"Not really." I shuffle a foot and pick up the Sprite can, set it on the counter. I slide the card into my front pocket. I grab some paper towels and begin to soak up the mess.

"Do you have a cell phone?" Dr. Bennett asks. "In case you change your mind?"

I press the folded sheets into the carpet. "Used to." I squint at the liquid spreading across the paper towels. "Ava gave it to me, but my dad dropped it. It's broken."

This time Dr. Bennett doesn't ask for details. "What about your home phone?" she says. "I know your father has one."

"Not allowed to use it. Except for emergencies." I ball up the soggy paper towels, toss them in the trash.

Dr. Bennett moves Sam to the dry section of the room, to stack blocks, which he promptly knocks down. The tower of red, blue, and green tumbles into a heap. I sit down next to them.

"So what's up this weekend?" Dr. Bennett asks. "Any big plans?"

I close my mouth tight and build a tower for Sam, pyramid-like. The top wavers and wobbles but balances with a tap of my finger. Just in time for Sam to swing. *Crash.*

"Bingo with Isabel?" she suggests. "Now that would be fun. Maybe they call out the numbers in Spanish."

"We're going out of town, I guess." I pick at the hem of the Grateful Dead T-shirt. "Tonight. I didn't want to say anything in front of Ava because Dad says it might upset her."

"True." Dr. Bennett purses her lips. "That might make her sad. Or worried."

"Right," I agree.

Gosh. She won't stop talking. Where is my dad?

Dr. Bennett tries again. "Going anywhere fun? A lake? A state park?"

"I dunno." I hold up a block, turn it over and over in my hand.

"Well, maybe it's a big surprise. Something really fun! How long will you be gone? Did your dad say?"

A floorboard creaks.

Sam pipes up. "Dadadada." He pushes up from the floor and stands.

Dad fills the doorway. He's holding Dr. Bennett's pharmacy bag. He's smiling, though he doesn't look truly happy.

CHAPTER 55
JACK

FRIDAY, APRIL 30

"Jack, what are you all talking about?" My dad shoots a laser-beam stare at me. I shrink into the beanbag chair.

"Oh, nothing. Thank you so much." Dr. Bennett jumps up and holds out her hand for the paper bag. "I've been waiting for this. Isn't it fabulous they deliver?" She tears open the package.

"Asthma?" Dad asks and kneels down to hug Sam.

"Since I was a kid." She flips open the canister, takes a hit.

"How unfortunate," Dad comments.

"Not unless you run out of this." She shakes the inhaler and takes a step into her office, slides it onto the desk.

He turns to me and rakes his eyes over my clothes. "How'd your pants get so dirty? And where'd you get that?"

"They've been riding bikes. Playing

outside," Dr. Bennett answers for me. "When we came in, we had a small Sprite mishap. He was soaked. I gave him a spare shirt."

"Thank you."

"The boys were at the house with Ava and me," she adds. Dr. Bennett jabs a thumb toward the wall calendar. "Dr. Carson, I guess you haven't had a free minute to call me back. Would you like to reschedule your home visit now? How about Monday?"

"Gosh, I'm so swamped with work and campus issues. That's just not going to work. You call my assistant next week. She'll set it up." Dad points a finger at Dr. Bennett and chuckles. "And next time give me a little reminder. Card in the mail? You know?"

She doesn't laugh.

"Why don't we head over to your place right now?" She checks her watch, gives Dad an innocent gaze. "I've got an hour. What do you say? We can even get pizza, since it's dinnertime."

Sam runs circles around me, pulls at my pant legs.

"Thank you so very much for the kind offer." Dad glances back at the door. "No can do, Dr. Bennett. The fellas and I have too much planned for the weekend. Some other time."

Dr. Bennett bites her lip, disappointed.

"Come on, guys. Time to load up. Gotta get a move on." Dad pushes me toward the door. "We'll get you that shirt back, Dr. Bennett."

"Not worried about that in the least," she replies and hands me something. It's that same package Ava tried to give me. I roll my eyes but take it anyway and shove it into my backpack. No way I want to make a big scene with Dad here. He'll probably rip whatever it is to shreds. Now I am kind of curious to see what's inside.

"I do have two other issues to discuss with you." Dr. Bennett raises an eyebrow.

Dad sighs. "Jack, can you get your brother in his car seat? Thanks."

"Okay," I say, but I take my time leaving with Sam so that I can listen to the conversation.

Dr. Bennett watches us, then turns to my dad. "Now where are you off to in such a hurry? Big trip?"

"Ah, that's a surprise." Dad says, "Shh!"

"The children are out of the room." She laughs. "They can't hear you."

But Dr. Bennett can see I'm still here. She knows.

Dad straightens his shoulders. "I don't care for your tone. They're my children. I have custody —"

"Temporary custody."

A warning bell sounds in my head. Are they going to fight?

"And if I feel like having some fun, getting away from all of this . . ." Dad waves his hands at the office walls, the posters, the games. "Then I will. We will." He grits his teeth and forces the corners of his mouth up. "Now if that's all, we'll be on our way. We have a lot to do. Thank you very much. I can't leave them out there sitting in the truck."

Dad tries to ease past her, but she blocks the door.

"One last thing, okay?" Dr. Bennett asks. "Those bruises on Jack's arm. What happened?"

Uh-oh.

"He didn't tell you? He's a little adventurous, that one." Dad rubs his jaw. "Fell off his skateboard doing this amazing stunt. We were lucky he didn't break his arm."

Dr. Bennett steps out of his way. Gives Dad a thoughtful look. "Lucky," she echoes. But she doesn't sound like she's agreeing. "And I'm so glad that you explained what happened." She pauses. "Anyone else might

393

jump to conclusions and call child protective services."

"That would be a monumental mistake," Dad says. His voice drips with poison.

There's dead silence. I want to disappear into a wall. Or vanish like the Invisible Kid in DC Comics Universe.

Dr. Bennett and Dad glare at each other.

I pick up Sam and my backpack and we hightail it out to the Range Rover.

Chapter 56
Mitchell

FRIDAY, APRIL 30

My blood smolders as I drive away from Dr. Bennett's office. I grip the wheel, sweaty-palmed, and squint at the dark road. All I can see is the smug look on her face. The veiled threat echoes in my throbbing head.

I turn sharply, slam on the brakes, and lay on the horn when an oncoming car veers into our lane.

"Idiot," I mutter.

Accelerating, I weave quickly around the sluggish traffic, urgency burning in my veins. I have to set this straight. Dr. Bennett's a loose cannon. A crazy feminist determined to advocate for women, no matter if they lie and cheat.

I wonder what Ava has told her, the sob stories spoon-fed to this quack of a psychologist. I should have immediately rejected a female custody evaluator when the court appointed her. Damn my stupid attorney for not thinking of it first.

We bump over a pothole, jarring the boys in the back. Sam starts to cry, and I can hear Jack trying to soothe him. I rub at my temple, trying to quiet the noise in my head.

Dr. Bennett could ruin everything. She's a stranger. How can she presume to know anything about what's best for my children? My mind spins like a merry-go-round on fast-forward. I clench my teeth, dizzy.

Her words replay. Over and over. Louder. Faster. *Anyone else might jump to conclusions. Call child protective services.*

I jerk the Range Rover around a slow-moving pickup truck, silently cursing at the driver, and take the next right, barely braking for the stop sign. As I turn into the apartment complex, rolling over the speed bumps, my pulse surges.

Dr. Bennett's going to try and win over the kids. She wants Ava to get custody. I have to stop her. My heart clenches and I struggle to take a deep breath. With one hand pressed to my chest, I force myself to exhale, blowing all of the air out of my lungs.

As I park and cut the engine, there's nothing but the sound of our collective breathing as I stare up at the black sky. Jack's. Sam's. Mine. An idea forms in my head. A solution.

This will end once and for all. It has to. Tonight.

Chapter 57
Ava

FRIDAY, APRIL 30

A sharp breeze blows through the backyard, and I shiver. The sky darkens as silver clouds roll across the horizon, blocking the sun. I head back inside the house, tamping down the urge to drive back to Moulton to talk to Frank or Birmingham to see Will Harris. Pieces of the puzzle swirl around me like random debris in a dark funnel cloud. Karen's itinerary, Jack's fight at school, Mitchell's escalating antics. Karen's book tour. Her accident. The epilepsy.

I pull out a blank notebook, use my calendar, and sketch out a timeline. I jot down every single snippet of anything Will Harris told me, then move on to Mitchell's father. The story about his mother. Her suicide. Mitchell running away to Phoenix, Arizona. How he was never the same. My breath catches and holds in my throat.

What if . . . what if Mitchell runs? With the

boys. I grope for my phone, fighting the urge to jump in the Jeep and head for Dr. Bennett's office. It's too risky. Mitchell will be there and won't hesitate to call the police. Quaking with worry, I dial Graham's cell, but the call goes straight to voice mail. I leave a shaky message. Trying to slow my breathing, I try Will Harris next. This time I'm in luck. His assistant puts me through right away.

"I wanted to say thank you. I met Frank," I say.

"Good," Will says, clipped but polite. "Did he help?"

"He was a little shell-shocked at first, but once he found out who I was, he answered a lot of questions. It's so sad, he hasn't seen Mitchell or Jack since Karen's funeral."

Harris clears his throat. "And, my dear, how do I play in to this?"

"I'm trying to figure out what Mitchell might do next," I say. "He's disappeared before. I'm afraid he might do it again with the boys."

There's silence on the other end.

I squeeze my eyes tight and keep on talking. "I was wondering if you remembered anything else?" I continue. "Did *you* see Karen that day? Before she had the accident?"

He waits a beat before answering. "Give me a moment. I want to make sure of something." From the sound of it, he's clicking through his office calendar.

I hold my breath.

"Yes, I did see her," he offers. "We had a brief meeting. About ten minutes. She was about to leave —"

"Leave?" I interrupt.

"For her book tour, dear. We were going over last-minute details," says Harris. "But Mitchell called and told her to cancel it. She went into my office and shut the door, but the argument was so loud I could hear almost every word."

I squeeze my eyes shut and rub my temples, remembering the pain of my last argument with Mitchell. "What was it about?"

"Karen stood up to him, told him she was going. Karen never, ever did that." He exhales.

"That's when he threatened her." Harris takes a breath. "I think he did, anyhow."

I almost choke. "Why do you say that?"

"Because all of a sudden, Karen got really calm. Collected. Hung up the phone, came out of my office, and said she was going back to the house to work it out, even if it meant postponing the tour. She told me she had to check on Jack. And then she left."

My palms begin to sweat. "Did you hear from her after that?"

Harris sighs. "Ava dear, that was it. The next time we saw her, it was at her funeral."

"We?" I ask.

"That would be me and my partner, Paul. He loved Karen, he wasn't about to miss paying his respects." Will Harris sounds almost offended.

Instantly, my face blazes. "Of course not," I rush to say. "That's very kind."

"Dear, that's just what kind of gentlemen we are . . ." His voice trails off.

I swallow. "But were you suspicious? You and Paul? Your staff? Did you think about talking to the police?"

Will Harris doesn't answer right away.

"Of course, dear. We thought about it, agonized over it. Paul and I had long since realized Mitchell wasn't exactly stable. But Karen was gone. It was over. I couldn't exactly go over and start pointing a finger in his face."

I rub my lips with my knuckle, thinking. "I understand."

Harris coughs. "How is Jack? He must be, what? Seven years old?" he asks.

"Eight, if you can believe it." I shake my head. "He's hanging in there. We have a court-appointed counselor who meets with him every week. She's looking out for him."

"Good." Will Harris resumes his professional mode. "Dear, I must rush off. May I offer you a piece of advice before I go?"

"Certainly," I say. "I'd be grateful."

"Please, get away from Mitchell Carson. As soon as you can."

CHAPTER 58
JACK

FRIDAY, APRIL 30

The ride back to the apartment is dead quiet. I rest my head against the cool glass of the window and pretend to fall asleep. When the truck stops, I jerk my body to look like I've woken up. Before my dad can ask me anything, I jump out the door, head for my room, and shove the package from Ava under my bed.

I think I hear my name but ignore it. I lock myself in the bathroom, fan running, and water on. Sam's almost asleep, and Dad wants help getting my brother inside and in bed. It makes me feel sort of bad to ignore him, but he's been kind of a jerk lately.

No, really a jerk. And the last thing I want is another fight. About anything. Especially about the box from Ava. Dad can't know about that.

What I need is for Dad to forget about the stuff at Dr. Bennett's office and move on to something else that makes him mad. Someone at the college might do something dumb. Or the guy outside blowing leaves might give him a headache. I can always say I have stomach cramps. Or a fever. Then my dad will get busy calling the pediatrician. And be angry trying to play Mr. Mom.

He'll also take the credit for dragging me to the doctor or handing me a bottle of medicine. He wants everyone to think he does everything — even though Isabel takes care of us around here. Laundry, dishes, beds, vacuuming. Changing diapers still makes Dad gag-vomit. He just thinks I don't notice or I'm not looking.

Whatever works for him. But the truth matters to me. Like the stuff about my grandpa. All of a sudden, he's not dead? I'm still freaked out about that. Trying to tell myself it's real. Trying to make myself believe it.

But, hey, superheroes can come back to life. Superman did it. No one blinks at that. Captain America did too. Marvel Comics killed off his real identity, Steve Rogers, a few years back. The head honcho guys thought the fan world would take it lying down, but boy, were they wrong.

Rogers/Captain America had been around for more than sixty years. He was an icon, a veteran in the truest sense — created to help the United States fight in World War II — using his combat and survival skills. Yes, he was a character in a comic book. But when the sniper bullet took him out, the world fought back. Captain America was reborn.

A miracle? Maybe. I think it's because people believed in him and wouldn't give up.

So what about real life? What about my grandfather? If I had known he was alive, I wouldn't have given up.

Right now all I know is that I am starving. Headache and stomachache starving. So much so that I can't think. About Grandpa, about Ava or Sam. About anything but food.

Dad's on the phone when I finally come out of the bathroom, and as predicted, he's onto some new crisis. He's pacing around like a caged tiger, eyes crazy. My throat parches and I creep backward, away from him, until my hand finds the door frame of my bedroom. I duck inside the darkness and let my eyes adjust as I stay still and listen for my father.

When he hangs up the phone, he heads for the bathroom and flicks on the light, bathing the hall in bright yellow. I blink against the glare, rubbing my eyelids while my dad opens and closes drawers, rummaging around. I can tell when he opens the vanity over the sink because the hinges creak. I hold my breath as he rattles pill bottles and pushes around boxes of medicine we keep out of Sam's reach.

While he's busy searching, I tiptoe into the kitchen and ease open the bottom cabinets. Inside there's nothing but filé powder to make gumbo and a yellow bag of shrimp boil seasoning. The cupboard next to it isn't much better.

Holding my arms tight to my body, I step toward the refrigerator and pull gently on the freezer door. A blast of chilled air hits my cheeks. Two long blue trays sit to one side, shiny and full of ice, but otherwise that space is bare too. When I move down to the larger door, my hope for dinner really fizzles, like someone's punctured my favorite balloon. Other than a squeeze-jar of mustard and a box of baking soda, it's empty.

I check the trash. Dad's tossed out every single thing Isabel made us for the weekend. *What was he thinking?*

Panicking a little, I look in the pantry. One box of mac and cheese, which may become dinner, unless my dad decides to at least get takeout. I swear the guys at Red Dragon Chinese Restaurant know our weekend order by heart: sweet and sour shrimp, three egg rolls, and pineapple fried rice.

Dad's gruff voice sounds behind me. "Gotta go out for a while, Jack."

I jump up and whirl around, chest heaving.

His eyes run over me, scanning my rumpled T-shirt, jeans, and bare feet. I wait for him to criticize something about my clothes or my hair, but he brushes past me, reaching over my head.

When I glance up, he's already found what he's looking for, a silver flask among a few tall bottles of liquor. Stuff I'm never, ever supposed to touch.

Keeping his back to me, Dad slides the container inside his jacket pocket. "Watch your brother," he says, his voice gravelly, turning around to face me. "He's asleep."

I wrench my eyes away from the bulge in his jacket pocket and focus on his face, the pulse thudding in my veins. "Yes, sir," I reply quietly.

Dad opens up the closet door, pulls down a tan canvas suitcase. "Put anything you might want or need in there."

I don't move.

"Jack, get it done," he snaps. "I have to take care of some things. For the trip." He pulls at his shirt and straightens his collar.

"We leave when I get back. Whether you're packed or not."

I nod and my robot self clicks on. I inch toward my bedroom. I don't want to wake up Sam. But I need clothes, shoes, and stuff. God, I hate my dad right now.

"Good. Be back soon."

The door clicks shut behind him. I lock it. My stomach heaves as if it's the *Titanic* breaking in half on the Atlantic. Then a thought hits me. The canisters with flour, sugar, and sometimes a forgotten treat. I haven't checked there. Maybe Isabel left something. I almost sprint to the counter. The tops clink as I pull it up. No food. No cookies. But there's something else. Something cold and hard. I pull it up and take it out.

It's a gun. And I think it might be real.

CHAPTER 59
LUCY

FRIDAY, APRIL 30
This is the time when an escape route to an alternate universe would come in handy. When you want to run but can't, when you suspect someone is crazy, when you absolutely would rather drink a bottle of wine than deal with the cold, hard truth.

Now I have to call her attorney. On a Friday night. With some serious concerns.

Damn.

I search for Graham's card, find it stuck to some Jolly Ranchers in my drawer. Stained cherry-red on the edges, I can still make out the number. I punch it in and wait.

Voice mail.

"Graham, hey. This is Lucy. Please call me back ASAP. I need to talk to you about Mitchell Carson. I'm worried. It sounds like he's planning a trip away — and they're leaving tonight. I have no information about where they're going or for how long."

Pause. I take a hit from my inhaler.

"Also the older boy has some bruises that are consistent with abuse. His story does not, I repeat, does not match Dad's. Someone's covering up and I don't like it. Dad didn't meet me for his home visit. Not sure if that information made it down the food chain to you yet."

Another hit. I clear my throat.

"As a mandatory reporter, I have to contact CPS next. Call me. Graham —"

A rattle at the door startles me. Someone is trying to open it. Then a knock.

Bleep. The voice mail cuts off with a sound loud enough to do hearing damage.

More banging. Louder this time.

"Hold your horses," I call out. "Don't break my window."

I almost stumble over my umbrella as I step into the murky hallway and yank open the office door. "It's Friday night. What in the world could be so important?"

A thick hand grabs my neck and squeezes.

CHAPTER 60
AVA

FRIDAY, APRIL 30

My body sags when I hang up with Will Harris. I press a hand to the counter to steady myself. My head pulsates with pain. I start walking to get some Advil when the rumble of a motorcycle engine startles me. I rush to the door and peek out. It's Graham on his Harley. In a very wrinkled, dirty coat and tie. He pulls off his helmet and walks up the front steps.

"Got your message," he says. "Figured it'd be easier to just head over and talk."

"What happened?" I demand. "You look awful."

He grimaces, grabs his briefcase and a sack from Miss Beulah's. "My very temperamental bike led to a very temperamental judge."

"Late for court?" I push open the door and usher him inside.

"You guessed it." He plops the paper bag

on the counter, which smells like heaven — cinnamon, sugar, thick white icing. "I offered to be in contempt so that my client didn't get the short end of the stick. The judge fined me a thousand dollars."

I gulp.

"Next time I'll set two alarms." Graham pushes the bag in my direction. "Here, eat up while you tell me what's going on."

I recount the visit with Jack and Sam, show him the timeline, and offer my theory about Mitchell running with the boys. "Think about it," I say. "He took off after his mother committed suicide, and Frank said he was never the same. After Karen dies, he leaves his job and everything — including his father — behind, basically wiping out the past." I stop and take a breath. "So what's to stop him from taking the boys now and disappearing?"

"Other than it's illegal?" Graham tips back in his chair, considering this. "Although, I don't know if he cares."

"Exactly."

Graham drums his fingers on the table. "We can't go accusing someone of just *thinking* about kidnapping their own children."

"I know." I frown and cross my arms. "So while I was waiting for you to call me back, I got in touch with Will Harris. Told him what I was thinking about Mitchell disappearing. I asked him if he remembered anything else about Karen — anything weird that happened right before she died."

"And?"

"She was in his office the morning of the accident. Harris said Mitchell called and demanded Karen come home. He thinks Mitchell threatened to hurt Jack if she didn't come back right away. So she did."

Graham springs to his feet, starts pacing, but stops abruptly to rub his knee. "Damn. Why didn't Harris go to the cops?"

"I guess he didn't know for sure about the threat. Mitchell would have denied it anyway. What could the police do? Karen was already gone."

Graham mulls this, head down. "Okay, I get it. What else?"

"There's no way Harris was Karen's boyfriend. No way."

"Did you ask him straight out?"

"Didn't have to. He's gay. Told me about his partner, Paul. How they went to the funeral together. How he and Paul adored Karen and Jack."

Graham is shocked. For a second. "Well, tickle me pink. I'll be damned."

"There's more. Frank called and said he'd found something. So I went to see him yesterday. We had quite the discussion."

"Hit me."

I rummage through my papers, yank out the itinerary. Hand it to Graham. "Take a look at this. I made about ten copies, just in case."

He scans it, rubs his jaw, then hands it back to me. "She wasn't leaving him."

"Nope." I slip the paper in my pocket for safekeeping and cross my arms. "It was a surprise. They were going on a trip. Mitchell didn't know anything about it. Still doesn't."

"All right, partner!" Graham slaps his hands together and rubs them. "Did I mention I could get you a job as a PI?"

I grin at the praise. "Maybe," I say. "Or maybe I'll go to law school and give you a run for your money, counselor."

Across the room in Graham's briefcase, his phone starts vibrating. He jumps up from the table but doesn't snatch it up fast enough.

"Dr. Bennett," he says, swiping at the screen. He attempts to call back, but his phone won't connect. "Come on."

"Maybe she's leaving a voice mail?" I suggest.

Thirty seconds later, Graham's phone beeps. "She did." Graham sticks his cell between his ear and shoulder, listening and watching me closely. His forehead wrinkles. "It's not good. Go ahead, listen to it."

The message is broken up and crackly. I can only catch bits and pieces. *Worried. Away. Bruises. Check on the kids.* I stifle a cry. Then there's a sound, like banging on wood or knocking. Then the voice mail ends.

My body goes numb. "Something awful's happened."

He nods and redials her number. I bite my lip and pace as he listens.

He hangs it up. "She's not answering."

"Let's go," I urge him.

Graham nods, and we race for the door. He hands me my phone as we jog to the Harley. I climb on the back, jam the phone in my jeans, and strap on Graham's helmet.

"Ready?" he yells.

When I squeeze his arm as a yes, he guns the engine to life. In seconds, we're speeding downtown.

CHAPTER 61
LUCY

FRIDAY, APRIL 30

My knees buckle under the weight of my surprise. Mitchell Carson's fingers pressing into the cords of my neck, his face outlined in the darkness. My hands jerk forward, pushing against Mitchell's chest. It's like pressing into the worn grooves of a boulder, solid and unyielding. I rake at his forearms, my fingernails finding his skin.

"Dammit," he growls, glancing down at the place I've scratched and torn. He shakes me, as if I'm a puppet made of cotton cloth, felt, and stitching.

As I draw a ragged breath, I smell sweat — Mitchell's? My own? And the distinct scent of cypress branches after a rainstorm. I force my brain there, into a forest of trees, hoping to calm my frantic pulse. *Stay calm, Lucy. Stay calm.*

"Leave us alone." Mitchell hisses into my ear. His breath, hot and wet, settles on my clammy skin. When he steps back, his fingers loosen on my neck.

I suck in air, big gasping breaths. My throat, full of fire, fights the oxygen. My lungs scream for relief. I press my spine against the drywall, willing my weak legs to straighten and stand. Mitchell stares at me, motionless, as I meet his eyes, dark as obsidian and unyielding. His face, mask-like, reveals no emotion.

"My medicine. I can't breathe," I gasp. His fingers tighten, close off my vocal cords. I can't scream. I can't make a sound.

It's then Mitchell turns and reaches for my inhaler. I watch as his fingers curl around the cylinder. His knuckles tighten, squeezing, before my medicine disappears into the depths of his pocket.

The light fades. Darker. Darker. My arms flail and jerk. I slump over. And see Mitchell Carson smile just before I hit the floor.

CHAPTER 62
JACK

FRIDAY, APRIL 30

What would Iron Man do? Please. He'd grab his brother, blast off into space, and leave this mess behind. His suit's awesome like that. Bulletproof, able to shoot repulsor rays, it protects him from anything.

Okay. So there's the heart issue. Never stopped Iron Man for long. Genius inventor, problem solver, supersmart guy. MIT grad. *Sheesh.* If he can't come up with some answers, the world's lost. For good.

I have to channel my inner Iron Man. There's work to do, solutions to find. I grab a pen and paper. Research possibilities: Dad's computer. Off-limits. House phone. Off-limits. Contacts: Ava. Dr. Bennett. The judge. Lawyers. My grandfather.

Clues: My dad's weird freak-out sessions. The box Ava gave me when Dr. Bennett was at our house. The box I stuffed under the bed. The gun in the kitchen. I don't want

418

anyone else getting hurt. Ava. Me. Especially Sam.

Like he knows I am thinking about him, Sam sighs in his sleep, stretches his arms overhead. He exhales and rubs his cheek against the mattress. I climb out of bed, steal into the kitchen, and lift up the cover of the canister. The gun is still there. The metal glints back at me in the soft light from the hallway. Before I change my mind, and knowing my dad might ground me forever, I reach inside and pull it out. It's heavy and solid in my hand. I squint, checking that the safety is on. Heart thumping, I replace the canister top and race back to my room. After wrapping the gun in a towel, I tuck it into my backpack and shove it under my bed.

While my cheek is pressed to the carpeting, I see the box from Ava. I hesitate, then pull it out, sit up on my knees, and examine the writing on the card. Flowery, like a girl wrote it. The box, a little banged up, is held shut with brittle tape and a plain yellowed ribbon. It breaks open when I tug. I lift off the cover, move the tissue paper aside, and pull out what's inside.

A children's book, with a drawing of a boy on the cover. He's six or seven years old, with a red cape flying in the breeze. It's me.

The same eyes, nose, mouth. My hair is a little darker now, and I'm bigger. But it's a picture of me. No doubt about it. Here's the title: *The Adventures of Jack Carson: Super Kid.* The author and illustrator? Karen Carson.

The book spine cracks as I open the pages. My mother's drawings tell the story: a regular boy in a regular neighborhood with a regular life. One day he finds a red cape in an old trunk in his grandfather's attic. Every time he puts it on, amazing things happen. He saves a baby from being hit in traffic, he climbs a tree to rescue a kitten, he helps the police find a bank robber.

On the last few pages, Jack finds out the cape doesn't have superpowers, but he can still do all kinds of good things without it. It's the magic inside his heart that counts. When I turn the final page, a card and a photo fall out into my lap. My throat gets tight.

Dearest Jack,

This book is one of many surprises I planned for your birthday. It's a little late getting back from the printer, but I hope you like it. I'll miss you every minute and will be home as soon as I can from the book tour! Here's a photo from last year. Look how much you've grown! I'm proud of you, my superhero son.

> I love you more than anything,
> Mommy

The photo's upside down, with names on the back. My mother's handwriting, because it matches the card. *Jack's birthday. Jack, Frank, Mitchell, Karen.* I flip it over.

I'm wearing a red cape. Sitting on my grandfather's lap. Beaming in the glow of candles. And I'm next to my mother, who *wasn't* going to leave me, after all.

Chapter 63
Graham

Dr. Bennett's office door is cracked open and the place is trashed. Garbage overturned, files knocked to the ground. The hallway's dark, so I can't see well. I grab for Ava's hand, fumble for the light switch and flick it on. Ava gasps. The light glares harsh on a crumpled body. Dr. Bennett's lying on her side. She's alabaster white, the color of drying plaster. Her cell phone is within inches of her outstretched hand. I crouch down and check her pulse. My fingertips catch a faint beat. Ava drops to her knees and holds her other hand.

I punch 9–1–1.

"What's your emergency?" the operator answers.

The woman records the address, sketchy details, and my name in the Mobile County EMS system. I grab the wrinkled pharmacy bag on the desk, turn it upside down, and shake out the empty Albuterol box.

"She has asthma. I can't find her medicine."

Where's the inhaler? On my hands and one good knee, we search the room. Ava starts opening drawers. I dump her purse, scattering pens and lipstick in all directions. Her wallet falls out last, a wad of cash stuffed in the pocket.

Though I don't say it to Ava, a voice in my head shouts. *This was no random break-in.*

"An ambulance is on the way, sir. Stay on the phone with me until the paramedics arrive, please."

"Of course." I keep my fingers on her pulse. Check her arms and legs for bruising. Anything unusual.

Dr. Bennett groans, shifts her neck. And I see the marks. Big enough to match a man's hand and fingers. Around her throat.

My brain jolts. "Look." I motion to Ava.

When she sees where I'm pointing, her face drains of color. She shrinks back, and her shoulders fold in.

Ambulance sirens blast. Doors slam. Voices yell.

"Mitchell," she mouths.

Footsteps drum in the hallway, but Ava doesn't move. She's in a trance, body rigid, eyes fixed on Dr. Bennett's face. I move out of the way, stand up, then reach over and jostle Ava's arm.

She clambers to her feet, pushes her hair back from her face. Her voice is low and strangely calm. "Graham, I have to do *something.*"

The EMS team jogs into the room.

I frown and glance over at her. "What are you talking about? We did. The paramedics are here."

Ava shakes her head.

One throws down a duffel bag and kneels next to Dr. Bennett. The rest jostle for room in the tight space. The first medic bends down his shaved head to check her vitals. His partner, a slight, dark-haired female, slips an oxygen mask over her face and starts an IV.

Ava pulls at my arm and motions toward the hallway. When we step out of the room, she starts pacing, her green eyes ablaze. "He's going to hurt the boys," she whispers. "That message from Dr. Bennett. She was scared."

I shake my head and lower my voice. "Look. No matter what happened here — whoever they find out is responsible — I don't think Mitchell will go so far as to hurt the kids. They're all he can hold over your head. He's using them to manipulate you. Why would he take his best weapon out of the mix? This way, he's in control, you're suffering. And he knows it."

Ava sets her jaw. "I don't know."

"Sir?" One of the paramedics calls out.

"Let me talk to them," I plead. "Then we'll call the police, do whatever we need to do." I reach down and squeeze her forearm. "But we have to be careful and do this right. There's too much at stake."

"Sir?" the voice repeats, this time, louder.

Ava bites her lip. "Go. I need some air."

She frowns, zips up her jacket, and jogs down the hallway. When I get back to the paramedics, they're loading Dr. Bennett on a stretcher. It's another five minutes before I realize Ava is gone.

CHAPTER 64
AVA

FRIDAY, APRIL 30

I walk away from Dr. Bennett's office. My hands tremble. I find my cell, punch in Mitchell's number, and pray. The battery is dangerously low. Enough to eke out a few minutes? I hit Send. The sharp ring jars my heart.

"Dr. Carson," he snaps.

I force my lips into a smile. Soften my voice. "Mitchell. It's me. Ava."

Nothing.

"Do you have a moment or two?"

I can hear the breath expel from his lungs in a deep gust. Music plays in the background. Shopping carts rattle by. A loudspeaker announcement blares.

He's out somewhere. Where are the boys?

"I'm pretty busy." He coughs, clearly distracted by the *bleep-bleep* of a checkout scanner.

"How are the children? They with you?"

426

Mitchell clears his throat. "Fine, fine. Home with Isabel."

She's at Friday night Bingo. Unless the kids are sick. But I just saw them. They're fine. I picture them in the apartment. It strikes me then. *They're alone.*

"Great!" I squeak, trying not to sound desperately chipper. "Then you could meet me. So I can just, you know, share some things with you. I need to tell you . . . um, I want to say this . . . in person. Apologize."

He's intrigued. "It's a little late. I don't know if it's going to change anything." Gruff. Stubborn. Typical Mitchell. But appealing to his sense of control definitely seems to be working.

"I know," I gush a little. "It's probably just to make *me* feel better. But I need to see you in person. It would be a huge favor to me. I'd owe you."

This gets him.

I scramble to think. Somewhere private. Somewhere safe for Mitchell, but not me. "How about the college? Your office?"

"Give me ten minutes."

I calculate the distance to Mitchell's apartment. If I sprint, I'll be there in a few minutes. I have to try. Once he realizes I've tricked him, it's all over.

I start to run.

CHAPTER 65
JACK

FRIDAY, APRIL 30

The computer hums to life under my fingertips. If Dad comes home and finds me on his laptop . . . But I can't think about that right now. I google my grandfather's first and last name, then Birmingham, Alabama. The usual Internet garbage pops up. Sites with flashy graphics that promise to find anyone, anywhere, and want you to pay money. With a credit card I don't own.

I try his name again with the army, Vietnam. Nothing.

Combine his name and my dad's. Add "Karen Carson." Hit return. A newspaper article. And my mother's obituary. I open the news story and read it. A few paragraphs sum up the last minutes of my mother's life. Dry, sunny day. Car accident. Investigation closed.

The obituary's twice as long. *Karen Carson. Beloved wife, mother, daughter.* Her picture stares back at me, empty, haunting, like a ghost. I'd almost forgotten the color of her eyes, the texture of her thick, shiny brown hair. She smelled like apples, crisp and fresh. Seeing her helps me remember what I've buried so deep inside my chest.

Graveside service at four o'clock. The memories zoom back, sharp and biting. *Donations in lieu of flowers.*

I check the name of the cemetery. I've never been back to the gravesite since the day she was buried. Dad refuses to take me. Won't talk about it. Acts like it never happened. We used to have photo albums and scrapbooks. Where are they now?

I can't look at my mother's face any longer. I force myself to scan the words, look for clues. Anything. We're all listed as next of kin. Wait. The obituary lists Grandpa Frank as from Moulton.

I close the window, try the Internet white pages. Type in Frank Carson with my wobbly fingers. In seconds his information pops up on the screen. I write down the number, wonder if he's home, guess at what he's doing. Eating dinner? Watching TV?

I grip the scrap of paper, carry it to the kitchen, and stare at the phone. As if it'll dial itself. One hand out, I reach a little further and punch the buttons with a shaky finger. *I can always pretend it's a wrong number. Except I'm a terrible liar. With stomach cramps and a headache.*

"Carson," the voice barks. An older version of my father, rough around the edges.

I choke on my fear.

"Hello?" he says. "Hello?" he snaps, then his voice deepens a few octaves. "I don't appreciate these prank phone calls —"

"Do you have a son?" I croak out. "Mitchell?"

The man stops his angry tirade. He's breathing hard. "Jack? Is this Jack? Talk to me."

But I cut him off. Hang up. Sink to the floor, pull my knees to my chest, bury my head.

Everything.

Everything my dad's told me.

Everything my dad's told me is a lie.

CHAPTER 66
AVA

FRIDAY, APRIL 30

My head hammers with every step. Storm clouds brew in the distance. The rain falls hard as I reach the door of Mitchell's place, a blessing and a curse. My socks are soaked through, they squish water as I pound my shoes on the pavement.

The lightning flashes across the wet parking lot. Mitchell's truck is gone. For now. There's a single bulb burning in the apartment window. Thunder booms and crashes, nearer now. The wind whips my hair. A gust tosses tree branches to the ground. Birds cry and flutter to safety. Soda cans spin in circles on the blacktop, their clatter like broken cymbals in a marching band.

I race up the stairs, pausing under the shelter of the porch roof to draw a ragged breath and call Graham. He's only minutes away.

"Where the hell are you?" he shouts.

"The apartment —" I cough out the words.

"Dammit, Ava!"

I bend over, chest heaving. "Get over here. And call Mike Kennedy."

The wind howls and Graham's question gets lost in the crackle of the connection.

"What?" I yell.

"What about Mitchell?" he repeats.

The phone goes dead.

I shove it back in my pocket and turn.

The apartment door is shiny-slick with water and humidity. I knock with my knuckles. Once, then harder. Mother Nature drowns me out.

"Jack," I call out, my cheek pressed to the metal frame. "Can you hear me? Open up!"

With my palm open wide, I slap at the barrier between my children and me. In the darkness, I feel for the bell. *Do I have the wrong apartment?* When no one answers, I creep around the corner, try to peer inside. Mitchell's tie and sport coat lie across the sofa. I shade my eyes and see Sam's blocks and his pretend radio. Jack's comic books. I rap against the glass. "Jack? Are you there, babe?"

Through the fogged-up glass, I think I see a figure crouched on the floor in the kitchen. Too small to be Mitchell. My fingertips

432

wipe at the window, trying to see better. It has to be Jack. I tap again and wave, trying to get his attention.

"Jack, please." I whisper. The wind carries my plea down the street, out of sight.

Finally, movement. A leg, then an arm. I see the edge of a head. With red earplugs in. Jack's earplugs for his iPod.

It is Jack. And he can't hear me between the music and the storm. I race back to the front and steady myself in front of the apartment. I take a few steps running start and hit the door with my shoulder. It creaks and gives a little, I can feel it. One more time. I ball up my fists, clench them across my chest, and summon all of my strength. This time the lock breaks apart. The door flies open.

Jack races into the living room, earphones flying. "Ava!" He yells.

He falls into my arms, buries his face.

"Oh, thank God." I gasp and clutch him to me. "Jack, are you okay? I'm so worried about you both. Is your brother okay?" We're both shaking.

"Yes," he answers and begins to sob. "Mom."

Mom.

I ease the door closed behind me. It won't shut all the way. The air-conditioner blasts a chill through my skin. I shiver and hold Jack close.

"I'm sorry I didn't believe you."

"No need to apologize, honey. There's nothing to be sorry about." I squeeze his hand. "I'm here."

Jack snuffles. "But he's taking us. We're leaving." He glances at the clock, wipes his eyes. "He's supposed to be back by now. I don't know where he is."

I know — at least, I pray I do.

He continues. "I called Grandpa Frank a little while ago. He answered but I hung up. I would have called you on the cell phone, but Dad —"

He gestures wildly to the open suitcase, chin trembling. "He took it and smashed it to pieces. He knew you gave the phone to me. He was really, really mad. And then I couldn't remember your new phone number. And —"

Finger to my lips, I shake my head. "We'll have time to talk later. I don't want you to worry about it. But we need to get your brother and get out of here now. Is he in bed?"

Jack nods and points to the back bedroom. *Hurry up, Graham, please. You should be here by now.* I calculate the logistics. One motorcycle. Two adults, one kid, and a baby.

A gust of wind pushes the door open. A floorboard creaks. "It's about time —" I spin around, ready to scold Graham for making me worry.

But it's Mitchell.

CHAPTER 67
AVA

FRIDAY, APRIL 30

Before I can cry out or react, Mitchell jerks me to the wall, his breath hot on my face.

I shift my gaze to Jack, signaling for him to leave the room. His face pinches in worry, but Jack moves quickly toward the kitchen. He can't leave the apartment and wouldn't leave Sam, but at least he'll be out of the line of fire if things get ugly.

With Jack out of sight, Mitchell pushes his forearm against my neck, cutting off my supply of air. I choke as he hisses at me. "Ava, this isn't just trespassing. It's attempted kidnapping. Punishable by law."

When he stands back, I grasp at my throat and suck in air, staring into Mitchell's dark eyes. Chest heaving, I manage to spit out six words. "I heard you're the one leaving."

Mitchell glowers at me and yanks my arm. "Your phone. Where is it?"

I grit my teeth and pluck it out of my

pocket. Though it feels like betrayal, I hand it over. It's no use to me now, anyway. Mitchell fumbles it, pressing the On button to no avail.

"It's dead, Mitchell," I whisper. "I can't call anyone."

His lips curl, and he tosses it onto the sofa, sending it bouncing across the cushions. "Jack," he snaps, shouting into the next room. "Get your brother."

My heart spasms.

Snatching his keys, Mitchell hustles me out the door. We wait there for the boys — Jack in just a T-shirt and jeans with his backpack on, Sam, bleary-eyed and wrapped in a fleece blanket. Rain drums on the roof, pooling on the walkway. As Mitchell prods us down the stairs and toward the parking lot, I yank off my own jacket, holding it over the boys' bare heads, letting the rain pelt my face in tiny needles. An icy rivulet of water trickles down the back of my neck as I help buckle the boys inside the Range Rover.

Sam is fussy from being woken up, and I stroke his head, murmuring to soothe him. Our eyes lock. My breath quickens. Today I want to lie. I want to tell Jack there's a backup plan. That everything will be fine, there's an elaborate escape route planned.

But I stay silent, give Jack an encouraging smile, and listen for the wail of sirens. For the roar of Graham's Harley rivaling the bellow of the storm. Neither come. As my seat belt clicks in place, the air around me crackles. My body tremors. And I send up a silent prayer. To the angels, to the heavens, to all that is good and true in the universe.

I am strong. I am scared as hell. But this isn't over yet.

Chapter 68
Ava

FRIDAY, APRIL 30

Rain pummels the Range Rover, beating the roof and windshield in a frantic pattern. We hydroplane, and my stomach lurches when the vehicle suddenly slides right. Gripping the armrest, I squint through the windshield, trying desperately to catch a glimpse of the road as the wipers strain to keep pace with the downpour.

Mitchell pulls at the wheel, slows, and turns. We're heading toward our own house now, not away from it. I blink, trying to filter all of the reasons he'd run here instead of Dallas, Atlanta, or Miami, cities so large it might be possible to disappear for a day or two.

Our headlights shine on the driveway, and I jump out and punch in the new code to open the garage. As Mitchell pulls into the sheltered space next to the Jeep, I squint at the glare from the fluorescent bulb

439

overhead, rubbing at my eyelids with my fingertips.

As I open the passenger doors to let the boys out, Mitchell motions for me to wait. "I want to talk, Ava." His voice, now steady and restrained, is almost kind. I hesitate, letting my hand rest on my thigh.

Thoughts pummel my brain in a constant beat of questions. Will Graham think to look here? Will Mike?

"Jack," he continues, "take your brother to his room. I'll be up in just a few minutes. Your mother and I need to talk."

I swallow and look back at the children. Jack doesn't say a word, just unbuckles Sam, pulls him onto his shoulder, grabs his backpack, and eases out of the SUV. With a last look at me, face pale, brow furrowed, Jack disappears inside.

An eerie calm falls over Mitchell. He backs out of the garage, parks outside, and cuts the engine.

"Let's go," he says, motioning that I should get out and head for the house.

Lightning bursts through the sky, illuminating the house and yard in an eerie glow. I don't move. "Are you leaving, Mitchell?" I ask. Moisture prickles the small of my back. My hands grow damp. "Whatever it is you have planned, it's not going to work."

Mitchell scoffs and shakes his head. He steps out, shuts the door, and jogs toward the soft yellow glow from the garage. The rain falls, silver, on his silhouette, water soaking his sport coat and skin.

Damn him. The boys are in the house. After a moment, I follow. Stepping over downed twigs and small, gnarled branches, I pick my way up the driveway. When the wind picks up, leaves swirl around my feet. Three steps later, I'm inside the garage, wiping the water from my cheeks.

Mitchell is waiting next to my Jeep. When he flexes his hands, an image of Dr. Bennett's face flashes in front of my eyes. Her neck with the finger marks.

I twinge with nausea but steady myself. My voice comes out stronger and clearer than I expect. "What is it that you want, Mitchell?"

He laughs, a stilted sound that reverberates in the garage. "I have what I want, Ava. Custody of the boys."

My heart twists like ribbon. "It's not over," I retort. "Nothing's been decided."

"Ah, but it has," he replies evenly. "Your little stunt tonight."

I exhale, trying to slow my racing pulse. I force my eyes to his. They're dark as charcoal, hot at the edges. "So now you're judge and jury?"

Mitchell smiles and walks over to the garage wall but doesn't answer. I follow his gaze to the smaller tools, neatly lined on a small shelf above my head.

My skin prickles. "You lied to me about your father. Frank's very much alive."

Mitchell whirls on me, and I jump. His face is purple-furious, contorted in pain. "That man is dead to me."

"He cares about you. And Jack," I protest.

"That's bull," he spits, clenching his fists. "He left us. He left my mother."

The rain slows, the thunder softens.

"Maybe he did," I say, my hand stealing to my back pocket. "But Karen wasn't leaving, was she?"

"Yes, she was," he argues. "Everyone leaves."

"She was going on a book tour, Mitchell." I keep my voice low, steady, and firm.

Mitchell's eyes flicker over me. "You're a liar. Just like she was."

I slide the paper from my back pocket. "Karen planned a trip for you, right after the book tour. It was a surprise." I hold it out. "Take it." The paper shakes.

He snatches it, scans the type. "Where did you get this? Frank?" Mitchell scoffs. "The

442

old man made it up." His face betrays him, though. He can't take his eyes away from the page.

"Mitchell, your father doesn't have a computer." A surge of frustration wells up and crests like an ocean wave. "Think about what you're saying."

Mitchell lashes out a whip-curl of outrage. "I know what I'm talking about." He rips the page in half, tears it again, and lets the pieces drift to the floor. "You're so naive. She was in love with Will Harris." He spits out the name.

I shake my head. "Will Harris has a partner. I met him."

Mitchell chortles. "That's the same thing Karen said. The two of you are just alike. Always plotting and lying." He's seething with fury now, starting to perspire. I back away, nearly tripping over my feet. In four quick strides, Mitchell catches up to me. He catches my shoulder, pushes me back, and punches the wall next to my head.

I ball up, cross my arms to cover my face. But when I lower my elbows, lift my chin, and meet his gaze, the action fuels his rage. He shakes his fists, bits of white drywall flecking his knuckles. A needle-thin shiver shoots up my back. *He can kill me, but he's not going to touch the kids. I'll die first.*

I make a run for the door to the house, ducking under his arm. Mitchell grabs me by the back of the head, balling my hair in his fist. My scalp burns, and I claw at his body, trying to wrestle away from his grasp. Mitchell lifts me off the ground and pushes me against the Jeep. I cough and kick wildly, trying to catch my breath.

"I didn't want it to come to this, Ava." Keeping one hand on my arm, he pulls a bottle of pills from his pocket and a silver flask.

He releases my hair. My chin falls forward and I shake my head vigorously.

"Drink it. Take the pills," he murmurs, popping the lid. "You're depressed. You don't have your children. Everyone will understand that you decided to take your own life."

I gasp and start shaking. The room tilts. Mitchell means to murder me. He cups a hand under my chin, gripping the skin with his fingers.

"Do it," he growls, "or the children get it too. I'll make sure it looks like you decided if you couldn't have them, I wouldn't be able to either."

"I called the police," I cry out. "They're coming."

Mitchell laughs. "While you were in the

truck, debating whether or not to come in the house, I called the sheriff's department. A little bomb threat on campus," he adds. "All of those students. They're on their way."

My body sags. Mitchell seizes the opportunity, grabs my jaw, and forces my mouth open. With a quick jerk, he upends the pills. I gag and retch, writhing underneath him. Mitchell uses his body to hold mine up, his forearm braced against my neck.

I hear the twist of metal and the slosh of liquid. There's the acrid smell of whiskey mixed with something medicinal, just before Mitchell empties the flask into my throat. The whiskey softens the pills and singes my windpipe. I try to cough, but I can't breathe. I swallow what I have to, my need for oxygen overtaking every other instinct.

"Don't fight it," Mitchell murmurs. He relaxes his grip on my mouth enough to pour more alcohol through my lips. The whiskey hits my belly, then warms every limb. I am dizzy from struggling.

I have to fight, I tell myself. I have to get the children. With a surge of energy, I reach for his face, scraping my nails down his cheek. The marks draw blood, bright red, in three angry streaks. Mitchell's body contracts in pain and he rears back and away, covering the wounds.

I seize the moment of distraction to swipe the remaining pills out of my mouth, tossing the handful as far into the dark edge of the garage as possible.

Mitchell's hands drop from his face and clench into fists. "Dammit, Ava," he says, clenching his teeth. In a swift motion he yanks open the door to the Jeep and drags me into the driver's seat. He finds my keys easily, slips the large one into the ignition, and turns. The engine purrs, and Mitchell grabs the garage remote, closing the door from the inside.

Oh my God. My brain fast-forwards. My pulse gallops, but I force my body still. "Is this what you did to Karen?" I whisper.

The corners of Mitchell's mouth twist. "She took the wrong medicine, that's all."

My heart stops. When I speak next, my tongue is thick, trying to trap the words. "Wh-what did you give her?"

He closes his eyes and starts to laugh. When I hear the sound filling the stale air — floating around my body — I know what I must do. When Mitchell catches his breath and looks at me, I tilt my head ever so slightly, jaw slack, and allow my eyelids to almost close. Abruptly, I straighten, as if rousing from a dream.

As if in slow motion, I wipe at my lips and let my hand drop. "Wh-what did you give her?"

Mitchell watches me. "Not these." He holds up the bottle of pills, shaking them so that the letters vibrate.

I let my chin drop and flutter my eyelashes, pretending not to focus. But I can read the label. Generic. Over the counter. Sleeping tablets. I let my head fall back against the seat and make my words slur. "What med-i-cine?"

Mitchell wipes off the container and tosses it into the Jeep. "She was taking Frank's blood pressure meds. They looked exactly the same as her epilepsy pills. An easy mistake to make. She took them for almost two weeks and never even knew a thing."

"How could you?" I want to yell. But I say it softly, slumping down in the seat as if battling for consciousness. I only have to half-pretend, though. The world is getting fuzzy.

"It was supposed to make her tired. Make her want to stay home, where she belonged," Mitchell adds, walking away from me, his footsteps echoing. "It wasn't supposed to kill her."

Fear stabs my chest and I want to scream,

but I close my eyes, feigning sleep. It is the only way I will live. The garage light flicks off, and we are bathed in darkness except for the faint glow from my dashboard. I hear Mitchell open and close the door. And I am alone at last.

CHAPTER 69
JACK

FRIDAY, APRIL 30

No superhero is going to jump in and web-sling my dad to the wall. Or swoop in and carry us off, red cape flying. There isn't a person alive who can break down walls with big green fists. Or wave a wand and make all of this disappear.

I'd love to pretend I'm living — here and now — in the pages of a comic book, but I can't. What's going on is real. I scoop up Sam, hold him close to my chest, and rock him. When he's sleepy enough, I settle him in his crib. Just like me, he's exhausted from the day, from the happiness of seeing Ava and the stress of Dad's car ride here.

It's time for me to step up and face what frightens me most. I unzip my backpack and feel for the grooved metal handle of the gun. I wrap my fingers around it and grip tightly. My dad and Ava have been down there talking for a long time. It's quiet. Too quiet, I think. Maybe everything's okay, but something in my brain scratches at me. Call 9–1–1. Now.

The phone's in my parents' room. I step into the hallway, holding the gun behind my back, just as my father's coming up the new staircase. His hand brushes over the smooth railing. The wood, glossed to perfection, shines in the light of the chandelier.

"Where's Ava?" I ask, heart racing. I walk toward him quickly, getting as far away from Sam as possible.

My father pauses. "Why, son, she's gone." His expression doesn't give anything away, but his shirt's dirty. He smells like sweat. His pants are wrinkled. And there's a fresh scratch on his face like a cat clawed him. The blood, smeared and dried, looks like war paint.

"Why?" I swallow back the bile in my throat. What did my father do? Did Ava run? Is she really gone?

Dad narrows his eyes at me and takes the last few steps. "I told you," he replies, looming over me. "She is not a part of our life anymore."

One hand under the other, I point the pistol, hold it steady, aim at my dad's chest.

Dad takes a step back, looking from me to the gun. "Put that down, son. Someone's going to get hurt."

My body quakes. "Did you hurt *her*?"

Dad shakes his head and reaches out a hand, his fingers beckoning me. "Jack, she wasn't happy."

Inside my head I scream. My eyes blind with tears. The words come out before I can stop them, tumbling end over end. "You killed her, didn't you? And you killed my mom." One tear escapes and trickles down my cheek.

My father inches toward me and I lift the pistol higher.

"Jack, forget about Ava. She doesn't matter." Dad spreads out his arms and shrugs, like we're talking about a glass of spilled milk. "We're all leaving tonight. One big, happy family."

"No."

Dad walks closer. "Right now."

My chest heaves. The muscles in my shoulder cry out. My brain aches, pounds. I raise the gun a little higher. And aim.

"You're not going to fire that thing," my father says. "You're a coward. Hand it over, Jack." His face mocks me, smug and sure.

"I'm not a coward," I hear myself say. *Not now. Not ever.*

There's a creak downstairs. My father and I both jump. From the corner of my eye, I

451

see a figure in the foyer. Like an apparition, Ava moves closer, until she is standing at the bottom of the staircase. Her shirt's torn, and her hair is a mess. She's pale, like the color of a marble statue, and one of her hands is clutching the banister for all she's worth. My father, rooted to the floor, just stares through narrowed eyes.

"He's not a coward, Mitchell," she says, taking the first step. Her voice is surprisingly strong. "And neither am I." She locks her eyes on me and gives me the faintest smile.

A faint siren wails in the distance.

Ava takes another step. "You're not leaving with the boys, Mitchell," she says, moving her eyes to him.

My father's hands curl into fists. I can see the muscles in his neck tighten. He's getting ready to pounce, and this time he will kill her.

"Wait," I yell and toss the gun sideways, releasing it into the air.

Dad lurches back in surprise and reaches for the pistol, which is tumbling end over end. It falls through his fingertips, hits the floor, and explodes, sending the scent of gunpowder into the air. My heart thuds like fists beating on the front door. There's a yell from outside. That's when I launch myself like a linebacker. Head tucked, shoulder forward. I collide with my father, sending him back against the staircase, over the balcony.

Then we're both tumbling.

Crashing.

Falling for what feels like forever.

EPILOGUE:
JACK

Three Years Later

The return address says Holman Correctional Facility. I grip the envelope in one hand. A page, maybe two. As always, I consider ripping it open and reading it, or just shredding it into a million pieces. After all, it's what he did to our family.

The door slams. Sam races in to meet me, carrying his soccer ball. Mom trails behind toting a few canvas shopping bags. She raises an eyebrow when she notices the mail. I shrug.

"Jack!" Sam jumps into my arms and almost knocks me over.

"How's my best bud?" I ask and give him a big squeeze. He's grown so much that I do a double take every time he walks into a room.

"Can we practice penalty kicks?" Sam begs and sets the ball on the floor. "You promised."

"Just a sec, honey." Mom walks over and hoists the bags onto the counter. "Can you be a big boy and put these away?" She hands Sam two tissue boxes and sends him trotting off to the back bedroom.

"Be right back," he yells, thundering down the hall.

We share a grin at Sam's enthusiasm, and then I hand over the envelope. As she's done a dozen times, Mom walks over to her desk, opens the top drawer, and slides the letter inside.

"Whenever you're ready," she says.

I want to answer but stay silent. *Not today or tomorrow. Maybe not ever. Would Superman go looking for trouble?* Dad's letters are Kryptonite.

As Mom slides the drawer closed, she turns and smiles. There's lots she's filed away, up in her bedroom, where she thinks I won't find it. Mom's not that great at hiding things. There's Judge Crane's divorce decree, an award of full custody for my mom, and the property settlement. There's a Final Protection from Abuse order for her, Sam, and me. And Dr. Bennett's custody evaluation. I've looked at it so much, reading and rereading the sentences.

No evidence that the mother of the minor

children is unfit. No evidence of alcoholism, risky behavior, or abuse of the minor children. In observing the father of the minor children, his behavior indicates that he suffers from acute anxiety and paranoia. His characteristics appear in line with sociopathic personality disorder, as described in the DSM-IV. In order to avoid further trauma to the minor children and mother, it is recommended that the father undergo a full psychiatric evaluation.

Until such time that the evaluation is completed and submitted to the court's satisfaction, it is further recommended that the father be restricted from having any contact with said minor children.

I don't know what the judge decided, really, or if the letters my dad sends count as "contact." I haven't asked.

When I close my eyes, I relive that night. The fury in Dad's face, his outrage. Mom — braver than I've ever seen — willing to die to protect Sam and me.

We landed at the bottom of the staircase. Dad's body, crumpled and twisted, cushioned my fall. I walked away with a broken arm and wrist, some bruised ribs. For several minutes I couldn't breathe or move or talk. I honestly thought I was dead.

Ava was crying and stroking my head. The paramedics said I was in shock.

Dad wasn't as lucky. He cushioned my fall and cracked his head on the marble floor of the foyer. Blood, dark and sticky, pumped out of his skull. The smell of it, coppery and sweet, haunts my thoughts.

And yeah, I didn't think first. It was a gut reaction. Panic. I had to get him out of the way, away from Sam and Ava. Away from me. Now the thought of it — what I did — what happened, still seems like a bad dream.

Everyone said it was self-defense. I wasn't charged with any crime, though my father spent weeks recovering. He was locked down in a private hospital room, making small but steady improvements. As soon as he was stable, the moment he was discharged, the police arrested him for Dr. Bennett's and my mom's attempted murders.

Attempts to plea-bargain the charges down to assault didn't work. I've lost track of the number of appeals he's filed. Dad's finished more than two years of his sentence. Almost eighteen more years to go. Meanwhile, Officer Mike Kennedy has pressed hard to reopen the investigation into my biological mom's death. He's sure it was no accident. The district attorney wants a charge of reckless homicide, which could mean another two to twelve years tacked on to Dad's sentence. My father could be eighty years old when he gets out of prison.

It's all surreal. Dad in Atmore, Alabama, another trial going on. There's always a news crew or someone lurking at the bottom of the driveway. We keep the TV and radio turned off.

Still, you hear things. At school, at the grocery store, at the soccer field. Things like Dad went insane, that he and Mom had a shoot-out in the house, and that Dad was going to poison all of us.

That last story came from my friend Mo. He overhead some cops tell his dad one of the detectives discovered a stash of sleeping tablets in the apartment, half a bottle of hard liquor hidden under the counter, and some medicine for epilepsy. I don't even want to think about it.

When I talk to Dr. Bennett about it, she says stopping the pain when you lose someone you love is difficult. Practically impossible, like trying to keep water in a sieve. You plug a few openings, but you can't close them all. There are too many memories, too many holes, and the emotions just keep seeping out. Eventually you have to let go.

I've done the best I can. Put all of my energy into doing well in school and on the soccer field. Spending time with Mo. With my mom and Sam. And really good things have happened.

After my arm and wrist healed up, Will Harris called and asked if he could release *The Adventures of Jack Carson: Super Kid* series. As it turns out, four stories were written. He found an illustrator to finish the drawings, which turned out better than I ever expected. Watch out, Stan Lee and Marvel Comics.

Book one came out last summer. Book two is scheduled for next month. The cool thing is that I get all of the proceeds, which go straight to my college fund. Mom even takes me to book signings when I'm not in school, and Grandpa Frank usually comes along. He says he's my biggest fan.

Six months ago Grandpa Frank finally sold his house and moved to Mobile. He's so much a part of the family now that I can't seem to remember what it was like without him. Mom's got him volunteering, tutoring elementary school kids in math and science.

I know Isabel loves having him over for dinner because he always cleans his plate. And he's become close buddies with Graham. Every time they're over at the house, it's a contest to see who can come up with the craziest stories. Graham about courtroom drama, Frank about his time in the army.

I hear the pounding of Sam's feet on the wood floor. He runs up, breathless, his green eyes sparkling.

"How about a story?" I ask my brother.

"Superheroes," he announces.

"My favorite," I agree with a grin.

I grab a comic book from my room and get us settled on the sofa. Sam snuggles close and I begin to read, though I could recite the words from memory.

As we sit together, my thoughts go back to the past. Through all of the pain, through all of the good and bad. Because of the path my father chose to take, I've learned this much: some heroes are made, not born. They don't wear costumes or special amulets. They are mothers, men, kids, and regular people. They might get bruised, broken, or beaten down.

But they don't give up.

DISCUSSION QUESTIONS

1. Jack is infatuated with all things superhero. Is this a typical phase or an unconscious way of dealing with his mother's death?
2. Ava seemed happy in her role as a student counselor and planned on returning after Sam's birth. Why does Mitchell send in her resignation to Mobile Prep?
3. Graham, as an outsider from Birmingham, seems able to observe the town objectively. How does this help him and hurt him as Ava's attorney?
4. Dr. Bennett is assigned to evaluate the child custody dispute. Is it possible for anyone to remain completely neutral in a case like this one?
5. Ava confesses to her mother that she and Mitchell are having marital problems. Why does her mother dismiss the conversation?
6. Mobile is Ava's hometown, yet she doesn't receive much emotional support

461

from many friends or former coworkers after Mitchell files for divorce. Why is that?

7. Jack finds himself torn between loyalty to his father and love for a stepparent. Have you ever experienced this?

8. Frank Carson is shocked to discover that his grandson believes that he is dead. Why didn't he try harder to find Mitchell and Jack?

9. Mitchell Carson is determined to keep in contact with Jack. What message do you imagine his letters contain?

10. Sam is four years old when the novel ends. How will his father's incarceration affect his emotional growth and development as a young adult?

ACKNOWLEDGMENTS

Deepest gratitude to my editor, Ami McConnell, and my associate editor, Karli Jackson, along with everyone at Thomas Nelson, especially Daisy Hutton, Amanada Bostic, Ansley Boatman, Katie Bond, Kristen Ingebretson, and Kristen Golden. From the moment I arrived in Nashville, I felt like part of the family. I am indebted, also, to my fabulous agent, Elizabeth Winick Rubinstein, for her guidance and advice.

I owe so much to author, editor, and friend Emily Heckman, who believed in Jack and Ava's story from page one. To my early readers, Jen McGee, Doug McCourt, Yvonne Edeker, Kelly McCulloch, Linda Moore, and Laura Pepper Wu, I can't thank you enough for your enthusiasm and encouragement. A Starbucks frappuccino and several lattes to Caroline Steudle for reading and reviewing the revised manuscript in record time on her way to St.

Simons Island.

To my author and blogger friends, Tracie Banister, Jen Tucker, Karen Pokras, Jessica Sinn, and Tobi Helton, I am blessed to know you! Hugs to my Mobile, Alabama family: April Sanders, Jenny Good, Tara Jones, Mary Steudle, Chris Hughes, Bob Stewart, Julie Flotte, Ellen Odom, Cecelia Heyer, Simone Armstrong, Valerie Case, Jana Simpson, and Lisa Emanuelli.

Much appreciation to the Friends of the Mobile Library and all of the folks at Page and Palette Bookstore in Fairhope, Alabama who've shown so much support for my work. Much love to my readers and friends throughout the world. Without you, none of this is possible.

A huge heartfelt thank you to my family. And to Patrick and John David — who mean everything.

ABOUT THE AUTHOR

Laura McNeil is a writer, web geek, travel enthusiast, and coffee drinker. In her former life, she was a television news anchor for CBS News affiliates in New York and Alabama. Laura holds a master's degree in Journalism from The Ohio State University and is completing a graduate program in Interactive Technology at the University of Alabama. When she's not writing and doing homework, she enjoys running, yoga, and spending time at the beach. She lives in Mobile, Alabama, with her family.